THEODOR FONTANE

Jenny Treibel

Translated, with introduction and notes,
by
ULF ZIMMERMANN

Frederick Ungar Publishing Co.
New York

Translated from the original German
Frau Jenny Treibel

Copyright © 1976 by Frederick Ungar Publishing Co., Inc.
Printed in the United States of America
Designed by Irving Perkins

Library of Congress Cataloging in Publication Data

Fontane, Theodor, 1819-1898.
  Jenny Treibel.

  Translation of Frau Jenny Treibel.
  I. Title.
PZ3.F7347Je4 [PT1863]   833'.8   76-15648
ISBN 0-8044-2209-5
ISBN 0-8044-6154-6 pbk.

Berlin, Fontane, and Jenny Treibel

THE Berlin of recent history, familiar from newspapers, novels, and films as a center of East-West diplomacy and intrigue, and the Berlin of the "Golden Twenties," famous for Bertolt Brecht's *Threepenny Opera* and Christopher Isherwood's stories, dramatized in *Cabaret*—this is the Berlin that matured, with all the excitement and growing pains symptomatic of a precocious but rambunctious youth, during Theodor Fontane's most creative age. His *Jenny Treibel* appeared in 1892, almost exactly at the midpoint of those years of the Empire, from 1871 to 1914, during which the provincial capital of Prussia became the cosmopolitan metropolis of modern Germany. And because of Fontane's penetrating vision, the novel offers a pivotal viewpoint from which one can survey the past and see a surprising distance into the future as well.

This Berlin, as the Treibels of the novel aspire to represent it, was now becoming a center of international politics, finance, and industry. It was also able to claim one of the finest universities anywhere, one which would soon attract such men as Max Planck and Albert Einstein. In this intellectual realm toward which the Schmidts of the novel look, Robert Koch had just discovered the TB bacillus, and Rudolf Virchow, whose medical and political career they followed, had just returned from helping excavate Troy. And for a time this realm of intellect and art joined forces with that of money and power, now allowing Corinna Schmidt to witness Edwin Booth's Shakespearean performances and later enabling men like Max Reinhardt to make Berlin into the theater capital of the world. Fontane himself had decisively encouraged this development with his clearsighted and forward-looking reviews of the emerging Naturalist dramas, such as Gerhardt Hauptmann's *Before Sunrise* (1889) and his later *Weavers*.

Berlin's sudden rise and far-reaching resonance in the world resulted in part from a peculiarly reciprocal relationship between the dynastic ambition of the ruling house of Hohenzollern and the boundless vitality of the amenably energetic Berliners. The Huguenots exiled by Louis XIV were easily able to make themselves at home among these hospitable Berliners after Frederick William, the Great Elector, had invited them with the Edict of Potsdam in 1685. To this act the city owes much of its refinement in commerce as in the arts—and by extension, its greatest chronicler, Theodor Fontane. For it was the subsequent mass of immigrants from France, like his ancestors, and from Flanders and Switzerland, with Slavs and Jews coming from the East, who mingled with the native population and ultimately produced that famous image of Berliners whom Goethe, when he visited the city in 1778, pronounced an "audacious breed" and of whom Fontane has given such an engaging specimen in Corinna Schmidt.

Several years later another famous visitor to Berlin, Madame de Staël (to whose most famous heroine Corinna is indebted for her name), also remarked on the happy social mixture that prevailed there. But when she then observed further that "the thinkers are soaring in the empyrean, and on the earth you encounter only grenadiers," she revealed the newly-widening chasm between the ruling aristocracy and the increasingly less amenable and more audacious bourgeoisie. The latter's demands for reform and liberalization grew more and more insistent until, by 1848, political pressures mounted to a revolutionary pitch, and the Berliners, Fontane among them, started to the barricades. And though their effort was initially victorious, its effects proved to be short-lived, for the erstwhile liberal bourgeoisie very quickly found itself preferring the secure rule of the Junker aristocracy to the domination by the masses that the "specter of communism" seemed to threaten.

It seems that the ambitious men of the liberal bourgeoisie, whose revolutionary energies were politically frustrated under Junker rule, now increasingly addressed them to economic aims, much as Treibel appears to have done. In so doing they helped to produce a boom that lasted twenty years and laid the economic foundations of modern Germany. What remained of the liberal bourgeoisie's political opposition was rendered bloodless by this unarguable economic success, and it allowed Bismarck the iron rule by which he unified Germany and made it into an empire with Berlin as its capital. And by the time this economic boom had abated, Bismarck had engineered the success of the Franco-Prussian War. The huge reparation sum that poured into Berlin from France proved to be every bit as intoxicating economically as the war victory had been politically. In the delirious years that followed, the *Gründerjahre* (founders' years), Berlin abounded equally with vitality and vulgarity, and even the soberest thirsted for money and glamor, as Fontane delightfully demonstrates.

The beginnings of Fontane's career as the chronicler of this Berlin and its society very nearly coincide with the foundation of the Empire in 1871. The coincidence is remarkable, for one thing, because at a time in life when most men are making retirement plans Fontane embarked on an entirely new literary course, and for another, because to do so he had to create a novel form to suit the new society of Imperial Berlin. His success, increasingly acknowledged in subsequent years, made him one of the greatest of German novelists and the only one of the nineteenth century to attain international stature, an achievement as unanticipated in his past as Berlin's sudden ascendancy had been in its history.

Fontane was born, in the same decade as Marx and Bismarck, on December 30, 1819, the first child of a couple proud of their French Huguenot heritage and of some prominence in the small town of Neuruppin, just northwest of Berlin. The father had acquired a pharmacy there that same year but, given to gambling, he had to sell it a few years later, and the family moved to another small town, Swinemünde on the Baltic. Here young Fontane received his early education, much of it through the entertaining methods of his father, as he fondly recalls in his autobiographical writings. After he had turned twelve he was sent back to Neuruppin to attend the Gymnasium there, but only a year later he was in Berlin at a trade school, preparing to become a pharmacist himself.

Here in Berlin his literary interests first developed and led to an early debut with the publication of a story and a few poems in 1839. A trip to London in 1844 expanded his literary horizon and allowed him some political insights; eventually it also proved a profitable background for later employment there. In Berlin he was invited to join a literary club because of his talent as a writer of ballads. The acquaintances he made here, artists as well as aristocrats, widened his social spectrum and also proved helpful as friends and influential intermediaries in his attempts to secure work.

Securing suitable work was a recurrent difficulty after Fontane decided to abandon his pharmacist's trade and to become a full-time writer; the difficulty was compounded when in 1850, after a five-year engagement to a woman who was never wholly sympathetic to his artistic ambitions, he finally married her and began to acquire a family that would need steady support. Moreover, there was the difficulty of

political principles—Fontane's pre-'48 liberal inclinations
were known and rather out of place in the reactionary press
that prevailed after 1848. For a time he contemplated the
popular expedient of emigrating to America, but finally he
was able to make an adequate compromise by going to London
in the service of the government's central press agency.

While there, he perfected his skills as a journalist in his
descriptions of London and the countryside of England and
Scotland. Returning to Berlin in 1859, he settled into a steady
position on one of the conservative papers and began to
explore and depict the historical terrain of his own countryside, the Mark Brandenburg province. The resulting series of
pastoral rambles, *Wanderungen durch die Mark Brandenburg*
(*Journeys Through the Mark Brandenburg*), which marks
Fontane's transition from ballads to the novel, was punctuated
by several reports from the battlefields of the Prussian wars.
The last of these gives an account of his own two months'
imprisonment in 1870 as a suspected spy, when, driven behind
enemy lines by his native curiosity, he had been apprehended
contemplating the statue of Joan of Arc in Domremy. (He
escaped execution only through the intervention of Bismarck
himself.)

In London, too, he had acquired the experience which he
now brought to the liberal *Vossischen* newspaper, in whose
pages he began to publish the theater reviews that were to
make him the celebrated champion of the young Naturalists.
This was the only newspaper work he continued after 1870,
and now that he had the time he wanted, he returned to a
fictional work he had begun in the mid-sixties, a historical
panorama of 1812–13, and completed it for publication in
1878. The historical novel somewhat in the manner of Walter
Scott did not, however, seem to be his métier; he came into
his own much more when he emphasized social and personal
elements, as he did in the work he began next, the historical
masterpiece *Schach von Wuthenow* (recently translated by

E. M. Valk as *A Man of Honor**). But while working on it
he was tempted into more contemporary storytelling by a
bit of scandal among the wealthier Berlin bourgeoisie: a
woman who was the wife of an important industrialist and
the mother of three had left her family and run off to König-
sberg with her lover. Titled *L'Adultera* after the painting by
Tintoretto, the resulting novel—the third of the seventeen
novels and *Novellen* he was to write—was the first of what
became a whole cycle of novels portraying Berlin society. In
these works Fontane not only leaves behind the historical
mode of the much-emulated Walter Scott, but he also departs
from the established German genres of the novels of individual
development and education (*Entwicklungsroman* and *Bil-
dungsroman*), and enters the great international tradition of the
century that extends from Jane Austen to Emile Zola. From
the genteel acrimony of Jane Austen to the social penetration
of Zola, one finds Fontane sharing a variety of the distinguish-
ing characteristics of his great contemporaries—the all-
embracing eye of a Balzac, the needle-sharp caricature of a
Thackeray, the affectionate mockery of a Trollope, and even
the attenuating sensibility of a James. But as Thomas Mann
(who is indebted to him for his *Buddenbrooks* title) attests
in his essay "The Old Fontane," he stands out as wholly himself in his easy charm and universal sympathy:

> If I may be permitted the personal confession: no writer of
> past or present stirs in me the kind of sympathy and grati-
> tude, that immediate, instinctive delight, that reflex gaiety,
> warmth, and satisfaction, which I feel reading any of his
> verses, any line of his letters, any scrap of dialogue.

Such charm and sympathy are the manifestations of Fontane's youthfully growing vigor as a writer and his increas-

* Published in 1975 by Frederick Ungar Publishing Co.

ingly forward-looking view of the world. In *Jenny Treibel* especially, the educated experience and critical intelligence of his years gracefully combine with the qualities of gentle humor and fine irony. While some, therefore, consider this novel Fontane's most outstanding, it is universally acknowledged among his readers that he reached the comic climax of his Berlin cycle in *Jenny Treibel*.

Reminiscent of *Pride and Prejudice* in the nuanced leisure of its initial exposition of character and setting, *Jenny Treibel* is similarly constructed like a traditional comedy in three acts and is likewise sustained by a comparably urbane use of dialogue. Dialogue, as developed in *L'Adultera*, had become for Fontane the quintessential medium to depict his society and his city. The characters' chatty conversations, with their touch or more of the sentimental and pretentious spiced with an occasional dash of the graphic or even vulgar, and studded with quotations, succeed as much in creating credible characters and authentic atmosphere as they do in imparting information. Fontane's realism results in part from having the reader join what are obviously continued conversations and long-standing social relationships among the characters and having him enter the city at the side of these persons with their particular backgrounds and attitudes. And with the eminently modern realism of this medium Fontane does indeed communicate his characters and his setting with such unprecedented directness and palpability that the reader is immediately at home with them in their city. Berlin need no more be described than the characters; it is experienced by and through these characters who are identified with its streets and quarters, and the reader becomes familiar with it through his intimate, conversational acquaintance with the characters.

Now to achieve this intimate familiarity between his reader and his fictive world—and Fontane is a master at establishing personal relationships—he exposes the reader, very gradually at first, to everyday existence in it. Beginning with Jenny's monologue, he lets his title character identify and characterize herself and her past with the pace and style appropriate to her age and position in life; through her, at the same time, he outlines Berlin's changing social and geographical stratification. Proceeding to the dialogue between Jenny and Corinna, Fontane slowly and circumspectly defines the antitheses of his narrative dialectic, from the social aspect of money and education, to the generational of youth and age, on to the psychological of sense and sensibility. From here he moves on to the orchestrated conversation of the larger sampling of society represented at the Treibels' dinner party—contrasting it then with the smaller group of Schmidt's evening gathering—and involves the reader in the complexities of its concerns, ranging from the trivialities of household gossip to the mysteries of national politics, and from the local pleasures of the palate to the far-reaching discoveries of modern archeology. And only now that the reader has been thoroughly initiated into this atmosphere and has adopted his own attitudes in it does Fontane draw him into the rush of events to come.

Behind the sudden developments in the novel is the character of Corinna who is, to some extent, equally reminiscent of Austen's Elizabeth Bennet in her like independence of mind as she is in the similar illusions of the heart. Yet like Fontane's more realistic dialogue, Corinna is more than merely a literary transposition from an English novel; she is rather an affectionate, if ironic, idealization of an actual person. For just as Fontane had employed his sister Jenny Sommerfeldt, whose name he also used, and her circle to model for his satiric portrayal of Jenny Treibel and her society, he modeled her antagonist Corinna on his daughter Mete. With a disposition akin to his, Mete was an intellectually sympathetic companion to Fontane during these later years, though she also remained something of a problem child. Using autobiographical detail like this was not Fontane's ordinary practice, but it may have been motivated by his particular concern for Mete, whom he wished to see securely and happily married before his death. He was greatly relieved when, at last, as she was approaching forty, she became engaged on September 16, 1898—four days before he died.

Such solicitude for his daughter is not, however, really characteristic of Corinna's untroubled father in whom, by extension, a parallel self-portrait of the author might have been suspected. Yet Fontane and his character Wilibald Schmidt do in fact share some other characteristics, besides having equally "audacious" daughters, that are equally typical of Berlin. Among these is the sense of irony which allows Fontane to project at least a part of himself into Schmidt and thereby to have some fun at his own expense. This typically "Berliner" irony stands out as a prime example of an indigenous perspectivism that sees everything that is said in relation to its source. In the novel the reader's perspective is accordingly varied in relation to the various conversational points of view presented, each of which evaluates and adjusts the other. From Schmidt's comments, for example, the reader thus knows where Corinna's statements are off the mark and where she is deluding herself, just as he knows the true character of Jenny from the ironic discrepancy between her sentimental chatter about her ideals and the sharp-tongued cynicism which characterizes her actions.

Fontane's own ironic distance allows him to portray Schmidt as a representative of an ingratiatingly vain bourgeoisie of education that is exactly parallel to a comically vulgar bourgeoisie of money represented by Jenny. The moneyed, like Treibel, the expediently patriotic manufacturer of Prussian blue dye, aspire to the idealistic respectability of titles that the Emperor—or even the populace—may bestow upon them.

And like Corinna, the educated and emancipated wish to share the material rewards of industrial progress—even if it might mean marrying the likes of a Treibel.

Though Fontane shows up his characters satirically by means of this irony, he also maintains a conciliatory and ameliorative tone throughout. For with the same ironic distance by which he dissociates himself from both types of the bourgeoisie, he associates himself with a more desirable alternative that he projects beyond them—an economically and socially more egalitarian society. Or as he has Schmidt put it: "If I weren't a Professor, I'd become a Social Democrat." And to the extent that such a society remains in the future, Fontane's portrait of Imperial Berlin has lost none of its timeliness and is still to be enjoyed with the same immediacy that made it both a critical and a popular success when the novel first appeared in 1892.

Because of *Jenny Treibel's* timeliness and immediacy, translating Fontane's Imperial Berlin idiom is as consistently gratifying as it is occasionally impossible. For though the characters and their concerns have sufficiently familiar equivalents in contemporary American society, the historical context, the local color, and more frequently the topics of conversations are very specifically those of nineteenth-century Berlin and Germany. And, as such, they cannot always be "translated" from their own language and time into modern English equivalents. For that reason, and to lead the curious reader further, it has seemed useful, wherever the importance of such less familiar elements exceeded that of simply adding flavor to the fiction, to provide a number of explanatory notes on immediately pertinent matters of history and society, political and literary figures, as well as the numerous quotations, allusions, and foreign phrases.

U.Z.

Northfield, Minnesota
1976

Chapter One

O N one of the last days of May, with the weather of early summer, an open landau turned from the Spittelmarkt into the Kurstrasse and then into the Adlerstrasse. Presently it stopped in front of an old-fashioned house which was rather stately despite its facade of only five windows, and somewhat cleaner if not more beautiful for its fresh coat of yellow-brown paint. In the rear seat of the carriage two ladies sat with a little Maltese spaniel that appeared to be enjoying the bright, warm sunshine. The lady sitting on the left, around thirty and evidently a governess or companion, now opened the carriage door from her seat and assisted the other lady in getting out. Then she immediately returned to her place while the older lady, who was dressed with taste and care and still looked very good though in her upper fifties, walked up to an entrance stairway and crossing it stepped into the hallway. From here she climbed, as quickly as her corpulence allowed, up the footworn steps of a narrow wooden staircase which was suffused with a very dim light at the bottom and a heavy air at the top, so heavy that one

might well term it a "double air." Immediately opposite the
point at which the stairs ended there was an apartment door
with a peephole and beside this a battered green metal plate
on which "Professor Wilibald Schmidt" could be read with
some difficulty.

Here the slightly asthmatic lady felt the need to rest and
accordingly took this opportunity to examine the hall—
familiar to her from long ago—with its four yellow walls, the
various hooks and rods, and the wooden half-moon for brush-
ing and beating coats. The atmosphere here took its character
from a singular kitchen odor wafting in from one of the back
corridors and indicating, if not deceptive, mashed potatoes
and cutlets, mingled with soapy steam. "So, washing finery—,"
the elegant lady said softly to herself, peculiarly touched by
all this. She recalled the long-past days when she herself had
lived in this very Adlerstrasse and had helped in her father's
grocery store directly across the street. There, on a board
laid across two coffee sacks, she had glued together small and
large paper bags, for which she was rewarded with "two
pennies for the hundred." "Really too much, Jenny," the old
man used to say, "but you must learn to manage money." Oh,
what times those had been! Noons, at the stroke of twelve,
when they went to the table, she sat between the clerk, Herr
Mielke, and the apprentice, Louis, both of whom, otherwise
so different, had the same high forelocks and the same frozen
hands. And Louis cast admiring glances at her out of the
corner of his eye but became embarrassed whenever he saw
he had been discovered. For he was of far too low a social
standing—from a fruit cellar in the Spreegasse.

Yes, all that was now in her mind again as she looked
around in the hallway and finally pulled the bell next to the
door. The thoroughly bent-up wire did indeed rustle, but no
ringing was to be heard, and so at last she grasped the bell
handle once again and pulled more strongly. Now a tinkling
did ring out from the kitchen into the hall, and a few moments

later it became apparent that a small wooden shutter behind the peephole was being pushed aside. Very likely it was the Professor's housekeeper now looking out for friend or foe from her observation post. When this observation had shown that it was "good friend," the doorlatch was pushed back rather noisily and a buxom woman in her late forties with an imposingly-constructed bonnet on her head, her face reddened by the fire of the stove, stood before the visitor.

"Oh, Frau Treibel. . . Frau Kommerzienrätin[1]. . . What an honor. . ."

"Hello, my dear Frau Schmolke. How is the Professor? And how is Corinna? Is the Fräulein at home?"

"Yes, Frau Kommerzienrätin. Just back from the Philharmonic. How happy she'll be!"

And with that Frau Schmolke stepped aside in order to clear the way to the entrance hall which, with its single window and narrow canvas runner, lay between the two front rooms. But even before the Kommerzienrätin could enter Fräulein Corinna came towards her and led the "maternal friend," as the Rätin liked to call herself, off to the right into one of the front rooms.

This was a pretty, high room, with the blinds down and the windows open to the inside and a planter with wallflowers and hyacinths in front of one of them. Exhibited on the tea table, side by side, were a glass bowl of oranges and the portraits of the Professor's parents, Rechnungsrat Schmidt from the Heralds' Chamber and his wife, née Schwerin, who were looking down upon the glass bowl. The old Rechnungsrat in a tailcoat with the red Order of the Eagle, his wife, née Schwerin, with strong cheekbones and a pug nose (which, in spite of its marked bourgeois quality, still suggested more the noble Pomeranian bearers of that famous name than the later, or if you will, also *much* earlier Posen line).

"My dear Corinna, how nicely you know how to do all this and how pretty it is here, so cool and fresh—and the beautiful hyacinths! Of course they don't go very well with these oranges, but that doesn't matter, it looks so nice. . . . And now, thoughtful as you are, you're even adjusting a pillow for me! But forgive me, I don't like to sit on the sofa; it's so soft and you always sink in so deeply. I'd rather sit over here in the armchair and look at those dear old faces there. Oh, that was a man—just like your father. But the old Rechnungsrat was perhaps even more courteous, and some always did say he was as good as from the Colony.[2] Which was true, because his grandmother, as you of course know better than I, was after all a Charpentier, Stralauer Strasse."

With these remarks the Kommerzienrätin had taken her seat in the tall armchair and with her lorgnette looked over at those "dear faces" which she had just recalled so benevolently while Corinna asked if she couldn't bring some Moselle and soda water—it was so hot.

"No, Corinna, I've just come from lunch, and soda water always goes to my head so. It's odd, I can take sherry and even port, if it's aged, but Moselle and soda water, that makes me giddy. . . . Goodness, child, I've known this room for forty years and more now, from the time when I was just a half-grown young thing with chestnut curls, which my mother —with all that she had to do—still always rolled up with touching care. For then, my dear Corinna, strawberry blond wasn't nearly the fashion it is now, but chestnut was quite the thing, especially if it was in curls, and people always noticed me for it. And your father too. He was a student then and wrote poetry. You'll hardly believe how charming and touching all that was, because children never want to accept that their parents were young once too and looked good and had their talents. And a few of the poems were addressed to me. I've kept them to this day, and when I feel heavyhearted I take the little book—which originally had a blue cover but I've now had it bound in green Morocco—

and I sit down by the window and look at our garden and quietly cry myself out, so that no one sees it, least of all Treibel or the children. Oh, youth! My dear Corinna, you just don't know what a treasure youth is and how those pure feelings, unclouded by rude gales, always are and remain the best part of us."

"Yes," Corinna laughed, "youth is a good thing. But 'Kommerzienrätin' is a good thing too, and actually it's even better. I'm for a landau and a garden around the villa. And when it's Easter and guests are coming—quite a number of course—then there'll be Easter eggs hidden in the garden, and every egg is an *attrappe*³ full of confectionary from Hövell or Kranzler,⁴ or there might even be a little *nécessaire*⁵ inside. And then when all the guests have found the eggs, each gentleman takes his lady and everyone goes to the table. I'm definitely for youth, but for youth with luxury and nice parties."

"I'm glad to hear that, Corinna, at least right now, because I'm here to invite you, and for tomorrow at that; it came up so quickly. This young Mr. Nelson has arrived at the Otto Treibels—though he's not staying with them—a son of Nelson and Co. from Liverpool with whom my son Otto has his chief business connection. And Helene knows him too. That's so like Hamburgers, they know all the English, and if they don't know them, they at least act as if they did. Inconceivable to me. So it's about Mr. Nelson, who's leaving the day after tomorrow, a dear business friend whom Otto and his wife absolutely had to invite to dinner. But they couldn't do it because once again Helene was having ironing day, which to her mind comes before anything else, even business. So *we* took it over, frankly not too enthusiastically, but not exactly unenthusiastically either. After all, Otto had been a guest at the Nelsons' house for weeks during his trip to England. So you can see how things stand and how important your coming is to me; you speak English and you've read everything, and last winter you even saw Mr. Booth[6] as Hamlet. I still remember quite well how you raved about it. And English politics and history you naturally know too—after all, you are your father's daughter."

"I don't know much about it, just a little bit. Everybody knows a little bit."

"Yes, nowadays, my dear Corinna. You've had it good, and everybody has it good now. But in my time it was different, and if I hadn't been given—thank heaven—a heart for the poetic, which is not to be rooted out once it's alive in you, I wouldn't have learned anything and wouldn't know anything. But, thank God, I've educated myself with poems, and if you know many of them by heart, there are quite a few things you know. And you see, next to God who planted it in my soul, I have your father to thank for this. He's the one who raised the little flower which otherwise might have languished over there in the store among all those prosaic people—and you wouldn't believe how prosaic people can be. . . . Well, how are things with your father? It must be three months or more since I've seen him—since the fourteenth of February, Otto's birthday. But he left early because there was so much singing."

"Yes, he doesn't like that. At least not when he's surprised with it. It's a weakness of his, and some think it's rude."

"Oh, don't, Corinna, you shouldn't say that. Your father is simply an eccentric man. I'm unhappy that he's so seldom to be gotten hold of. I would have liked to invite him along for tomorrow too, but I doubt that Mr. Nelson would interest him, not to mention the others; our friend Krola will probably sing again tomorrow and Assessor Goldammer will probably tell his police stories and do his trick with the hat and the two talers."

"Oh, that will be fun. But, of course, Papa doesn't like to feel constrained, and he prefers his comfort and his pipe to a young Englishman who may even have travelled around the world three times. Papa is good, but one-sided and obstinate."

"I can't agree with that, Corinna. Your Papa is a jewel, I know that better than anyone."

"He underestimates everything external, property and money, and generally everything that adorns and beautifies."

"No, Corinna, don't say that. He looks at life from the proper side; he knows that money is a burden and that happiness lies in an entirely different direction." She fell silent at these words and only sighed softly. But then she continued: "Oh, my dear Corinna, believe me, it's only in modest circumstances that you can find happiness."

Corinna smiled. "That's what all those say who aren't familiar with modest circumstances."

"I'm familiar with them, Corinna."

"Yes, from earlier days. But that's far behind you now and it's been forgotten or even transfigured. But actually it's like this: everybody wants to be rich, and I don't blame anyone for it. Papa, naturally, still swears by the text about the camel and the eye of the needle. But the young world. . ."

". . . is unfortunately different. Only too true. But as certain as that is, it's still not as bad as you think. And it would be too sad if the sense for the ideal were to be lost, especially among youth. There is, for example, your cousin Marcell, whom you'll see tomorrow too, incidentally—he's already accepted—with whom I could find no fault but that his name is Wedderkopp. How can such a fine man have such an unmanageable name! But however that may be, whenever I meet him at Otto's, I always enjoy talking with him so much. And why? Because he has the attitude one should have. Why, even our good friend Krola told me just the other day that Marcell had a basically ethical nature, which he placed even higher than the moral; and I had to agree with him, after some explanation on his part. No, Corinna, don't give up your sense for the higher things, the sense which expects salvation from them alone. I have only my two sons, businessmen, who are going the way of their father, and I must let it happen; but if God had blessed me with a daughter, *she* would have been mine, in spirit too, and if her heart had favored a poor, but noble man, let's say a man like Marcell Wedderkopp. . ."

". . . then they would have made a match of it." Corinna laughed. "Poor Marcell! Now there he could have found his happiness, but it just happens there's no daughter."

The Kommerzienrätin nodded.

"It's altogether too bad that things work out so rarely," Corinna continued. "But thank God, Madam still has Leopold, young and unmarried, and since you have such power over him—at least he says so himself, and his brother Otto says it too, and the whole world says it—and since now an ideal son-in-law is an impossibility, perhaps he could bring home an ideal daughter-in-law, a charming young person, perhaps an actress. . . ."

"I don't care for actresses. . ."

"Or a painter, or a pastor's or professor's daughter. . ."

The Kommerzienrätin started at this last word and cast a rather sharp, if fleeting glance at her. Observing, however, that Corinna remained serene and unaffected, her feeling of alarm vanished as quickly as it had come.

"Yes, Leopold," she said, "I still have him. But Leopold is a child. And his marrying is still in the far-distant future. But if he were to come. . ." And here—perhaps because it did seem in the so "far-distant future"—the Kommerzienrätin appeared in all seriousness about to indulge in the vision of an ideal daughter-in-law, but at that moment the Professor, coming from his junior class, entered and greeted his friend the Rätin with great courtesy.

"Am I disturbing you?"

"In your own home? No, my dear Professor; you could never disturb one at all. You always bring light with you. And you're still as you've always been. But I'm not satisfied with Corinna. She talks in such a modern way and denies her own father, who always lives only in a world of ideas. . . ."

"Well, yes, yes," the Professor said. "One can call it that. But I think she will find her way back. Of course, she'll always keep a touch of the modern. Too bad. That was different when we were young, when life was still imagination and poetry. . ."

He said this with a certain pathos, as if he had to demonstrate a particularly beautiful point in Horace or *Parzival*[7]— he was a classicist and a romanticist at the same time—to his juniors. But his pathos was somewhat too theatrical and had been mixed with a fine irony which the Kommerzienrätin was clever enough to distinguish. Still she considered it advisable to show good faith and therefore she only nodded and said:

"Yes, beautiful days that will never return."

"No," Wilibald said, continuing in his role with the earnestness of a Grand Inquisitor. "It's all over with that; but one has to live on."

An awkward silence followed, and suddenly the sharp crack of a whip could be heard from the street.

"That is a reminder," the Kommerzienrätin now spoke up, actually glad of the interruption. "Johann is getting impatient downstairs. And who would have the courage to fall out with such a powerful authority!"

"No, no," Schmidt replied. "Life's happiness depends on the good humor of our surroundings; a minister means little to me, but Frau Schmolke. . ."

"You've hit the mark as usual, my dear friend."

And with these words the Kommerzienrätin rose and gave Corinna a kiss on the forehead while extending her hand to Wilibald. "With us, my dear Professor, things will stay the same, come what may." And with that she left the room, accompanied to the hallway and the street by Corinna.

"Come what may," Wilibald repeated when he was alone. "Wonderful phrase of fashion, and it's already found its way to the Villa Treibel. . . . Actually my friend Jenny is just as she was forty years ago when she would toss her chestnut

curls. Even then she loved the sentimental, but always second
to her preference for flirting and whipped cream. So now
she has become plump and almost educated, or in any case
what one tends to call educated, and Adolar Krola performs
arias from *Lohengrin* and *Tannhäuser* for her. At least I
imagine that those are her favorite operas. Oh, her mother, the
good Frau Bürstenbinder, who always knew how to dress up
the little doll so nicely over there in the orange store, she had
certainly reckoned quite correctly in her woman's wisdom.
Now the little doll is a Kommerzienrätin and can afford
everything—even the ideal, and even 'come what may.' A
paragon of a bourgeoise."

And with that he stepped to the window, raised the blinds
a bit and saw Corinna shut the carriage door after the Kommerzienrätin had seated herself. Another exchange of greetings
in which the companion took part with a sweet-sour mien,
and the horses pulled out and slowly trotted towards the
Spree end of the street, since it was too difficult to turn
around in the narrow Adlerstrasse.

When Corinna was back upstairs she said: "You don't object, do you, Papa? I've been invited to dinner at the Treibels'
tomorrow. Marcell will be there too, and a young Englishman
whose name is really Nelson."

"I—object? God forbid. How could I object when a person
wants some enjoyment! I assume you'll enjoy yourself."

"Certainly I'll enjoy myself. It's something different for a
change. What Distelkamp says, and Rindfleisch and that little
Friedeberg, all that I already know by heart. But what Nelson
—imagine, Nelson—will say, I have no idea."

"Probably nothing very intelligent."

"That doesn't matter. I sometimes yearn for something un-
intelligent."

"There you're right, Corinna."

Chapter Two

THE Treibel villa was situated on a large property that extended spaciously from the Köpenick Strasse to the Spree. Here in the immediate vicinity of the river there had once been only factory buildings in which every year uncounted tons of potassium ferrocyanide, and later, as the factory expanded, not much smaller quantities of Berlin blue dye[1] had been produced. But after the war of 1870, as billions poured into the country and the newly-founded empire began to dominate the views of even the soberest heads, Kommerzienrat Treibel found his house in the Old Jakobstrasse no longer suited to his times nor his rank—though it was supposed to have been the work of Gontard, and according to some, even that of Knobelsdorff.[2] He therefore built himself a fashionable villa with a small frontyard and a parklike backyard on his factory property. The house was built with an elevated first floor, yet because of its low windows it gave the impression of a mezzanine rather than a *bel étage*.[3] Here Treibel had lived for sixteen years and still couldn't understand how he had been able to endure it for such a long time in the

Old Jakobstrasse, unfashionable and without any fresh air, just for the sake of a presumptive Frederickan architect. These were feelings more than shared by his wife. Although the closeness of the factory, when the wind was unfavorable, could bring a good deal of unpleasantness with it, the north wind, which drove the smoke fumes over, was notoriously rare, and one didn't after all have to give parties during a norther. Besides, Treibel had the factory chimneys built up higher every year and thereby removed the initial nuisance more and more.

The dinner had been set for six o'clock, but even an hour earlier one could see carts with round and square baskets from the caterer Huster[4] stop in front of the lattice entrance. The Kommerzienrätin, already in full toilette, observed all these preparations from the window of her boudoir and again took offense, not without a certain justification:

"If only Treibel hadn't neglected seeing to a side entrance! If he'd only bought a four-foot-wide piece of ground from the neighboring property, we would have had an entrance for people like that. Now every kitchen boy marches through the front yard, right toward our house, like an invited guest. That looks ridiculous and pretentious, as if the whole Köpenick Strasse were meant to know the Treibels are giving a dinner today. Besides, it's unwise to nurture people's envy and their Socialist[5] inclinations so uselessly."

She told herself this quite earnestly, but she was one of those fortunate individuals who take very little to heart for long, and so she turned from the window back to her toilette table to arrange a few things and to question the mirror whether she would be able to hold her own beside her Hamburg daughter-in-law. Helene, of course, was only half as old, why hardly that, but the Kommerzienrätin knew quite well that years meant nothing and that conversation and the expression of the eyes and particularly "matters of form," in more than one sense, were normally the decisive factor. And in this the Kommerzienrätin, already pressing the bounds of *embonpoint*,[6] was unconditionally superior to her daughter-in-law.

In the room corresponding to the boudoir at the other end of the front hall Kommerzienrat Treibel meanwhile sat and read the *Berliner Tageblatt*.[7] It happpened to be an issue containing the humor supplement, the "Ulk." Amused, he gazed at the end picture and then read a few of Nunne's philosophical observations.

"Excellent. . . very good. . . . But I'll still have to put this section aside or at least put the *Deutsches Tageblatt*[8] over it. Otherwise I think Vogelsang will give me up altogether. And the way things stand, I can no longer do without him, even to the point of having to invite him for dinner today. Odd group anyway! First this Mr. Nelson whom Helene has passed on to us because her girls are once again at the ironing board, and on top of Nelson this Vogelsang, this retired second lieutenant and *agent provocateur* in election matters. He understands his *métier*, I'm told everywhere, and I have to believe it. In any case, one thing seems certain to me—once he's seen me through in Teupitz-Zossen[9] and on the banks of the Wendish Spree, he'll see me through here too. And that's the main thing. Because in the end the main point is that, when the time has come, I will have shoved aside Singer[10] or somebody else of that color in Berlin itself. After the oratorical trial at Buggenhagen's[11] the other day a victory is very well possible, and so I've got to keep him warm. He's got a speechifying mechanism I could envy him for even though I wasn't exactly born and raised in a Trappist monastery myself. But next to Vogelsang? Zero. And it can't be any other way, because when you look closely the fellow has only three tunes in that organ of his and grinds them out one after another, and when he's finished with them he begins over again. That's the way it is with him, and that's where his power is. *Gutta cavat lapidem*[12]

—Wilibald Schmidt would be happy if he heard me quote like that, assuming that it's right. Or maybe the other way around —if there are three mistakes in it he'd be even more amused; scholars are like that. . . .

"Vogelsang, I've got to admit, has one other thing that's more important than that eternal repetition—he has faith in himself, and he's actually a genuine fanatic. Wonder if fanaticism is always like that? Seems very likely to me. A moderately intelligent individual just can't be fanatical. Anybody who believes in a particular means and a cause is a *poveretto*[13] in any case, and if he himself is the object of that faith, then he's a public danger and ready for the madhouse. And that happens to be the exact character of the man in whose honor— if I disregard Mr. Nelson—I'm giving my dinner today. And it's for him that I've invited two noble ladies. Blue blood like theirs is virtually unavailable here on Köpenick Strasse and I had to send off to Berlin West[14]—why, for half of it even to Charlottenburg—to get it here. Oh, Vogelsang! Really, the fellow's just abominable. But what one won't do as a citizen and a patriot!"

And with that Treibel looked down at the little chain suspended between his buttonholes with the three miniature medals, of which a Rumanian one was the most valuable, and he sighed while laughing at the same time.

"Rumania, before that Moldavia and Wallachia. It's really not enough for me."

The first carriage that drove up was that of his elder son, Otto, who had established himself independently. At the very end of Köpenick Strasse between the pontoon storage building that belonged to the Engineers' barracks and the Silesian Gate he had built a lumberyard, naturally of a more dignified sort: he dealt in dyewoods, Pernambuco and Campeachy. And for about eight years now he had been married. The very moment the carriage stopped he assisted his wife in getting out, obligingly offered her his arm, and after crossing the yard strode up the garden steps that led to the verandalike portico of his father's villa. The old Kommerzienrat was already standing in the door and received the children with his habitual joviality. From the adjoining room, separated from the reception hall only by curtains, the Kommerzienrätin now also appeared and proffered her cheek to her daughter-in-law while her son Otto kissed her hand.

"Good that you've come, Helene," she said with a happy mixture of pleasantness and irony which she was master of when she wanted to be. "I was beginning to be afraid you would find yourself prevented from coming."

"Oh, Mama, forgive me—it wasn't just because of ironing day. Our cook has given notice for the first of June, and when they're no longer interested they become unreliable; and there's no relying on Elizabeth at all anymore. She's inept to the point of indecency and always holds the bowls so closely over people's shoulders, especially the gentlemen's, as if she wanted to rest on them. . . ."

The Kommerzienrätin smiled, halfway placated, because she liked to hear that sort of thing.

"And to put it off," Helene continued, "was out of the question. Mr. Nelson, as you know, is leaving tomorrow evening. A charming young man, incidentally; you'll like him. A little abrupt and taciturn, perhaps because he doesn't quite know whether he should express himself in German or English; but what he says is always good and shows perfectly the composure and good breeding most English have. And always immaculate. I've never seen cuffs like that, and it almost depresses me when I then look at what my poor Otto has to make do with, just because even with the best intentions one can't have the proper help. And as clean as his cuffs are, everything else on him, I mean on Mr. Nelson, is too, even his head and his hair. It's probably because he brushes it with honey-water or maybe it's just from shampooing."

The person so creditably characterized was the next one who appeared at the garden gate. And even at that distance he rather astonished the Kommerzienrätin. After her daughter-in-law's description she had expected a marvel of elegance, but coming along instead was a fellow who, except for the cuffs lauded by the younger Frau Treibel, provoked criticism in virtually every respect. With an unbrushed top hat on the back of his head and a yellow and brown checked travelling suit hanging on him, he climbed up the garden stairs, swaying from left to right, and greeted everyone with the familiar English mixture of self-confidence and bashfulness. Otto came towards him to introduce him to his parents.

"Mr. Nelson from Liverpool—the very same, dear Papa, with whom I. . ."

"Ah, Mr. Nelson, a pleasure. My son still talks about his happy days in Liverpool and of that excursion he made with you to Dublin and, if I'm not mistaken, to Glasgow as well. That's almost nine years ago now; you must have been very young then."

"Oh, not very young, Mr. Treibel—about sixteen. . ."

"Well, I would have thought sixteen. . ."

"Oh, sixteen, not very young—not for us."

These assurances sounded all the funnier since even now Mr. Nelson seemed like a boy. But there was no time for further observations on that because just now a second-class cab drove up, and a tall, gaunt man in uniform got out. He seemed to be having a dispute with the driver, but he did not for a moment lose his enviably sure bearing; and now he turned about and shut the garden gate. He was in full uniform, but even before one could note the rank insignia on his shoulders, it was certain to anyone equipped with the least bit of a military eye that he had been out of the service for at least thirty years. For the pomp with which he approached was more the stiffness of an old peat or salt inspector of some rare sect than the correct bearing of an officer. Everything appeared more or less mechanical, and the mustache, which ended in two twirled points, not only seemed dyed—which it of course was—but also seemed glued on. And the same held for the goatee. On top of that, the lower portion of his face lay in the shadows of two protruding cheekbones. With the calmness that characterized his whole being he now mounted the front steps and walked up to the Kommerzienrätin.

"You have commanded, Madam. . ."

"Delighted, Lieutenant. . ."

In the meantime old Treibel had also joined them and said: "My dear Vogelsang, allow me to acquaint you with the other guests: my son Otto you know, but not his wife, my dear daughter-in-law—from Hamburg, as you'll easily recognize. . . . And here,"—and with that he stepped up to Mr. Nelson who was talking leisurely and without any consideration for the rest of the company to Leopold Treibel, who had also appeared meanwhile—"and here, a dear young friend of the family, Mr. Nelson from Liverpool."

Vogelsang started at the word "Nelson" and seemed to believe for a moment—because he had never been able to rid himself completely of the fear of being teased—that they were playing a joke on him. But everyone's calm expression soon told him otherwise, and he therefore politely bowed and said to the young Englishman: "Nelson. A great name. Pleased to meet you, Mr. Nelson."

The latter rather unceremoniously laughed at the old and stiffly-poised lieutenant, since he had never encountered quite such a funny person. That he appeared equally funny in his own way would never have occurred to him. Vogelsang bit his lip, and with this encounter confirmed his long-nurtured conviction of the impertinence of the English nation. But now the time had come when the appearance of more and more new arrivals supplanted every other consideration and soon let the peculiarities of an Englishman be forgotten.

A few of the invited factory owners from Köpenick Strasse,

coming in their carriages with the tops down, quickly and almost forcefully displaced Vogelsang's hovering cab; then Corinna came along with her cousin Marcell Wedderkopp (both on foot). Finally Johann, the Kommerzienrat's driver, drove up in the landau with the blue satin interior—the same in which the Kommerzienrätin had made her visit to Corinna the day before—and from it two elderly ladies alighted, whom Johann treated with very particular and almost surprising respect. But this was to be explained very simply by the fact that, right at the beginning of this important acquaintance, which now went back two and a half years, Treibel had said to his driver: "Johann, once and for all, with the ladies you always keep your hat in your hand. The rest, you know what I mean, is *my* business." After that there was no question about Johann's good manners. Treibel now came out to the middle of the front yard to meet both ladies, and after a lively exchange of compliments in which the Kommerzienrätin also participated, everyone went up the garden stairs and stepped from the veranda into the large reception room, which until then almost no one had entered because the pleasant weather had invited lingering out of doors. Almost all knew one another from earlier Treibel dinners; only Vogelsang and Nelson were strangers, which caused the partial act of introduction to be repeated.

"May I," Treibel addressed the two elderly ladies who had been the last to come, "may I acquaint you with two gentlemen who are giving me the honor of their company for the first time today: Lieutenant Vogelsang, the president of our election committee, and Mr. Nelson from Liverpool." They bowed to one another. Then Treibel took Vogelsang's arm and whispered to him to give him a bit of an orientation: "Two ladies from the Court; the corpulent one, Frau Majorin von Ziegenhals; the not so corpulent one—you'll agree— Fräulein Edwine von Bomst."

"Strange," said Vogelsang. "To tell the truth, I would have . . ."

"You would have considered it expedient for them to trade names.[15] There you've hit it Vogelsang. And I'm pleased that you have an eye for such things. That's evidence of that old lieutenant's blood. Yes, that Ziegenhals. She must have a yard's expanse of chest, and all sorts of speculation on it can be— and probably has been—indulged in at one time. For the rest, it's droll contradictions like that that brighten one's life. A man with a name like Klopstock was a poet, and another whom I knew personally was named Griepenkerl. . . . It so happens that both ladies can provide us salutary services."

"How so? How?"

"The Ziegenhals woman is a cousin of the county assessor of Zossen, and a brother of the Bomst woman married a pastor's daughter from the Storkow region. Something of a *mésalliance*, but we have to ignore it because it's advantageous for us. Like Bismarck, one should always have a dozen irons in the fire. . . . Ah, thank God. Johann has changed jackets and is giving the signal. High time. . . . Waiting for a quarter of an hour is all right; but ten minutes more than that is too much. . . . Without even listening too anxiously I can hear 'the hart panting after water.'[16] Please, Vogelsang, escort my wife. . . . Corinna, dear, take possession of Nelson. . . Victory and Westminster Abbey:[17] getting on board is up to you this time. And now, ladies. May I take your arm, Frau Majorin, and yours, my dear Fräulein?"

And with Frau Ziegenhals on his right and Fräulein Bomst on his left arm, he went towards the folding doors which had opened with a certain slow ceremoniousness.

Chapter Three

THE dining room corresponded exactly to the reception room in the front and it had a view of the large, park-like backyard with a splashing fountain very near the house. A little ball was going up and down on the water-jet, and on the crossbar of a stand off to one side a cockatoo sat and glanced, with that familiar profound eye, alternately at the water-jet with the bouncing ball and into the dining room where the upper sash window had been let down a bit for ventilation. The chandelier was already lighted but the little flames were turned down low and were hardly visible in the afternoon sun; they were leading this weak preexistence only because the Kommerzienrat did not enjoy, to use his own words, "having his dinner atmosphere disturbed by manipulations of the lamplighter's sort." Nor could the little puffs audible when the lamps were lighted, which he liked to call a "moderated gun salute," alter his attitude towards the matter. The dining room itself was of a nice simplicity: yellow stucco inlaid with a few reliefs—charming pieces by Professor Franz.[1] When the decor here had first been discussed, the

Kommerzienrätin had suggested Reinhold Begas, but this had been rejected by Treibel as exceeding his means.

"That's for the day when we'll have become General-konsuls. . ."

"A day that'll never come," Jenny had answered.

"Certainly, Jenny, certainly; Teupitz-Zossen is the first step up there." He knew how dubiously his wife viewed his electioneering activities and all the hopes attached to them, and he therefore liked to intimate that he fully expected branching out into politics to produce golden fruits for her female vanity.

Outside, the water-jet continued its play. Inside, in the dining room, old Treibel sat at the center of the table, which today displayed a little mosaic of flowers instead of the usual giant vases of lilac and laburnum; beside him sat the two noble ladies, and across from him sat his wife between Lieutenant Vogelsang and the former opera singer Adolar Krola. For fifteen years now Krola had been a friend of the family, a position to which he was entitled by three equally valuable assets: his good appearance, his good voice, and his good finances—for just shortly before his retirement from the stage he had married a millionaire's daughter. And it was generally admitted that he was a man of great charm which was as great an advantage over many of his former colleagues as was his financial security.

Frau Jenny presented herself in full glory, and in her appearance the very last trace of her origins in the little shop on Adlerstrasse had been obliterated. Everything seemed rich and elegant; but the lace on her violet brocade dress, it must be said, did not do it alone, nor the little diamond earrings that flashed with every movement; no, more than anything else it was the sure calmness with which she sat enthroned among her guests that lent her a certain refinement. Not a trace of agitation—for which there really wasn't any occasion—revealed itself. She knew what competent servants signified in a house that was rich and attuned to display, and therefore anyone who was good in this regard was retained by means of high wages and good treatment. In consequence everything went like clockwork, today too, and Jenny's glance ruled the whole affair—helped not a little by the air cushion underneath her that gave her a dominating position. And in her feeling of security she was charm itself. With no fear that something would go awry in the household she was able to devote herself to the duties of pleasant conversation, and because she might have found it disturbing not to have had a single intimate word—discounting the brief moment of greeting—with the noble ladies, she now addressed herself to Fräulein Bomst across the table and, full of apparent or perhaps even real solicitude, asked her:

"My dear Mademoiselle, have you heard anything about the little Princess Anisette recently? I've always had a lively interest in this young princess, for that matter in the whole House. She is supposed to be happily married. I like so much to hear of happy marriages, especially in the higher spheres of society, and I'd like to be permitted to remark that it seems to me a foolish assumption that marital bliss is impossible in these high circles."

"Certainly," interrupted Treibel playfully, "such a renunciation of the most sublime imaginable. . ."

"My dear Treibel," the Rätin continued, "I was addressing Fräulein von Bomst, and with all due respect for your general knowledge of other things, she seems to me considerably more competent in everything pertaining to the Court."

"No doubt," Treibel said. And Fräulein Bomst, who had followed this conjugal intermezzo with visible relish, now spoke about the Princess who was just like her grandmother —she had the same complexion and especially the same good disposition. That, she could safely say, no one knew better than she, because she had enjoyed the advantage of beginning her life at Court under the eye of that noble departed lady who had truly been an angel; and it was as a result of having had this opportunity that she had properly comprehended that naturalness was not only best but also most refined.

"Yes," Treibel said, "the best and the most refined. There, Jenny, you can hear it from a party that you—pardon me, Mademoiselle—yourself just described as the most competent."

Now Frau Ziegenhals also joined in, and the conversational interest of the Kommerzienrätin, who like all native Berlin women was full of enthusiasm for the Court and the Princesses, seemed to turn more and more toward the two ladies across the table. But a gentle wink from Treibel gave her to understand that there were other people at the table too, and that it was customary here, as far as conversation was concerned, to pay attention to one's neighbors on the left and right rather than on the other side. The Kommerzienrätin was more than a little dismayed when she perceived how right Treibel was with his quiet and half-facetious reproach. She had meant to make up for earlier neglect and had thereby fallen into new, weightier negligence. The neighbor on her left, Krola—well, that might be all right, he was a friend of the family, and harmless and considerate by nature. But Vogelsang! It suddenly came to her that during her conversation about princesses she had kept feeling something like a penetrating stare. Yes, that had been Vogelsang; Vogelsang, this terrible man, this Mephisto with a cock's feather and a limp—even if neither could really be seen. He was loathsome to her, but still she had to speak with him; it was high time.

"Lieutenant, I've heard about your intended trip through our fine Mark Brandenburg; you plan to go as far as the banks of the Wendish Spree, why even beyond that. A most interesting area, as Treibel tells me, with all sorts of Wendish gods, who to this very day supposedly manifest themselves in the dark minds of the populace."

"Not so far as I know, Madam."

"As they seemed to do in the little town of Storkow, for example, whose Burgomaster was, if my information is right, Burgomaster Tschech, that rightist political fanatic who shot at King Frederick William IV without any regard whatsoever for the Queen next to him. It's been a long time, but I remember the details of it as if it had been yesterday, and I also remember the peculiar song composed on this incident."[2]

"Yes," Vogelsang said, "a pitiful street ballad completely under the spell of the frivolous spirit that dominated the poetry of those days. Anything that pretends otherwise in that poetry, and particularly in the poem under discussion, is just sham, falsehood, and deceit. 'He would by a hair have shot our royal pair!' There you have the whole perfidy. That was supposed to sound loyal, perhaps even supposed to cover the retreat, but it is more despicable and disgraceful than anything else that mendacious age produced, not excepting the greatest sinner in this field. I mean Herwegh, of course, Georg Herwegh."[3]

"Oh, Lieutenant, there you've touched—even if you didn't mean to—a very sensitive spot with me. Because in the middle of the forties, when I was confirmed, Herwegh was my favorite poet. I was always delighted, because I felt very much a Protestant, when he brought out his 'Curses upon Rome'— you might agree with me there. And I read another poem, in which he called on us to tear the crosses out of the earth, with almost the same pleasure. Of course I have to admit that it was not the proper reading for a girl in confirmation classes. But my mother said: 'Go ahead and read it, Jenny; the King has read it too, and Herwegh even visited him in Charlottenburg, and the better classes are all reading it.' My mother— and I'll thank her forever for it—was always for the better classes. And every mother should be, because it determines the course of our lives. What is base and low can't get at us then and is left behind."

Vogelsang knit his brow, and everyone who before this

had just barely perceived the Mephistophelian in him would
have had to look for his cloven hoof after that grimace. But
the Kommerzienrätin continued:

"Other than that it won't be difficult for me to admit that
the patriotic principles this great poet preached may very well
have been highly disputable. Even though what is found in
the mainstream isn't always the right thing either. . ."

Proud of definitely not belonging in the mainstream, Vogelsang now nodded in agreement.

"But let's leave politics, Lieutenant. I'll abandon Herwegh
as a political poet to you, since politics was just a drop of
alien blood in his veins. Yet he remains great where he is
purely a poet. Do you recall, 'I want to pass on like the red
sunset, like the day with its last glow. . .' "

" '. . . bleeding away in the lap of eternity.' Yes, my dear
lady, I know that; in those days I prayed along with that too.
But when it counted, the one person who decidedly didn't
want to 'bleed away' was the Lord Poet himself. And that's
the way it will always be. That's what comes from these hol-
low, empty words and this rhyme hunting. Believe me, Frau
Rätin, those are notions that have been overcome. The world
belongs to prose."

"Everyone according to his own taste, Lieutenant Vogelsang," said Jenny, somewhat hurt by these words. "If you're
going to prefer prose, I can't keep you from it. But for me
the poetic world counts, and the forms in which the poetic
traditionally finds expression are especially important to me.
That alone is worth living for. Everything is vain, but the
vainest is what the whole world pursues so greedily: external
possessions, fortune, gold. 'Gold is only a chimera.' There you
have the pronouncement of a great man and artist who, to
judge by his fine fortune—I'm talking about Meyerbeer[4]—
was surely in a position to distinguish between the eternal
and the transitory. For my own part, I shall remain faithful
to the ideal and will never abandon it. And the purest form

of the ideal I find in a lyric, especially in the lyric that's sung. For music lifts it into an even higher sphere. Isn't that right, my dear Krola?"

Krola smiled with good-natured uneasiness because as a tenor and a millionaire he was caught right in the middle. But finally he took his friend's hand and said:

"Jenny, when ever have you not been right?"

The Kommerzienrat had meanwhile turned wholly to the Majorin von Ziegenhals whose days at Court went even further back than those of Fräulein Bomst. But to Treibel this was of course immaterial; for however much of a certain polish the appearance of the ladies-in-waiting, though retired, lent to his party, he himself was above such considerations, a fact which the two ladies rather reckoned to his credit than otherwise. Certainly Frau Ziegenhals, who was exceedingly inclined towards the pleasures of the table, took nothing in her Kommerzienrat friend amiss; least of all was she annoyed when he touched upon, besides questions of birth and nobility, all sorts of problems of morality which, as a born Berliner, he felt a particular calling to solve. The Majorin would then tap him with her finger and whisper something to him that would have been risqué forty years earlier, but *now* (both constantly paraded their age) would only cause amusement. Most of the time it would be a harmless saying from a book of familiar quotations or other winged· words to which only the tone would—very decidedly—lend an erotic character.

"Tell me, *cher* Treibel," Frau Ziegenhals began, "where did you get that ghost over there? He seems to be a pre-forty-eighter; that was the era of peculiar lieutenants; but this one is overdoing it. A caricature throughout. Do you still remember a picture from those times that showed Don Quixote with a long lance and thick books all around him? That's him all over."

Treibel ran his left index finger back and forth along the inner edge of his cravat and said: "Yes, where did I get him, my dear Madam. Well, in any case, more from heeding necessity than my own impulse. His social merits are no doubt slight and his human ones are probably on the same level. But he's a politician."

"That's impossible. He could stand only as a sign of warning against those principles that have the misfortune of being represented by him. Anyway, Kommerzienrat, why are you straying into politics? What will be the result? You'll ruin your good character, your good morals, and your good society. I hear you're going to be a candidate for Teupitz-Zossen. Fine, for all I care—but what for? Why not leave things be? You have a charming wife, with feeling and a highly poetic sensibility, and you have a villa like this, in which we're now eating a *ragoût fin* that defies comparison, and outside in the garden you have a fountain and a cockatoo —for which I could envy you because mine, a green one, is just now losing his feathers and looks like a bad day. What do you want with politics? What do you want with Teupitz-Zossen? Why, even more—to give you full proof of my complete lack of bias—what do you want with conservatism? You're an industrialist and live on Köpenick Strasse. Why don't you just leave this area to Singer or Ludwig Loewe[5] or whoever else happens to have the advantage here? For every position in life there are also certain corresponding political principles. Junkers are agrarian, professors are in nationalist center parties, and industrialists are progressive. Why don't you be a progressive? What do you want with the Order of the Crown? If I were in your place, I would launch into city politics and contend for the burgher crown."

Treibel, who was usually restless when someone spoke for a long time—an indulgence he allowed only himself—had, however, listened attentively this time, but before replying signalled a servant to offer the lady another glass of chablis. She took some more, as did he, and then they clinked glasses and he said:

"To good friendship and another ten years like today! But that about progressivism and the burgher crown—what can I say there, my dear Madam? You know that our sort calculates and calculates and never gets beyond the rule of three, beyond the old statement, 'If that and that make this much, how much do that and that make?' And you see, my friend and benefactress, according to that same statement I've also made calculations on the progressive and the conservative and have found out that conservatism—I don't want to say pays me more, that would be wrong of course—suits me better and is more becoming to me. Particularly since I've become a Kommerzienrat, which is a title with a rather fragmentary character that naturally still looks toward some further fulfillment."

"Ah, I understand."

"Now you see, *l'appétit vient en mangeant*,[6] and whoever says A must say B. But aside from that, I perceive the wise man's life task primarily in the achievement of so-called harmony, and this harmony, the way things are—or perhaps I should say the way the signs point—as much as precludes the progressive burgher crown in my particular case."

"Are you saying that in all seriousness?"

"Yes, my dear Madam. Factories in general incline toward the burgher crown, but particular factories—and that's expressly what mine is—demonstrate the exception. Your look demands proofs. Now then, I'll give it a try. I ask you if you can imagine a commercial gardener, let's say in the Lichtenberger or Rummelsburger area, who raises cornflowers in quantity—cornflowers, this symbol of royal Prussian sentiment—and who is at the same time an incendiary and dynamiter? You're shaking your head and thereby confirming my 'no.' And now I ask you further, what are all the cornflowers in the world to one Berlin blue factory? In Berlin blue you have Prussia symbolized to the highest power, so to speak, and the more certain and indisputable that is, the more indispensable is it for me to stay on the ground of conservatism. The most natural thing in my particular case is to aim for an improvement on my status as a Kommerzienrat . . . at any rate, for more than the burgher crown."

Frau Ziegenhals appeared conquered and laughed, while Krola, who had listened with one ear, nodded in agreement.

Thus went the conversation at the center of the table; but it took an even more cheerful course at the lower end of it where the young Frau Treibel and Corinna sat opposite one another, the young wife between Marcell Wedderkopp and the junior civil servant Enghans, Corinna between Mr. Nelson and Leopold Treibel, the younger son of the house. Placed at the foot of the table with her back to the wide garden window sat the companion, Fräulein Honig, whose sharp features appeared to protest her name. The more she tried to smile, the more visible became her consuming envy, which was directed against the pretty Hamburg woman on her right and almost more expressly against Corinna on the left, who, though her partial colleague, nevertheless behaved with such assurance as if she were the Majorin von Ziegenhals or at the very least Fräulein von Bomst.

The young Frau Treibel looked very good—blond, bright, calm. Both neighbors paid court to her, though Marcell's was only an affected ardor since he was actually observing Corinna who for one reason or another seemed resolved on the conquest of the young Englishman. During this coquettish procedure she spoke so vivaciously, so loudly, that it seemed she was concerned that every word should be heard by the whole company and particularly by her cousin Marcell.

"You have such a fine name," she addressed Mr. Nelson, "so fine and famous that I would like to ask if you've never had the desire. . ."

"Oh yes, yes. . ."

". . . to give up forever the Pernambuco and Campeachy wood business—in which you too are engaged so far as I know? I feel distinctly that if my name were Nelson I wouldn't have a moment's rest until I'd also fought my battle of the Nile. Naturally you know the details of the battle. . . ."

"Oh, to be sure."

"Well, then I've finally come to the right source—because hereabouts no one knows anything definite about it. Tell me about the plan, Mr. Nelson, the disposition of the battle? I read the description of it some time ago in Walter Scott and since then I've always been in doubt as to what turned the scales, whether it was more a brilliant disposition of forces or more a heroic courage. . . ."

"I should rather think, a heroical courage . . . British oaks and British hearts. . . ."

"I'm pleased to see this question settled by you and in a manner that corresponds to my sympathies, because I favor the heroic since it's so rare. But I would also like to assume that the brilliant command. . ."

"Certainly, Miss Corinna. No doubt. . . England expects that every man will do his duty. . . ."

"Yes, those were glorious words, which until today, by the way, I believed had been spoken at Trafalgar. But why not at Aboukir too? A good thing can always be said twice. And then. . . one battle is after all like the next, particularly sea battles—a bang, a column of fire, and everything goes up in the air. It must be grand and fascinating for all those who can watch, a wonderful sight."

"Oh, splendid. . . ."

"Yes, Leopold," Corinna continued, suddenly turning to her other neighbor, "there you sit now and smile. And why do you smile? Because you want to hide your embarrassment behind that smile. You just don't have that 'heroical courage' which dear Mr. Nelson professed so unconditionally. Quite the contrary. You have withdrawn from your father's factory,

which still represents in some sense—if only commercially—
the blood and iron theory. . . why a little while ago it sounded
to me as if your Papa had been telling Frau Majorin von
Ziegenhals about these things. . . as I was saying, you've withdrawn from the potassium prussiate business, where you should
have stayed, into the lumber business of your brother Otto.
That wasn't good, even if it is Pernambuco wood. You see
my cousin Marcell over there, he swears every day when he's
fidgeting with his dumbbells that as far as heroism is concerned it's a matter of gymnastics and the horizontal bar, and
that Father Jahn[7] is certainly more important than Nelson."

Half in earnest and half in fun Marcell shook his finger at
Corinna and said: "Cousin, don't forget that a representative
of another nation is sitting by your side and that it is more or
less your duty to set a good example of German womanhood."

"Oh, no, no," Mr. Nelson said, continuing in his awkward
mixture of English and German, "nothing about womanhood;
always quick and clever. . . that's what we love in German
women. Nothing about womanhood. Fräulein Corinna is
quite on the right way."

"There you have it, Marcell. Mr. Nelson, for whom you've
interceded so carefully so that he won't take any false impres-
sions along into his seagirt Albion, why Mr. Nelson is leaving
you in the lurch, and Frau Treibel, I imagine, will leave you
in the lurch too and Herr Enghans too and my friend Leopold
too. And so my courage is up and there remains only Fräulein Honig. . ."

The latter bowed and said: "I'm accustomed to going along
with the majority," and the tone of her agreement contained
all her embitterment.

"But nevertheless I'll keep my cousin's admonition in mind,"
Corinna continued. "I'm a little pert, Mr. Nelson, and from
a chatty family besides. . . ."

"Just what I like, Miss Corinna. 'Chatty people, good people,' as we say in England."

"And I say the same, Mr. Nelson. Can you imagine a constantly chatting criminal?"

"Oh, no, certainly not. . ."

"And to show that in spite of my eternal prattling I still have a feminine nature and am a genuine German, Mr. Nelson should know that I can cook, sew, and iron besides, and that I've learned invisible weaving in the Lette Institute. Yes, Mr. Nelson, that's how it is with me. I'm completely German and completely feminine and that just leaves the question—do you know the Lette Institute and do you know what invisible weaving is?"

"No, Fräulein Corinna, neither the one nor the other."

"Now you see, dear Mr. Nelson, the Lette Institute is an institution or a club or a school for feminine handicrafts.[8] After the English model, I think, which would be a special merit."

"Not at all; German schools are always to be preferred."

"Who knows; I wouldn't want to put it that sharply. But let's drop that to occupy ourselves with something far more important, with the question of invisible weaving. First of all, would you please say the word for me. . ."

Mr. Nelson smiled good-naturedly.

"Well, I see, it's difficult for you. But these difficulties are nothing against those of invisible weaving itself. You see, here is my friend Leopold Treibel and he's wearing, as you see, a faultless coat with a double row of buttons, and really buttoned up too, as is proper for a gentleman and a son of a Berlin Kommerzienrat. And I would estimate that the coat cost at least a hundred marks."

"Overestimated."

"Who knows. You forget, Marcell, that there are different scales in this area too, one for an assistant master and one for a Kommerzienrat. But let's drop the question of price. In any case, it's a fine coat, first-class. And now when we get up, Mr. Nelson, and the cigars are passed around—I imagine you do smoke—I'll ask you for your cigar and I'll burn a hole into my friend Leopold Treibel's coat, right here where his heart is, and then I'll take the coat home in a cab, and tomorrow at the same time we'll all gather again in the garden and place chairs around the basin of the fountain, as for a performance. And then I'll make my entrance like an artist—which I indeed am—and will let the coat make the rounds, and if you, dear Mr. Nelson, are still able to find the spot where the hole was, then I'll give you a kiss and will follow you to Liverpool as your slave. But it won't come to that. Should I say, unfortunately? I've won two medals for invisible weaving, and you'll surely not find the spot. . ."

"Oh, I will, no doubt, I will find it," Mr. Nelson replied with shining eyes. And because he wanted to express his constantly growing admiration—fitting or not—he concluded with a rhapsodic series of exclamations about Berlin women, followed by the frequently repeated assurance that they were 'deucedly clever.'

Leopold and the young civil servant joined with him in this praise, and even Fräulein Honig smiled, perhaps because as a native herself she felt flattered too. Only in the young Frau Treibel's eye was there a trace of resentment at seeing a Berlin woman and a little professor's daughter celebrated in this fashion. Cousin Marcell, too, as much as he agreed, wasn't completely pleased, because he felt that his cousin had no need to put on such an act; to him she seemed too good for the role she played. Corinna herself saw quite clearly what was going on in his mind and would have taken pleasure in teasing him if at that very moment—the ice cream was already going around—the Kommerzienrat had not tapped his glass and risen from his seat to give a toast. Addressing them in English and German, he began: "Ladies and Gentlemen. . ."

"Ah, he's doing that for you," Corinna whispered to Mr. Nelson.

". . . I have let the joint of lamb come and go and have

waited until this relatively late hour to propose a toast—a
novelty which in this moment confronts me with the question
of what should be avoided more, a red and white ice cream
dessert melting or a joint of lamb solidifying. . . ."

"Oh, wonderfully good. . ."

"But however that may be, there is in any case at present
only one expedient for keeping an evil that may have already
been done to a minimum: Brevity! Permit me then, Ladies and
Gentlemen, collectively, to give you my thanks for coming
here, and allow me further, and particularly in view of two
dear guests whom I have the honor to see here for the first
time today, to express my toast in the almost sanctified British
formula 'on our army and navy,' which we have the good
fortune to see represented here at this table: on the one hand"
—he bowed towards Vogelsang—"by profession and position
in life; on the other"—bow to Nelson—"by a world-famous
hero's name. Once more then: 'our army and navy.' Long
live Lieutenant Vogelsang, long live Mr. Nelson."

The toast met with universal approval, and Mr. Nelson, in
some nervous anxiety, wanted to speak immediately in order
to return thanks. But Corinna held him back, saying that
Vogelsang was the older and would perhaps express thanks
for him too.

"Oh, no, no, Fräulein Corinna, not he. . . not such an ugly
old fellow. . . please, look at him," and the fidgety namesake
of a hero made repeated attempts to get up from his seat and
to speak. But Vogelsang really did get ahead of him, and
after he had wiped his beard with his napkin and had nerv-
ously unbuttoned his tunic and then buttoned it up again, he
began with a dignity that was not without a tinge of the
comic:

"Gentlemen! Our kind host has toasted the army, and he
has connected my name with the army. Yes, Gentlemen, I
am a soldier. . ."

"Oh, for shame!" Mr. Nelson muttered, sincerely disgusted

at his repeating 'gentlemen' and at the same time ignoring all the ladies present, "oh, for shame," and a tittering could be heard from all sides which continued until the more and more darkly glowering eye of the speaker had reestablished a truly churchlike silence. Only then did he continue:

"Yes, Gentlemen, I *am* a soldier. . . but more important than that, I am also a warrior in the service of an idea. There are two great powers that I serve: the people and the King. Everything else is disturbing, damaging, and confusing. England's aristocracy, which conflicts with me personally, not to mention with my principles, illustrates such damage and confusion; I detest intermediate levels and the feudal pyramid altogether. Those are medieval notions. I conceive of my ideal as a plateau with but a single peak, but one that towers above everything."

Here Frau von Ziegenhals exchanged glances with Treibel.

"Let everything be by the grace of the people up to the point at which the grace of God begins. And that with strictly separated powers of authority. What is common, what pertains to the masses, should be determined by the masses; what is uncommon, what is great, should be determined by the great. That is throne and crown. According to my political judgment, all that is good, all that promises improvement, lies in the establishment of a royal democracy— which, so far as I know, our Kommerzienrat also professes. And in this feeling in which we are as one, I raise my glass and ask you to drink with me to the health of our highly honored host, our *gonfaloniere*,[9] who bears our standard. Long live Kommerzienrat Treibel!"

Everyone rose to clink glasses with Vogelsang and to congratulate him on the invention of royal democracy.[10] A few could be considered sincerely captivated, particularly the word *gonfaloniere* seemed to have had its effect; others were laughing softly to themselves, and only three were truly dissatisfied: Treibel, because he did not expect much that was practical from Vogelsang's principles; the Kommerzienrätin, because the whole thing did not seem refined enough to her; and Mr. Nelson, because he had imbibed new hatred for Vogelsang out of the statement he had directed against the English aristocracy.

"Stuff and nonsense! What does he know of our aristocracy? To be sure, he doesn't belong to it! That's all."

"Well, I don't know," Corinna laughed. "Doesn't he have something of the Peer of the Realm about him?"

Imagining this, Mr. Nelson almost forgot all his anger, and now took an almond from one of the dishes on the table and was about to engage Corinna in a flirtatious little game with it when the Kommerzienrätin pushed her chair back and thereby signalled that the meal was concluded. The folding doors opened up, and in the same order in which they had gone to table they now walked back to the front room, which had meanwhile been aired, and there the gentlemen, Treibel at their head, respectfully kissed the hands of the older and some of the younger ladies.

Only Mr. Nelson abstained, because he found the Kommerzienrätin "a little pompous" and the two ladies-in-waiting "a little ridiculous," and he contented himself, as he came up to Corinna, with shaking hands vigorously.

Chapter Four

ALTHOUGH the large glass door that led to the outside stairway was standing open, it was still rather stuffy, and so the company preferred to take their coffee outdoors—some on the veranda, others in the yard itself—and those who had been neighbors at the table gathered together again and continued chatting. The conversation, richly spiced with gossip and scandal, was interrupted only when the two noble ladies took their leave of the company, and for a little while everyone looked after the landau driving up Köpenick Strasse on its way first to Frau von Ziegenhals' apartment directly by the Marschall Bridge and then on to Charlottenburg. Quartered in a wing of this palace for thirty-five years, Fräulein Bomst derived her life's happiness as well as her greatest pride from the reflection that she had breathed the same air here with His late Majesty the King, then with the Queen Widow, and lastly with the ducal family of Meiningen. All this gave her a touch of the *spirituel*—which also rather suited her figure.

Treibel, who had accompanied the ladies to the carriage

door, had meanwhile come back from the street to the veranda where the momentarily forsaken Vogelsang had maintained his place with unforfeited dignity.

"Now for a word among ourselves, Lieutenant, but not here. I think we should absent ourselves for a moment and try a very special little smoke."

With that he took him by the arm and led the happily obedient Vogelsang into the next room, his study, where the well-schooled servant, who was long familiar with this favorite moment in the dinner party habits of his master, had already set out everything: the cigar box, the liqueur case, and the carafe with ice water. But the good schooling of the servant was not limited to the pre-arrangements; at the very moment both gentlemen had taken their seats he stood before them with the tray and presented the coffee.

"That's good, Friedrich, everything else here is set up to my satisfaction too, but why don't you give us the other box there, the flat one. And then tell my son Otto I'd like him to join us. . . . All right with you, Vogelsang, isn't it? Or if you don't find Otto, then the Police Assessor, yes, better *him*, he's more in the know. Strange, everybody who's grown up in the Molkenmarkt[1] area is superior to the rest of mankind by a considerable bit. And on top of that this Goldammer has the advantage of being a genuine pastor's son, which gives all of his stories a peculiarly piquant savor."

And with that Treibel snapped open the case and said: "Cognac or Kümmel?[2] Or a bit of both?"

Vogelsang smiled and rather demonstratively pushed aside the cigar cutter and bit the tip off with his protruding teeth. Then he reached for a match. For the rest he seemed inclined to wait for what Treibel would care to begin with. And he was not kept waiting long.

"*Eh bien*, Vogelsang, how did you like the two ladies? Something special, yes? Particularly Fräulein Bomst. My wife would say *spirituel*. Well, she is transparent enough. But frankly, I prefer Frau Ziegenhals, full and firm, a capital woman—must have been a downright formidable fortress in her time. Class, temperament, and if I've heard right, her past was spent shuttling back and forth between various little courts. A Lady Milford,[3] but less sentimental. All old stories, all settled now—one might say unfortunately. During the summer she's now regularly at the Kraczinskis', in the Zossen area—where the devil have all those Polish names been coming from recently? Well, it doesn't matter, after all. In view of her acquaintance with the Kraczinskis, what would you think if I tried to make her useful for our purposes?"

"Can't lead to anything."

"Why not? She has an appropriate attitude."

"At the very least I'd have to say an inappropriate one."

"How's that?"

"She has a thoroughly one-sided attitude, and if I choose that word I'm still being chivalrous. This 'chivalrous,' by the way, is being subjected to a growing and downright horrendous abuse because I don't believe that our knights were very chivalrous, that is, chivalrous in the sense of polite and obliging. All that's historical falsification. And as for this Ziegenhals woman, whom we're supposed to make useful for our purposes, as you say, she represents the viewpoint of feudalism, of the pyramid. That she's on the side of the Court is good, and it's what connects her with us, but that is not enough. Individuals like this Majorin, and of course her noble acquaintance—whether they're of Polish or German origins— all of them more or less live in a chaos of delusions, of medieval class prejudices, which precludes our going together despite having the royal flag in common. And having this in common doesn't benefit us, it just harms us. When we shout 'Long live the King!' it's done perfectly unselfishly to secure the sovereignty of a great principle. I'll vouch for myself, and I hope that I can do the same for you. . . ."

"Certainly, Vogelsang, certainly."

"But this Ziegenhals woman—and I'm afraid, incidentally, that you may be only too right with your intimations about her defiance of morality and propriety; thank God that's at least far in the past now—this Ziegenhals and her kind, when they shout 'Long live the King' it always just means long live whoever takes care of us, our provider. They think of nothing but what's to their own advantage. To be wholly absorbed by an idea is denied them, and to prop ourselves on people who think only of themselves means to give up our cause as lost. Our cause doesn't just consist of fighting against the progressive dragon, it also consists of fighting the vampire nobility that just sucks and sucks. Away with all this special interest politicking! We must win under the banner of absolute selflessness, and to do that we need the people, not the likes of the Quitzows[4] who have been on top again since the play of the same name appeared and who just want to get their hands on the helm again. No, Kommerzienrat, no pseudo-conservatism, no kingdom on a false basis; the kingdom—if we want to conserve it—must rest on something more solid than a Ziegenhals or a Bomst."

"Now listen, Vogelsang, Ziegenhals at least. . ."

And Treibel seemed seriously intent on pursuing this line, which suited him, further, but before he could do so the Police Assessor entered from the drawing room, his little Meissen cup still in his hand, and sat down between Treibel and Vogelsang. Right after him Otto appeared, perhaps notified by Friedrich or perhaps just of his own accord, because he was long familiar with the erotically oriented paths that Goldammer pursued regularly, and often so rapidly, over liqueur and cigars, that missing any was a punishment in itself.

The older Treibel naturally knew this even better but considered it appropriate to speed up the procedure himself and thus began:

"And now tell me, Goldammer, what's going on? How

are things with the Lützowplatz? Is the Panke River going to be filled in, or, to put it in other terms, is the Friedrichstrasse going to be morally cleansed? Frankly, I'm afraid that our most piquant traffic artery won't gain much from it, it'll become slightly more moral and considerably more boring. Since my wife's ear does not reach this far we can talk about such things here; for the rest, all my quizzing is not meant to limit you. I've lived long enough to know that everything that comes out of a policeman's mouth is always good subject matter, always a fresh breeze—occasionally a sirocco, or even a simoom. Let's say simoom. So what's floating on top?"

"A new soubrette."

"Capital! You see, Goldammer, every form of art is good because each one has an ideal in sight. And the ideal is the main thing, that much I've learned from my wife by now. But a soubrette is always the most ideal. Name?"

"Grabillon. Delicate figure, somewhat large mouth, mole."

"For God's sake, Goldammer, that sounds like an arrest warrant. But a mole is charming; large mouth—a matter of taste. And a protégée of whom?"

Goldammer was silent.

"Ah, I see. Upper spheres. The higher up, the closer to the ideal. By the way, since we're on the upper spheres, how is it with the salute story? Did he really not salute? And is it true that he—the one who didn't salute, of course—had to take a leave? It would actually be the best thing, because then it would be tantamount to a renunciation of all Catholicism,[5] two birds with one stone, so to speak."

Goldammer, a secret progressive, but openly anti-Catholic, shrugged his shoulders and said: "Things are unfortunately not that good, and not likely to be either. The power of the counter-current is too great. The one who declined to salute, the William Tell[6] of the situation, if you like, has too much backing. Where? Well, that'll have to stay up in the air; certain things can't be called by their right names, and before we have stamped out the heads of the familiar Hydra or—to put it another way—have helped the old Frederickan '*écrasez l'infâme*'[7] to victory. . ."

At that moment they heard singing next door, a familiar composition, and Treibel, who had just started to take a new cigar threw it back into the box and said: " 'My peace is gone. . .'[8] And it won't go much better with yours, Gentlemen. I believe we'll have to join the ladies again in order to partake of the Adolar Krola era, because *that* is beginning now."

With that all four of them rose and, Treibel preceding, returned to the drawing room where Krola was indeed sitting at the grand piano and giving his three main pieces. These he usually disposed of in rapid succession and with perfect virtuosity, though with a certain intentional rattling quality. The songs were "The Elf-King," "Lord Henry sat by the Fowling Floor," and "The Bells of Speier."[9] This last number, with the ding-dong of the bells mysteriously chiming in, always made the greatest impression and caused even Treibel momentarily to listen quietly. But then he said with a somewhat more elevated expression:

"That's Löwe, *ex ungue leonem*;[10] that is, by Karl Löwe—Ludwig doesn't compose."

When Krola had begun, many of those who had taken their coffee in the garden or on the veranda had likewise stepped into the drawing room to listen; others, however, who knew the three ballads from twenty other Treibel dinners, had preferred to remain outdoors and to continue their garden promenade. Among them was Mr. Nelson who, as a thoroughbred Englishman, was not the least musical and flatly declared that what he liked best was a "native with a drum between his legs": "I can't see what it means; music is nonsense." Thus he walked up and down with Corinna, Leopold on the other side, while at some distance Marcell followed with the young Frau Treibel, both of them half angered and half amused by Nelson and Leopold who, as at the table, were unable to leave Corinna.

It was a splendid evening outside, with no trace of the stuffy warmth predominating inside, and diagonally above the tall poplars that cut off the backyard from the factory buildings stood the crescent moon; the cockatoo still sat on his stand, earnest and disgruntled at not having been put back in his cage at the right time, and only the water-jet rose up high as gaily as before.

"Let's sit down," said Corinna, "we've been promenading for I don't know how long," and without further ado she settled herself on the edge of the fountain. "Take a seat, Mr. Nelson. Just look at the cockatoo, how angry he looks. He's upset that no one pays any attention to him."

"To be sure, and looks like Lieutenant Sangevogel, doesn't he?"

"We normally call him Vogelsang. But I have nothing against rebaptizing him. Of course, it won't help very much."

"No, no, there's no help for him: Vogelsang, ah, an ugly bird, no 'Singevogel,' no finch, no thrush."

"No, he's just a cockatoo, just as you say."

But these words had hardly been spoken when there was a loud shriek from the stand—as if the cockatoo wanted to protest this comparison—and then Corinna too screamed out loudly, though only to break immediately into bright laughter in which Leopold and Mr. Nelson promptly joined her. For a sudden gust of wind had directed the water-jet exactly towards the place they sat, showering all of them, including the bird on his stand, with a flood of spraying water. And now they brushed and shook themselves off, and though the cockatoo did the same, it did not improve his humor.

Inside, Krola had meanwhile concluded his program and got up to make room for other talents. According to him there was nothing worse than such monopolizing of art—besides, one shouldn't forget that the world belonged to the young. Bowing towards them he thus paid homage to several young ladies with whose families he was as intimate as with the Treibels. But the Kommerzienrätin for her part translated this completely general homage to youth into more specific language and enjoined the two Misses Felgentreu to sing a few of the charming things that they had performed so well recently when Ministerialdirektor Stoeckenius had been in the house; surely friend Krola would have the goodness to accompany the ladies on the piano. Very pleased to have escaped the further vocal demands that were usually the rule, Krola immediately expressed his agreement and sat back down in the place he had only just given up, without even waiting for a yes or no from the two Felgentreus. His whole being bespoke a mixture of benevolence and irony. The days of his own fame lay far behind; but the further they lay behind, the higher his artistic requirements had become, and since these remained totally unfulfilled it seemed to be a matter of complete indifference to him *what* came to be performed and *who* ventured the enterprise. Enjoyment there was none in it for him, only amusement, and since he had an inborn sense of the comic one could say that his pleasure reached its high point when his friend Jenny provided the conclusion of the musical soirée, as she loved to do, by performing a few songs herself. But that was still to come; for the time being there were still the two Felgentreus, of whom the elder sister—or "the far more talented one," as was always said to Krola's invariable delight—always started right in with "Brooklet leave your murmuring be."[11] It was followed by "I'd carve it into every tree" which, as a general favorite, and to the great though unvoiced annoyance of the Kommerzienrätin, was accompanied by several indiscreet voices in the garden. Then the concluding number followed, a duet from *The Marriage of Figaro.*

Everyone was enraptured, and Treibel said to Vogelsang,

"I can't recall having seen or heard anything so lovely from a pair of sisters since the days of the Milanollos,"[12] to which he added the unconsidered question of whether Vogelsang still remembered the Milanollos.

"No," said the latter harshly and peremptorily.

"Well, then let me apologize."

A pause set in, and a few carriages, among them the Felgentreus', had already driven up; nevertheless they hesitated to break up and leave because the party still wanted a proper conclusion. For the Kommerzienrätin had not sung yet, why she hadn't even been—it was unheard of—asked to perform one of her songs, a state of affairs that had to be changed as quickly as possible. No one perceived this more clearly than Adolar Krola who, taking the Police Assessor aside, urgently impressed upon him that something absolutely had to happen and that what had been overlooked with Jenny had to be made up immediately.

"If Jenny is not asked, I can see the Treibels' dinners—or at least our participation in them—jeopardized for all time, and that would after all signify a loss."

"Which we must prevent under all circumstances. You can count on me."

And taking the two Felgentreus by the hand, Goldammer resolutely approached the Kommerzienrätin in order to ask her, speaking, as he put it, for the whole party, for a song. The Kommerzienrätin, who could not help noticing the contrived nature of the affair, wavered between anger and desire, but the eloquence of the proposer at last proved victorious; Krola took up his place again and a few moments later Jenny's voice—rather thin in contrast to her fullness otherwise—sounded out through the drawing room and one heard the words of a song very well known to the members of this circle:

Fortune, of your thousand dowers
There is only one I want.
What good is gold? I love flowers
And the rose's ornament.

And I hear the rustling branches,
And I see a flutt'ring band—
Eye and eye exchanging glances,
And a kiss upon your hand.

Giving, taking, taking, giving,
And the wind plays in your hair.
That, oh that alone is living,
When heart to heart is paired.

It need not be said that resounding applause followed, to which old Felgentreu added the remark that the songs of those days—he avoided a specific reference to time—had after all been nicer, more heartfelt. Asked directly for his opinion, Krola confirmed the remark with an amused smile.

Mr. Nelson for his part had listened to the performance from the veranda and now said to Corinna: "Wonderfully good. Oh, these Germans, they know everything. . . even such an old lady."

Corinna put her finger on his mouth.

A short time later everyone was gone, the house and the park empty, and one could hear only busy hands pushing together the expanding table in the dining room and the jet of water splashing into the basin in the garden.

Chapter Five

AMONG the last to leave the Kommerzienrat's house were Marcell and Corinna who were now crossing the frontyard. The latter was still chatting in her exuberant mood, which only increased her cousin's painstakingly repressed ill humor. Finally they were both silent.

They had walked like this side by side for a good five minutes when Corinna, who knew very well what was going on in Marcell's mind, picked up the conversation again.

"Well, my friend, what is it?"

"Nothing."

"Nothing?"

"Well—why should I deny it—I'm in a bad humor."

"What about?"

"About you. About you, because you have no heart."

"I? I certainly do. . ."

"Because you have no heart, I say, no family feeling, not even for your father. . ."

"And not even for my cousin Marcell. . ."

"No, leave him out of it, no one's talking about him. With

me you can do what you like. But your father—today you just left the old man alone and lonely and didn't really concern yourself about anything. I don't think you even know whether he's home or not."

"Of course he's at home. He's holding his 'evening' tonight, and even if all of them don't come, a few from high Olympus will surely be there."

"And you go out and leave everything to good old Schmolke?"

"Because I can leave it to her. You know that as well as I do; everything goes like clockwork, and at this very moment they're probably eating Oder crayfish and drinking Moselle. Not a Treibel Moselle, but a Professor Schmidt Moselle, a noble Trarbacher that Papa claims is the only pure wine in Berlin. Are you satisfied now?"

"No."

"Then go on."

"Oh, Corinna, you take everything so lightly, and you think if you've taken it lightly you've gotten it out of the way. But you don't succeed. Things stay what and how they are after all. I was watching you at the table now. . ."

"Impossible, you were paying court to young Frau Treibel very intensively, and a couple of times she even turned red. . . ."

"I was watching you, I say, and I was genuinely shocked at the excesses of coquetry you tirelessly used to turn that poor boy's, Leopold's, head. . . ."

Just as Marcell was saying this they reached the end of Köpenick Strasse, which broadened almost to a square towards the Insel Bridge, a place without traffic and almost completely emptied of people. Corinna withdrew her arm from her cousin's and said, pointing to the other side of the street:

"Look, Marcell, if that lone policeman weren't standing over there, I'd stop in front of you, arms crossed, and laugh at you for a good five minutes. What is that supposed to mean

—I never tire of turning the poor boy's, Leopold's, head? If you hadn't been so totally absorbed in your attentions to Helene you would have had to see that I hardly spoke two words with him. I talked only with Mr. Nelson, and a couple of times I expressly addressed you."

"Oh, you can say that, Corinna, but you know how wrong it is. Look, you're very smart, and you know it too; but you make the same mistake that many smart people make—you consider others less smart than they are. And so you think you can tell me what's black is white, and twist and prove everything the way you want to twist and prove it. But some of us have eyes and ears too and are therefore—if you'll permit me—sufficiently equipped to see and hear."

"And what is it now that the Herr Doktor has seen and heard?"

"The Herr Doktor has seen and heard that Fräulein Corinna has come down upon the unfortunate Mr. Nelson with her verbal cascades."

"Very flattering. . ."

"And that she—to give up the image of verbal cascades and replace it with another—that she, I say, balanced the peacock feathers of her vanity on her chin or on her lips for two whole hours and otherwise achieved the utmost in the finer acrobatic arts. And all this in front of whom? Mr. Nelson perhaps? Not at all. This good fellow Nelson was just the trapeze on which my cousin performed; the one for whose sake all this happened, his name is Leopold Treibel, and I noticed very well how correctly my little cousin had calculated, because I can't recall having seen a person so—if you'll forgive the expression—smitten, for a whole evening, as this Leopold."

"You think so?"

"Yes, that's what I think."

"Well, I could say something about that. . . . But look at that. . ."

And with this she stopped and pointed to the enchanting

view that spread out before them on the other side of Fischer Bridge which they were just crossing. Thin mists were lying across the stream, but they did not completely absorb the gleaming lights that fell on the wide water surface from left and right, while the crescent moon stood above in the blue expanse, not two hands' breadth distant from the somewhat ponderous tower of the Parochial Church silhouetted very distinctly on the other bank.

"Look at that," Corinna repeated, "never have I seen the singing clock tower so sharply. But to find it beautiful, as has become the fashion recently, that I can't do; there's something half or unfinished about it, as if it had lost its strength on the way up. I'd rather have the tapered, ordinary shingled spires that just want to be tall and point into heaven."

And at the same moment that Corinna said this the little bells there began to play.

"Oh," said Marcell, "don't talk about the tower like that, and whether it's beautiful or not. It's all the same to me, and to you too; let the experts decide that among themselves. And you're just saying all that because you want to get out of the actual discussion. But you'd better listen to what the little bells over there are playing. I think they're playing 'Be always true and honest.' "[1]

"Could be, and it's only too bad that they can't also play the famous passage about the Canadian who wasn't familiar with Europe's whitewashed politeness yet.[2] Something good like that doesn't get put to music, or perhaps it doesn't work. But tell me, my friend, what is all that supposed to mean? 'True and honest.' Do you really think I'm not? Whom have I sinned against by being untrue? Against you? Have I made any vows? Have I promised you something and then not kept the promise?"

Marcell was silent.

"You're silent because you can't say anything. But I want

to say quite a bit more to you, and then you can decide for yourself whether I'm true and honest, or at least upright, which means about the same."

"Corinna. . ."

"No, now I want to speak, in all friendship but in all seriousness too. True and honest. Now I know very well that you're true and honest, which doesn't really say very much; for myself I can only repeat that I am too."

"And still play at comedy all the time."

"No, I don't. And if I do, then in such a way that everyone can tell. After careful consideration I have set myself a definite goal, and if I don't say 'this is my goal' in such bare words, it's only because it doesn't suit a girl to come out with such plans. Thanks to my upbringing I enjoy a good amount of freedom—some will perhaps say emancipation—but in spite of that I'm definitely not an emancipated female. On the contrary, I have no desire to upset old traditions, good old maxims such as 'a girl does not court, a girl *is* courted.' "

"Good, good, all that goes without saying. . ."

"But, of course, it's our ancient Eve's right to try to glitter and sparkle and to use our strengths until what we're here for happens, in other words, until we are courted. Everything has this purpose. Depending on your inclination, you call that launching fireworks, or comedy, sometimes even intrigue, and always coquetry."

Marcell shook his head. "Oh, Corinna, you shouldn't want to give me a lecture about that and to talk to me as if I were born yesterday. Naturally I've often spoken of comedy and even more often of coquetry. What all doesn't one talk about? And if one says that sort of thing, then one contradicts oneself too, and what's criticized one moment is praised the next. To put it plainly, play as much comedy as you like, be as coquettish as you like, I won't be so stupid as to want to change the ways of women or of the world in general; I really don't want to change it, even if I could. There's only one thing I must say to you about it: you should sparkle and glitter, as you put it earlier, at the right times, that is, in front of the right people; where it's suitable, where it belongs, where it's worthwhile. But you're not going to the right address with your arts because you can't be seriously thinking of marrying this Leopold Treibel."

"Why not? Is he too young for me? No. He's born in January and I in September, so he even has a lead of eight months."

"Corinna, you know very well how things are, and that he simply isn't suitable for you because he is too insignificant for you. You're a rather special individual, and he's barely average. A good fellow, I'll have to admit, with a good, soft heart, not one of the pebbles these moneymen usually have instead of a heart, and he can probably distinguish a Dürer engraving from a Ruppin print;[3] but you'd be bored to death at his side. You, your father's daughter and actually even smarter than the old fellow, you wouldn't want to throw away your real happiness in life just to live in a villa and to have a landau that now and then picks up a couple of ladies-in-waiting or to hear Adolar Krola's worn-out tenor singing the 'Elf-king' every couple of weeks. It's not possible, Corinna. For such mammon trifles you wouldn't throw yourself into such an insignificant man's arms."

"No, I wouldn't throw myself; I don't care for importunities. But if tomorrow Leopold approached my father—I'm afraid he's still one of those who make sure of the secondary person's favor before the main one's—anyway, if tomorrow he approached and asked for this right hand of your cousin Corinna, then Corinna would take him and would feel like 'Corinne au Capitole'."[4]

"That's not possible, you're deceiving yourself, you're playing with the affair. It's some of that fantasy you indulge in."

"No, Marcell, *you're* deceiving yourself, I'm not; I'm perfectly serious, so much so that I'm a little bit scared of it."

"That's your conscience."

"Perhaps. Perhaps not. But I'll readily admit this much to you: what God really created me for has nothing to do with a Treibel factory business or with a lumberyard, and perhaps least of all with a Hamburg sister-in-law. But there's a bent for good living that's dominating the whole world now and that has me in its power too, just like all the others. And ridiculous and contemptible as it may sound to your schoolteacher's ear, I'm more for Bonwitt and Littauer[5] than a little seamstress who comes as early as eight o'clock and brings a peculiar backyard and backroom atmosphere into the house with her, and then for her second breakfast gets a roll with sausage and maybe even a little shot of liquor. All that is repugnant to me to the highest degree. The less I see of it, the better. I find it immensely charming when little diamonds sparkle on one's ear—as on my prospective mother-in-law's. 'Limit yourself' —oh, I know the tune that's always sung and preached, but when I dust off Papa's thick books that nobody looks at, not even he, and when Schmolke sits down on my bed in the evening and tells me about her late husband, the policeman, and that he would have had a district of his own by now if he were still alive because Madai,[6] the Police Commissioner, thought very highly of him, and when she finally says, 'But my little Corinna, I haven't even asked what we want to eat tomorrow. The Teltow turnips are so bad right now and they've actually gotten maggoty, and I'd like to suggest boiled pork and kohlrabi, Schmolke always liked to eat that so much'—yes, Marcell, at moments like that I get a very peculiar feeling, and then suddenly Leopold Treibel becomes the sheet anchor of my life, or, if you like, the topsail to be raised with which a good wind will carry me to distant happy shores."

"Or to wreck your happiness if there's a storm."

"Let's wait and see, Marcell."

And with these words they turned from the old Leipziger Strasse into Raule's courtyard from which a little passageway led to the Adlerstrasse.

Chapter Six

AT the same time that dinner was over at the Treibels',
Professor Schmidt's "evening" began. This "evening,"
sometimes also called the "little club," gathered—if
everyone was there—seven secondary school teachers, most
of whom had the title of Professor, together about a round
table and an oil lamp provided with a red shade. Aside from
our friend Schmidt, there were the following: Friedrich
Distelkamp, Director Emeritus of the Gymnasium[1] and senior
member of the circle; after him Professors Rindfleisch and
Hannibal Kuh, joined by the Assistant Master Immanuel
Schultze, all of them from the Great Elector Gymnasium.
Lastly there was Doctor Charles Etienne, a friend and fellow
student of Marcell, now a French teacher at a refined girls'
boarding school, and the art teacher Friedeberg to whom just
a few years ago the title Professor had also fallen—no one
really knew why or from where—but it nonetheless failed to
raise his standing. Rather, he was viewed now as before as
not quite being of right mind, and for a time they had very
seriously discussed "harassing" him, as his main opponent

Immanuel Schultze suggested, out of their circle. Our Wilibald Schmidt fought against this with the remark that for their "evening" Friedeberg had a significance not to be underestimated in spite of not belonging there as a scholar.

"You see, my dear friends," had been his approximate words, "when we're among ourselves we actually follow the discussions chiefly out of consideration and politeness, and we more or less live in the conviction that we could say everything that is said by others *much* better or—if we're modest— at least as well. And that always hampers things. For my own part, at least, I confess openly that whenever it was my turn for a talk, I was never able to get rid of a certain feeling of discomfort, at times even a really high degree of anxiety. And at such a moment of pressure I would see our forever tardy friend Friedeberg come in, naturally with an embarrassed smile, and I would feel immediately how my soul got its wings again: I would speak more freely, more intuitively, more clearly, because I had an audience again, even if only a very small one. *One* devoted listener, apparently so little, is still something and now and then even quite a lot."

Upon this warm defense by Wilibald Schmidt, Friedeberg was kept in the circle. For Schmidt could really consider himself the soul of the little club, whose name, "The Seven Foolosophers of Greece," could be traced back to him as well. Immanuel Schultze, usually in the opposition and a Gottfried Keller enthusiast besides, had himself suggested "The Banner of the Upright Seven,"[2] but he had not prevailed with it because, as Schmidt stressed, this designation would constitute a borrowing. "The Seven Foolosophers" of course also sounded borrowed, but that was just a deception of the ear, of the senses: the first little syllable that made all the difference not only changed the significance at a single stroke but also brought it to the highest conceivable level, that of irony.

It goes without saying that the little society, like every

association of this sort, fell into almost as many factions as it had members, and it could only be attributed to the circumstance that the three from the Great Elector Gymnasium, aside from belonging together because of this common post, were also relatives and in-laws (Kuh was the brother-in-law, Immanuel Schultze the son-in-law of Rindfleisch)—owing only to this circumstance the four others, out of some instinct of self-preservation, likewise formed a group and mostly went along with one another when resolutions were made. In regard to Schmidt and Distelkamp this wasn't particularly surprising since they had been friends for a long time; but between Etienne and Friedeberg there usually gaped a deep abyss which was apparent as much in their divergent appearances as in their different living habits. Very elegant, Etienne never neglected to go on leave to Paris during the long vacation, while Friedeberg, ostensibly for the sake of his painting studies, withdrew to the Woltersdorfer Lock (unsurpassed as a landscape). Naturally all this was just a pretext. The real reason was that Friedeberg, with rather limited financial means, seized the next best thing within reach and chiefly left Berlin in order to have a few weeks away from his wife, with whom he had lived just on the brink of divorce for years. In a circle that examined the deeds as well as the words of its members critically, this subterfuge would necessarily have been annoying; but then openness and honesty in dealing with and among one another was in no way a conspicuous feature of the "Seven Foolosophers," rather the contrary. Thus each one, for example, declared "not to be able to live without the 'evening,' " which in truth did not preclude that it was always only those who had nothing better planned that came; theater and cards took precedence by far and assured that partial gatherings were the rule and did not surprise anyone.

But today it seemed it would be worse than usual. The Schmidts' wall clock—a piece inherited from grandfather— was already striking the half hour, half-past eight, and still no one was there but Etienne who, like Marcell, counted among the intimates of the house and was hardly considered a guest or visitor.

"What do you say, Etienne," Schmidt now addressed him, "what do you say to this dilatoriness? Where is Distelkamp keeping himself? If he can't be counted on anymore either—the Douglasses were always faithful[3]—the 'evening' will go out of joint and I'll become a pessimist and for the rest of my days take Schopenhauer and Eduard von Hartmann[4] under my arm."

While he was still saying this, the bell sounded outside and a moment later Distelkamp entered.

"I'm sorry, Schmidt, I'm late. I'll spare you and our friend Etienne the details. Discussions of why one has come late, even if true, are no better than stories about one's illnesses. So let's forget it. Meanwhile I'm surprised that in spite of my tardiness I'm still actually the first. Etienne after all as much as belongs to the family. But the Great Elector fellows? Where are they? I won't even ask about Kuh and our friend Immanuel, they're just their brother- and father-in-law's clientele. But Rindfleisch—where is he keeping himself?"

"Rindfleisch wrote to say he had a meeting of the Classical Society today."

"Oh, that's foolishness. What does he want in the Classical Society? The 'Seven Foolosophers' comes first. He'd really find more here."

"Yes, that's what you say, Distelkamp. But it's a little different after all. Because Rindfleisch has a bad conscience, perhaps I should say, he once again has a bad conscience."

"Then he belongs here all the more; here he could confess. But what is it about? What is it?"

"He's once again made a slip, confused something—Phrynikos the tragedian with Phrynikos the comedian, I think. Wasn't that it, Etienne"—who nodded—"and his students promptly made a joke of it. . . ."

"And?"

"And so he's got to make good the damage as best he can, for which the Classical Society with its luster is, after all, the best expedient."

Distelkamp, who had meanwhile lighted his meerschaum pipe and had sat down in the corner of the sofa, cozily smiled to himself during the whole story and then said:

"That's all twaddle. Do you believe it? I don't. And if it were true, it wouldn't mean much, actually nothing at all. Such slips are always occurring, happens to everybody. I want to tell you something, Schmidt, something that, when I was still young and had to lecture on the history of Brandenburg to my students—something, I say, that then made a great impression on me."

"Well, let's hear it. What was it?"

"Yes, what was it. Frankly, my field—at least as far as our good Electorate of Brandenburg is concerned—did not amount to much, nor does it now, and whenever I'd be sitting at home and preparing myself as best possible, I would read—we had just gotten to the first king—all sorts of biographical things and among them something by the old General Barfus who, like most men of his time, wasn't all that remarkable but as good as gold otherwise. And this Barfus presided at a court-martial during the siege of Bonn at which a young officer was to be tried."

"So, so. Well, what was it?"

"The fellow to be tried had, to say the least, behaved rather unheroically, and all of them were for 'guilty' and 'execute.' Only old Barfus didn't want to hear of it and said: 'Let's look at it a bit differently for a moment, gentlemen. I've been through thirty skirmishes, and I must tell you that no day is like another, and man varies, as does his heart and his courage especially. I've felt like a coward many a time too. As long as it's possible, one should exercise clemency, because everyone can use it.' "

"Hear, Distelkamp," Schmidt said, "that's a good story. I thank you for that, and as old as I am I'll take a lesson from it. Because, Lord knows, I've made a fool of myself too, and though the boys didn't notice it—at least I couldn't tell—I did notice it myself and was awfully angry and ashamed afterwards. Isn't that right, Etienne, something like that is always awkward, or doesn't it happen in French, or at least not if one goes to Paris every July and brings home a new volume of Maupassant? That's the latest now, isn't it? Forgive the bit of malice. Besides, Rindfleisch is as good as gold, *nomen est omen*,[5] and actually the best fellow, better than Kuh and particularly better than our friend Immanuel Schultze. He's a sly one and a sneak as well. He's always grinning and trying to give the impression that somehow and somewhere he's looked behind the veil of Saïs.[6] And he's a long way from that because he can't even solve the riddle of his own wife who is supposed to have quite a few things veiled better—or perhaps not at all—than he, the spouse, could be happy about."

"Schmidt, you're having another one of your gossipy days today. Just now I rescued poor Rindfleisch from your clutches —why you even promised to better yourself—and right away you pounce on the unfortunate son-in-law. Besides, if I were to criticize Immanuel for anything, it would be for an entirely different matter."

"And that would be?"

"That he has no authority. If he doesn't have it at home, well, that's sad enough. But then that's none of our business. But that he has none, according to everything I hear, in the classroom either, *that* is bad. You see, Schmidt, that is what mortifies and pains me these last years of my life—that I see the categorical imperative declining more and more. And if I think of old Weber then! It's said of him that when he entered the classroom one could hear sand fall through the hourglass, and not a single student even remembered that it was at all possible to whisper or otherwise to speak. And besides his own voice, I mean Weber's, there was nothing audible other than the crackling of pages turning in Horace. Yes, Schmidt, *those* were times, then it was worthwhile being a teacher and a Director. Now the boys come up to you at the coffee shop and say: 'When you've finished reading, Sir, I'd like to. . .' "

Schmidt laughed. "Yes, Distelkamp, that's the way they are now, that's the new times, it's true. But I can't really get too bitter about it. Looked at closely, what were the great dignitaries with their double chins and their red noses? They were gluttons who knew their Burgundy far better than their Homer. Everybody is always talking about older, simpler times; silly nonsense. They must have tippled pretty generously—you can still see that on their pictures in the auditorium. All right, self-confidence and a straitlaced *grandezza*,[7] all that they had, that much should be admitted. But how did it look otherwise?"

"Better than today."

"I can't see that, Distelkamp. When I was still supervising our school library—thank God I don't have anything to do with it anymore—I frequently looked into the School Programs and into the dissertations and ceremonial speeches as they flourished then. Now I know very well that every age thinks it's something special, and those to come may well laugh about us too as far as I'm concerned. But you see, Distelkamp, from the standpoint of our present knowledge, or of our taste I might say, it can certainly be said that all that old-fashioned, bewigged learning was ghastly, and the stupendous importance it displayed can only amuse us now. I don't know in whose time it was, I think in Rodigast's,[8] that the fashion came up—perhaps because he himself had a garden outside the Rosentaler Gate—to take the subjects for public speeches and the like from gardening, and so I read dissertations about the horticulture of Paradise, the nature and condition of the

Garden of Gethsemane, and the supposed landscaping of the garden of Joseph of Arimathaea. Gardens and nothing but gardens. Well, what do you say to that?"

"Yes, Schmidt, it's bad to cross swords with you. You've always had an eye for oddities. And you pick them out, impale them on your needle, and show them to the world. But what lies alongside and is much more appropriate you leave lying. Very rightly you've already pointed out that we'll be laughed at later too—and who'll guarantee us that we're not daily entering into investigations that are even more absurd than those horticultural investigations of paradise. My dear Schmidt, the decisive factor will always be character; not vain, but good, honest faith in ourselves. *Bona fide*—we must proceed in good faith. But with our eternal criticism, even self-criticism, we get into a *mala fides* and mistrust ourselves and what we have to say. And without faith in ourselves and our purpose, there is no genuine pleasure and joyfulness, nor any blessing, least of all authority. And that's what I'm lamenting. For just as there is no military system without discipline, there is no school system without authority. It's the same with faith. It's not necessary that there be a belief in the right thing, but that there be a belief at all, that is what matters. Every belief harbors mysterious powers and authority does too."

Schmidt smiled. "Distelkamp, I can't follow you there. I can only let that count in theory, but in practice it becomes meaningless. Surely it's a question of one's standing in the eyes of the students. We just part ways as to the roots of that standing. You want to trace everything back to character and you think, even if you don't say it, 'if you just have faith in yourself, other souls will have faith in you too.'[9] But, my good friend, that is just what I'm disputing. Mere faith in oneself or, if you'll permit the expression, swollen self-importance, pomposity, doesn't do anymore. This obsolete power has been replaced by the actual power of real knowledge and ability.

You only need to look around and you'll see every day that Professor Hammerstein, who helped storm Spichern[10] and has preserved a certain officer's air from it, Hammerstein, I say, does not rule his class, while our Agathon Knurzel, who looks like Mr. Punch and has a double humpback, but a doubly good head too, holds his class in the fear of God with his little hawk's face. And especially with our Berlin boys who can spot right away how much there is to anyone. If one of those old fellows came out of his grave, done up with his pride and grandeur, and asked for a horticultural description of Paradise, how would he fare with all his dignity? Three days later he'd be spoofed in *Kladderadatsch* magazine and the boys themselves would have written the verses."

"But all the same, Schmidt, the higher studies will stand or fall with the traditions of the old school."

"I don't believe it. But if that were the case, if the higher world view—or whatever we call it—if all that would have to fall, well, then let it fall. Long ago Attinghausen, who was old himself, said: 'The old order is collapsing, the times are changing.'[11] And we're standing directly before such a transformation process, or better, we're already in it. Do I have to remind you that there was a time when matters of the church were still the business of churchmen alone?[12] Is it still that way? No. Has the world lost anything? It's over with the old ways, and our scholarly methods won't be an exception. Look here. . ." and he lugged a large luxurious volume over from a little side table, ". . .look here at this. Sent to me today, and I'm going to keep it, expensive as it is: Heinrich Schliemann's[13] Excavations at Mycenae. Well, Distelkamp, what's your opinion of it?"

"Dubious enough."

"I can imagine. Because you don't want to get away from the older views. You can't imagine that somebody who has glued up paper bags and sold raisins has dug up old Priam, and if he then even moves on to Agamemnon and looks for the cleft skull—Aegisthus' remembrance[14]—you'll become highly indignant. But I can't help myself, you're wrong. Of course, one has to achieve something; *hic Rhodus, hic salta;*[15] but whoever can leap will leap, no matter whether he's gotten through the university at Göttingen or just through grade school. But I want to leave off here; I don't feel in the least like irritating you with Schliemann whom you've denied from the start. The books are lying here just because of Friedeberg whom I wanted to ask about the enclosed drawings. I can't understand why he's not coming, or rather why he's not here yet. Because it's unquestionable that he's coming; he would have written otherwise, polite man that he is."

"Yes, that he is," said Etienne, "that comes from his Jewish background."

"Very true," Schmidt continued, "but where he got it from doesn't matter in the end. I sometimes regret, arch-Teuton that I am, that we don't have some supply source for a bit of polish and civility; it wouldn't exactly have to be the same kind. This terrible association of the Teutoburg forest[16] with rudeness really is disturbing at times. Friedeberg is a man who, like Max Piccolomini[17]—not exactly his model otherwise, not even in love—always cultivated 'friendliness of manner' and the only thing to be lamented is that his students don't always have the proper understanding for that. In other words, they play around right under his nose. . ."

"The ancient fate of writing and drawing teachers. . ."

"Of course. And ultimately that's the way it has to go and it's going well enough. But let's drop that ticklish question. Let me instead get back to Mycenae and you tell me your opinion of the gold masks. I'm sure we've got something very special there, something very much the essence. Not just anyone could have worn a gold mask at his burial, it was always just the princes, so there is the highest probability that they were Orestes' and Iphigenia's direct ancestors. And if I reflect that these gold masks were shaped precisely after the face, just as we now shape a plaster or wax mask, my heart skips at the barely admissible idea that *this*"—and he pointed to an open page—"that this is the face of Atreus or his father or his uncle. . . ."

"Let's say his uncle."

"Yes, you're being sarcastic, Distelkamp, even though you've forbidden me sarcasm. And all that just because you mistrust the whole business and can't forget that he—I mean Schliemann of course—never got out of little towns like Strelitz and Fürstenberg in his school years. But just read what Virchow[18] says about him. And Virchow is someone you would accept after all."

At that moment the bell was heard outside. "Ah, *lupus in fabula*.[19] There he is. I knew he wouldn't leave us in the lurch. . . ."

And hardly had Schmidt spoken these words when Friedeberg indeed came in, and a handsome black poodle, his tongue hanging far out from strenuous running, leapt towards the two old gentlemen and alternately fawned upon Schmidt and Distelkamp. He didn't dare approach Etienne, who was too elegant for him.

"Good heaven, Friedeberg, where are you coming from so late?"

"Of course, of course, and very much to my regret. But Fips here has been carrying on too much, or he's going too far in his love for me, if going too far in love is at all possible. I imagined I had locked him in and got underway on time. Good. When I get here, who's here, who's waiting for me? Fips naturally. I take him back again to my apartment and hand him over to the porter, my good friend—in Berlin one should actually say, my benefactor. But, but what is the result of all my efforts and kind words? I'm hardly back here and Fips is back again too. What was I supposed to do finally? For better or worse I brought him in with me and apologize for him and for me."

"Doesn't matter," Schmidt said, cheerfully occupied with the dog. "Handsome animal, and so jolly and devoted. Tell me, Friedeberg, how is his name written? with an 'f' or a 'ph'? Phips with 'ph' is English, hence more refined. Other than that, whatever the spelling may be, he's invited for this evening and is a perfectly welcome guest provided he has nothing against taking his place at the kitchen table, so to speak. I'll vouch for my good Schmolke. She's very partial to poodles, and if she just hears how faithful he is too. . ."

"Then," Distelkamp threw in, "she'll hardly deny him a special tidbit."

"Certainly not. And there I'll heartily agree with my good Schmolke. Because faithfulness, which everyone is talking about these days, is in fact becoming rarer and rarer, and in his part of town Fips is preaching it, so far as I know, for nothing."

Though otherwise he virtually protected him, Schmidt's words now, spoken with apparent lightness and as if in jest, were directed rather earnestly at Friedeberg, whose notoriously unhappy marriage was among other things characterized by a decided lack of faithfulness, especially during his painting and landscape studies at the Woltersdorfer Lock. Friedeberg distinctly felt the taunt and wanted to pull himself out of the affair with an obliging word to Schmidt, but he did not get to it because at that moment Schmolke entered and, bowing to the other gentlemen, whispered into her Professor's ear that "everything's ready."

"Well, my friends, come. . ." And taking Distelkamp by the hand he crossed the hallway and walked towards the drawing room where (since there was no actual dining room in the apartment) the supper table had been set. Friedeberg and Etienne followed.

Chapter Seven

THE room was the one in which Corinna had received the visit of the Kommerzienrätin the day before. Well provided with candles and wine bottles, the table stood in the middle with places set for four; over it was a hanging lamp. Schmidt sat down with his back to the window pier, across from his friend Friedeberg, who for his part had a view into the mirror as well. Between the polished brass candelabra stood a pair of porcelain vases won at a bazaar; out of their half-tooth and half-wave shaped opening—*dentatus et undulatus* Schmidt said—grew little market bouquets of wallflowers and forget-me-nots. In front of the wine glasses lay long caraway-seed buns to which the host ascribed, as he did to everything with caraway, a particular abundance of healthy gifts.

The main dish was still lacking, and Schmidt, after he had twice poured himself some of the "evening's" statutory Trarbach and had also broken off both of the crisp tips of his caraway-seed bun, was obviously at the point of showing strong signs of ill humor and impatience when finally the door leading to the hall opened and Schmolke, red from agitation and the hot stove, entered carrying a mighty bowl of Oder crabs.

"Thank God," Schmidt said, "I was beginning to think everything had gone crab-walking"—an incautious remark that only made Schmolke all the more flushed and likewise caused the degree of her good mood to sink. Quickly recognizing his error, Schmidt was a clever enough strategist to try to balance things by a few obliging remarks. But of course they were only half successful.

When they were alone again Schmidt did not neglect to play the obliging host. In his own way, of course.

"Look, Distelkamp, this one here is for you. It's got a large and a small claw, and those are always the best. Nature plays games that are more than just games, and they serve the wise man as guides; the blood oranges and the Borsdorf apples with their scab spots, for example. And it's an established fact that the more scab spots they have, the nicer they are. . . . What we have before us here are Oder Marsh crabs; from the Küstrin area, if I'm rightly informed. It seems that the marriage of the Oder and the Warthe rivers produces especially good results. By the way, Friedeberg, aren't you actually from there? Half Neumarker or Oderbrücher?"

Friedeberg confirmed this.

"I knew it; my memory rarely deceives me. And now tell me, my friend, can we presume to view this as strictly local production or are the Oder Marsh crabs like the Werder cherries whose growing region will soon extend over the whole province of Brandenburg?"

"I do believe," Friedeberg said, while he lifted a glistening white and pink crab tail out of its shell with an adept turn of the fork that betrayed the virtuoso, "I do believe that these are sailing under the proper flag and that we have real Oder crabs in this bowl before us, the most genuine article, not just according to the name but also *de facto*."

"*De facto*," Schmidt repeated with an easy smile since he was familiar with the extent of Friedeberg's Latin.

But Friedeberg continued: "Masses of them are still caught around Küstrin, even though it's no longer what it used to be. I myself was still able to see marvelous specimens of them, but of course nothing in comparison to what people described from the old days. Then, a hundred years ago, or even more, there were so many crabs throughout the whole Marsh that they were shaken from the trees, hundreds of thousands of them, when the flood waters subsided in May."

"That's enough to make one's heart rejoice," Etienne, the gourmet, said.

"Yes, here at this table; but there in that area they didn't rejoice. The crabs were like a plague and naturally completely devalued. They were despised by the servant population that was to be fed with them, and so repulsive to their stomachs that it was forbidden to serve the help crabs more than three times a week. A shock of crabs cost a penny."

"It's a good thing Schmolke can't hear that," Schmidt broke in, "otherwise her disposition would be spoiled a second time. Because as a proper Berliner she's forever wanting to save, and I don't believe she could calmly overcome the fact that she missed the epoch of 'a penny a shock' altogether."

"You shouldn't make fun of that, Schmidt," Distelkamp said. "That's a virtue that the modern world is losing more and more, among other things."

"Yes, you're right there. But my good Schmolke on this point too has *les défauts de ses vertus*.[1] That's the phrase, isn't it, Etienne?"

"Yes, of course," said the latter, "from George Sand. And one could almost say '*les défauts de ses vertus*' and '*comprendre c'est pardonner*'[2]—those are quite the very words she lived for."

"And perhaps she also lived for Alfred de Musset," Schmidt added, since he didn't like to pass up an opportunity to display

—quite apart from his classical learning—his acquaintance with modern literature.

"Yes, if you wish, for Alfred de Musset too. But those are things that literary history fortunately passes by."

"Don't say that, Etienne, not fortunately. History almost always passes by what it should record most. That Frederick the Great, toward the end of his days, threw his crutch at the head of the President of the Supreme Court—I've forgotten his name—and, what's even more important to me, that he definitely wanted to be buried alongside his dogs because he despised men, this '*méchante*[3] *race*,' so thoroughly—you see, my friend, that is worth at least as much to me as the Hohenfriedberg or Leuthen victories.[4] And the famous Torgau address, 'You rogues, do you want to live forever,' is more to me than the Torgau battle itself."

Distelkamp smiled. "That's more Schmidtiana. You've always liked anecdotes, intimacies. In history only the great counts for me, not the small, the incidental."

"Yes and no, Distelkamp. The incidental, that much is right, doesn't count if it is merely incidental, if there is nothing in it. But if there is something in it, then it's the main thing, because it always reveals the human essence."

"Poetically you may be right."

"Poetry—assuming one understands it in a way other than does my friend Jenny Treibel—poetry is always right; it far exceeds history."

This was one of Schmidt's favorite topics, one on which the old romantic in him fully came into his own. But before he could engage in a weighty discussion, the riding of his hobbyhorse today was prohibited by voices heard in the hallway. A moment later Marcell and Corinna entered, Marcell ill at ease and almost cross, Corinna still in the best of moods. She went over to Distelkamp who was her godfather and always paid her little compliments. Then she shook hands with

Friedeberg and Etienne and concluded with her father whom she gave a hearty kiss after he had, on her order, wiped his mouth with the napkin draped down from his collar.

"Well, children, what have you got? Move in here. There's plenty of room. Rindfleisch wrote that he couldn't come. . . Classical Society. . . and the other two, as hangers-on, are naturally absent too. But not another insinuating word; I've taken an oath to improve after all and want to keep it. So, Corinna, you over there by Distelkamp, Marcell here between Etienne and me. Schmolke will set the table for you right away. . . So, that's good. . . . And how different it looks right away! Whenever there are gaps yawning like that I always think Banquo is arising. But thank God, Marcell, you don't have much of a Banquo about you, or if you do, you know how to hide your wounds. And now tell us, children, what's Treibel doing? What's my friend Jenny doing? Did she sing? I bet, the eternal song, *my* song, the famous passage 'When heart to heart is paired,' and Adolar Krola accompanied her. If I could just once read Krola's mind then. But perhaps he's more charitable and humane about it. Anybody who is invited to two dinners a day and takes part in at least one and a half. . . But please, Corinna, ring the bell."

"No, I'd rather go myself, Papa. Schmolke doesn't like to be rung for; she has her notions of what she owes herself and her departed. And I don't know whether I'm coming back— you gentlemen will excuse me—I don't really think so. When you have such a Treibel day behind you, the nicest thing is to recall how it all came about and what all you were told. Marcell can report for me after all. And now just this much— a most interesting Englishman was my neighbor at the table, and if you don't want to believe that he was so very interesting, I just need to tell you his name—it was Nelson. And now, good night."

And with that Corinna left.

The table was set for Marcell, and when he had asked for a sample crab, just in order not to disturb his uncle's good mood, Schmidt said:

"Go ahead and start. One can always eat artichokes and crabs, even after coming from a Treibel dinner. Whether the same is to be said for lobster we can leave open. I personally have always enjoyed lobster too. It's an odd thing that one never outgrows questions of that sort, they just change in the course of one's life. If you're young, it's 'pretty or ugly,' 'brunette or blonde,' and if that's behind you, there's perhaps the more important question, 'lobster or crabs.' We could of course take a vote on it. But then again, I must admit, voting always has something dead, mechanical about it, and doesn't suit me that well besides. Actually, I'd like to draw Marcell into the conversation, he's sitting there as if he's been left out in the rain. So let's rather discuss the question, debate—tell me, Marcell, which do you prefer?"

"Naturally lobster."

"Youth is quick at hand with words! Right at the outset, with very few exceptions, everybody is for lobster, especially because one can always cite Kaiser Wilhelm. But that's not all there is to it. Of course, when such a lobster is lying there cut up, and the wonderful red roe, a picture of blessing and fertility, gives one the additional certainty that 'there will always be lobster,' even after eons, just as today. . ."

Distelkamp cast a sidelong glance at his friend Schmidt.

"That gives one the certainty that even after eons one will enjoy this heavenly gift—yes, friends, if this feeling of the infinite pervades you, the humanitarian aspect of it doubtless will benefit the lobster and our position regarding it. Because every philanthropic impulse—for which reason philanthropy should be cultivated just out of egotism—signifies the increase of a healthy and at the same time refined appetite. Everything good has its rewards within itself, that much is indisputable."

"But. . ."

"But nevertheless providence keeps the trees from growing into the heavens, and alongside the great the small not only has its justification but its advantages as well. Certainly, the crab lacks this and that; it does not, so to speak, have the size which in a military state like Prussia does indeed mean something, but notwithstanding that, it too may say that it has not lived in vain. And when it—the crab—appears in front of us, coated in parsley butter and most appetizingly attractive, then it has moments of true superiority, especially because its best part isn't actually eaten, but rather sipped, sucked. And who would want to dispute that precisely this, in the world of pleasure, has its special merits? It is, so to speak, the most natural thing. First of all we have the sucking infant, for whom sucking is the same as living. But then too in the later semesters. . ."

"That's fine, Schmidt," Distelkamp interrupted. "But to me it always seems strange that besides Homer and even besides Schliemann you have such a liking for dealing with cook-book matters, pure menu questions, as if you belonged among the bankers and money lords who, I generally assume, eat well. . . ."

"I have no doubt whatsoever."

"Now, you see, Schmidt, these gentlemen of high finance, I would be willing to bet, don't talk about a turtle soup with half as much pleasure and eagerness as you."

"That's right, Distelkamp, and quite natural. You see, I have this freshness that does it; freshness makes the difference, in everything. Freshness gives one the pleasure, the eagerness, the interest, and where there is no freshness, there is nothing. The poorest life that man can lead is that of the *petit crevé*.[5] That's just floundering about—nothing behind it. Am I right, Etienne?"

The latter, always called upon as an authority in all matters Parisian, nodded in agreement, and Distelkamp let the question drop, or rather he was adept enough to give it a new direction. From the culinary in general he turned to specific famous culinary personalities, first to Freiherr von Rumohr[6] and then to Fürst Pückler-Muskau,[7] who had been his personal friend. And he talked about the latter with particular enthusiasm. If someday one should want to characterize the nature of modern aristocracy by means of a historical figure, one would always have to take Prince Pückler as a model specimen. He had been perfectly charming, a bit capricious, vain, and haughty, yes—but always thoroughly good. It was unfortunate that such figures were dying out. And after these introductory sentences he began to tell specifically of Muskau and Branitz where in the past he had often visited for days and had talked about things far and near with the fairy-tale-like Abyssinian woman brought home from "Semilasso's World Travels."

Schmidt liked nothing better than to hear experiences of this sort, and especially from Distelkamp for whose knowledge and character he had an altogether unfeigned respect.

Marcell fully shared this liking for the old Direktor and knew besides—even though a born Berliner—how to listen well and with interest. But today he asked question after question, which demonstrated his complete distraction. His mind was simply occupied with other things.

Thus it came to be eleven o'clock, and at the stroke of the bells—cutting one of Schmidt's sentences right through the middle—they rose and stepped out of the dining room into the hallway where Schmolke had laid ready their summer overcoats along with their hats and walking sticks. Everyone reached for his coat, but Marcell took his uncle aside for a moment and said: "Uncle, I'd like to have a word with you," a request to which the latter, jovial and cordial as always, fully assented. Then with Schmolke leading, the brass candelabrum held above her head in her left hand, Distelkamp, Friedeberg, and Etienne proceeded downstairs and then stepped out into the muggy warmth of the Adlerstrasse. Upstairs meanwhile, Schmidt took his nephew's arm and walked with him to his study.

"Well, Marcell, what is it? You won't be wanting to smoke, you look much too clouded already, but let me stuff a pipe for myself." And at that he pushed the tobacco box over and settled down in one corner of the sofa. "So, Marcell! ... And now take a chair and sit down and fire away. What is it?"

"The same old thing."

"Corinna?"

"Yes."

"Well, Marcell, don't take it amiss, but it's a poor suitor that always requires father's help to make any progress. You know I'm in favor of it. You seem to be made for one another. She looks beyond you and all of us, the Schmidt in her not only strives towards perfection, but—I must say it even though I am her father—comes very near the goal. Not every family can bear that. But a Schmidt is composed of such ingredients that the perfection I'm speaking of never becomes oppressive. And why not? Because the sense of irony, in which we, I believe, are great, always puts a question mark after this perfection. That is essentially what I call the Schmidt quality. Do you follow?"

"Certainly, Uncle. Just keep talking."

"Now look, Marcell, you suit one another excellently well. She has the more original nature, ready with an answer for everything, but that hardly carries enough weight in life. It's almost the opposite: the originals always stay half children, caught up in vanity, and always rely on intuition and *bon sens* and sentiment and whatever all those French words are. Or we can also say in plain German, they rely on their good inspirations. But that's only so-so; sometimes they flash like lightning for half an hour or even longer, sure, that happens; but all at once the electricity has run out and then not only the *esprit* stops like tap water but common sense does too. Yes, that especially. And that's the way it is with Corinna. She needs understanding guidance, that is, she needs a man of education and character. That's you, you have that. And so you have my blessing; everything else you have to provide for yourself."

"Yes, Uncle, that's what you always say. But how can I do that? I can't spark a blazing passion in her. Perhaps she's not even capable of such passion; but even if she is, how should one cousin stimulate such passion in another? That never happens. Passion is something sudden, and if they've always, from their fifth year on, played together and, let's say, have hidden countless times for hours behind the sauerkraut barrels of a little shop or in a peat and wood cellar, always together and always so blissfully happy that Richard or Arthur couldn't find them even though they were close by—yes, Uncle, then one can't speak of suddenness, this precondition for passion, anymore."

Schmidt laughed. "You've said that well, Marcell, you've actually outdone yourself. But it just increases my love for you. There's something of a Schmidt in you too, it's just a bit buried under that Wedderkopp stiffness. And this much I can tell you—if you keep up that tone with Corinna, then you're there, then you'll have her for sure."

"Oh, Uncle, don't think that. You're misjudging Corinna. One side of her you know precisely, but the other side you don't know at all. Everything that's clever, skillful, and especially what's spirited in her you see with both eyes, but what is external and modern about her you don't see. I can't say that she has that low desire to charm, to conquer everyone, no matter who it is—there's none of that in her. But she relentlessly sets her sights on one individual, one whom she is especially interested in conquering, and you won't believe with what fierce resolution, with what infernal virtuosity she weaves her web around her chosen victim."

"You think so?"

"Yes, Uncle. Today at the Treibels' we had another perfect example of it. She sat between Leopold Treibel and an Englishman, whose name she's already told you, a Mr. Nelson, who, like most Englishmen of good family, has a certain naive charm but is otherwise rather insignificant. Now you should have seen Corinna. She appeared to be occupied with no one else but this son of Albion, and she did succeed in amazing him. But don't think that she was in the least interested in this flaxen-haired Mr. Nelson; she was interested only in Leopold Treibel, to whom she didn't address a single word, or at least not very many, directly, but in whose honor she performed a sort of French play, a little comedy, a dramatic scene. This unfortunate Leopold has long been hanging on her every word and imbibing that sweet poison, but I've really never seen him quite as he was today. He was full of admiration from head to toe, and every expression seemed to want to say: 'Oh, how boring Helene is'—that is, as you may remember, his brother's wife—'and how wonderful is this Corinna.' "

"That's fine, Marcell, but I can't find those things to be all that bad. Why shouldn't she entertain her right-hand neighbor to make an impression on her left-hand neighbor? That happens every day, those are the little caprices that abound in woman's nature."

"You call them caprices, Uncle. Yes, if things were like that! But they're different. Everything is calculation: she wants to marry Leopold."

"Nonsense, Leopold is a boy."

"No, he's twenty-five, just as old as Corinna herself. But even if he were still a mere boy, Corinna has her mind set on it and will carry it through."

"Not possible."

"Yes, it is. And not just possible, but quite certain. She told me so herself when I called her to account. She wants to become Leopold Treibel's wife, and when the old man dies—

which could at most take another ten years, as she assured me,
and if he's elected in his Zossen district, hardly five—then she
wants to move into the villa, and if I've assessed her correctly,
she'll also get a peacock to go with the gray cockatoo."

"Oh, Marcell, those are fantasies."

"Perhaps hers, who is to say? But surely not mine. Because
those are all her very own words. Uncle, you should have
heard the disdain with which she spoke of 'modest circumstances' and how she depicted the meager, humble life for
which she just wasn't made; she's not for bacon and kohlrabi
and the like. . .and you should have heard just *how* she said
that, not just more or less lightly, no, there was a distinct
tone of bitterness sounding through, and it hurt me to see how
much she values externals and how these damned new times
have her in their grip."

"Hm," said Schmidt, "I don't like that—that about the
kohlrabi. That's just silly snobbery and culinary foolishness
as well; why, my dear Marcell, who can go against all the
dishes Frederick William I loved, cabbage with mutton or
tench with dill, for example? To oppose it is simply a want of
judgment. But believe me, Corinna doesn't really, for that
she's far too much her father's daughter. And if she indulged
herself by talking of modernity to you and by perhaps describ-
ing a Parisian hatpin or a summer jacket that's *chic* over and
over, and by acting as if there were nothing in the whole
world to compare to that in value and beauty, then that's all
sparkle, glitter, active imagination, *jeu d'esprit*;[8] and if tomorrow it suits her to describe a seminarian in a jasmine bower
blissfully reposing in Lottchen's arms, she'll carry it off with
the same aplomb and the same virtuosity. That's the Schmidt
in her. No, Marcell, don't let that give you any gray hairs;
all that isn't meant seriously. . ."

"It is meant seriously. . ."

"And if it is meant seriously—which for now I still don't
believe, because Corinna is a peculiar individual—this serious-

ness is of no avail, none at all, and nothing will come of it
anyway. You can depend on that, Marcell. Because it takes
two to marry."

"Certainly, Uncle. But Leopold wants to, if anything, more
than Corinna. . . ."

"Which is of no importance. For let me tell you—and these
are weighty words spoken lightly—the Kommerzienrätin does
not want to."

"Are you so sure of that?"

"Completely sure."

"And do you have any indications of that?"

"Indications and evidence, Marcell. Indications and evidence, in fact, that you can see before you in the flesh in your
old uncle Wilibald Schmidt. . . ."

"And that would be?"

"Yes, my friend—that you can see before you in the flesh.
For I've had the good fortune to be able to study the nature
of my friend Jenny with myself as the object and victim.
Jenny Bürstenbinder, that's her maiden name, as you may
already know, is the perfect bourgeoise type. She had the
talent for it when she was still snacking on the raisins over
there in her father's shop when the old man happened not to
be looking. Then she was already just as she is today and
declaimed the 'Diver' and 'To the Iron Hammer'[9] and other
little songs as well, and if it was something really moving she'd
be in tears even then. And when one day I had composed
my famous poem—you know, the unfortunate thing that she's
been singing ever since and perhaps even sang again today—
she threw herself into my arms and said: 'Wilibald, my one
and only, that comes from God.' A bit abashed I said something of my feelings and my love, but she maintained it came
from God and sobbed in such a way that I, happy as I was in
my vanity, nevertheless got quite a scare from the power of
those feelings. Yes, Marcell, that was more or less our quiet
engagement—very quiet, but an engagement nonetheless; at

least I took it for that and made gigantic efforts to get to the end of my studies and to take my examinations as quickly as possible. And everything did go excellently. But when I came to make the engagement final she put me off, alternately acting intimate and then again strange. And while she continued to sing that song, my song, she made eyes at everyone that came into the house until finally Treibel arrived and succumbed to the magic of her chestnut curls and, even more, to her sentimentalities—for the Treibel of those days was not yet the Treibel of today—and then I got the card announcing their engagement.

"All in all a strange story, which could have, I think I can safely say, caused our friendship to founder; but I don't hold a grudge nor am I a spoilsport. And in that song in which, as you know, 'heart to heart is paired'—a heavenly triviality, incidentally, and just as if made for Jenny Treibel—in that song our friendship lives on to this day, just as if nothing had happened. And after all, why not? I personally got over it, and Jenny Treibel has a talent for forgetting whatever she wants to forget. She's a dangerous person and all the more dangerous for not really knowing it herself, and she sincerely imagines she has a feeling heart, especially a heart for 'the higher things.' But she has a heart only for what has weight, for everything that counts and bears interest, and she won't let Leopold go for much less than half a million, no matter where the half million comes from. And poor Leopold himself? You know yourself that he is hardly the person to rebel or to elope to Gretna Green. I can tell you, Marcell, for a Treibel ceremony no one less than Brückner will do, and they'd even rather have Koegel.[10] Because the more it smacks of the Court the better. They constantly talk liberal and sentimental, but that's all a farce; and when it comes to showing one's true colors, then it's 'Gold is Trump' and nothing else."

"I think you underestimate Leopold."

"I'm afraid I'm still overestimating him. I know him from his junior year. He didn't get any further—and why should he? A good fellow, middling good, and in character rather below the middle."

"If you could speak with Corinna."

"Not necessary, Marcell. By interfering one just disturbs the natural course of things. Everything may waver and seem uncertain, but one thing is definite: the character of my friend Jenny. There lie the roots of your strength. And if Corinna keeps cutting mad capers, let her; I know the end of the affair. You should have her and you will have her, and perhaps sooner than you think."

Chapter Eight

TREIBEL was an early riser, at least for a Kommerzienrat, and never entered his study later than eight o'clock, always fully dressed, always immaculate. He would then look through his private correspondence, glance into the newspapers, and wait until his wife came to have the first breakfast with her. As a rule, the Rätin would appear very soon after him, but today she was late, and since the letters delivered were few and the newspapers, already foreshadowing the summer, contained little, Treibel became slightly impatient and, after rising quickly from his little leather sofa, strode through the two large adjoining rooms in which the previous day's party had taken place. The upper sash windows in the dining room had been lowered completely so that he could look down into the garden below him while resting comfortably on his arms. The scenery was the same as yesterday, only that instead of the cockatoo, who was still absent, one could see Fräulein Honig who was walking around the fountain leading the Kommerzienrätin's Maltese spaniel on a leash. This took place every morning and lasted each time until the cockatoo took up his place on the bar or was set outside in his shining cage, whereupon Fräulein Honig would withdraw with the Maltese to avoid an outbreak of hostilities between the two equally spoiled darlings of the house.

But today all that was yet to come. From his window Treibel inquired, polite as ever, after Fräulein Honig's health —an inquiry which the Kommerzienrätin, when she heard it, always found quite superfluous—and, receiving satisfactory reassurances, he asked how she had found Mr. Nelson's pronunciation. For he was more or less convinced that it must be an easy matter for any governess examined by a Berlin school director to determine that sort of thing. Fräulein Honig, who did not in the least want to destroy this belief, confined herself to questioning the correctness of Mr. Nelson's 'a' and to giving this 'a' of his a not quite admissible middle position between the English and the Scottish pronunciation of that vowel. Treibel accepted this comment quite seriously and would have pursued it further had he not at the same moment heard the latch of one of the front doors shut, which presumably meant that his wife had come in. Perceiving this, he considered it expedient to part from Fräulein Honig and walked back to his study which the Rätin had indeed just entered. The breakfast was already there, nicely arranged on a tray.

"Good morning, Jenny. . . . Sleep well?"

"Only tolerably. That dreadful Vogelsang haunted my bed."

"I'd really try to avoid that particular figure of speech. But your opinion. . . Anyway why don't we have breakfast outside?"

Agreeing, Jenny pressed the button for the bell, and the servant appeared again in order to carry the tray out to a small table on the veranda.

"That's fine, Friedrich," Treibel said and personally pulled up a footstool to make it as comfortable as possible for his wife—and himself too, for Jenny required such attentions to stay in a good mood.

Nor was this effect lost on her today. She smiled, moved the sugar bowl closer to herself, and holding her well-cared-for white hand over the large sugar cubes asked:

"One or two?"

"Two, Jenny, if you please. I can't see why I shouldn't enjoy these times of cheap sugar since I'm not in the sugar beet business, thank God."

Jenny agreed, put the sugar in, and then pushed the little cup, filled just to the gold rim, over to her husband with the remark:

"You've looked through the newspaper already? How are things with Gladstone?"

Treibel gave an unusually hearty laugh.

"If it's all right with you Jenny, let's stay on this side of the channel for the time being, let's say in Hamburg or at least in the Hamburg sphere, and let's transpose the question about Gladstone into a question about our daughter-in-law Helene. She was evidently out of sorts, and I'm just not sure what was at fault in her eyes. Was it that she herself had not been placed well enough? Or was it that Mr. Nelson, the guest of honor she kindly left to us—or to say it in the Berlin way, the guest of honor she saddled us with—was it because he was so unceremoniously put between Fräulein Honig and Corinna?"

"You just laughed, Treibel, because I asked you about Gladstone, and you shouldn't have done that. We women can ask a question like that even if we mean something entirely different. But you men shouldn't try to imitate us in that—just because you don't succeed, if for no other reason. I'm sure—and this certainly couldn't have escaped you—that I've never seen a more enchanted person than this good Mr. Nelson. So Helene surely won't have had anything against our placing her protégé just as we did. And even if there is this eternal jealousy between her and Corinna, who in her opinion takes too many liberties, and. . ."

"And is unwomanly and unhamburgian, which in her opinion is pretty much the same thing. . ."

"Then she probably forgave her yesterday for the first time because it was to her own benefit or at least to that of her hospitality, of which she has personally, of course, given such deficient examples. No, Treibel, there's no ill feeling about Mr. Nelson's place. Helene is pouting because we ignore all her hints and still haven't invited her sister Hildegard. Hildegard, incidentally, is a ridiculous name for a Hamburg girl. Hildegard is a good name in a castle with ancestral portraits or one that's haunted by a woman in white. Helene is pouting because we're so hard of hearing concerning Hildegard."

"Which she's right about."

"And I think she's not right about it. It's a presumption bordering on insolence. What's it supposed to mean? Are we here to do the honors for the lumberyard and its relations constantly? Are we here to encourage Helene's and her parents' plans? If Madam our daughter-in-law absolutely must play the hospitable sister, she can write off to Hamburg for Hildegard any day and can let the spoiled little doll decide whether the Alster at the Uhlenhorst or the Spree at Treptow is the prettier. But what concern of ours is that? Otto has his lumberyard just as you have your factory, and a lot of people find his villa to be nicer than ours—which is true. Ours is almost old-fashioned and in any case much too small, so that I often see no way in or out. I'm lacking at least two rooms, that's all there is to it. I don't want to say much about it, but why should we invite Hildegard as if we were anxious to cultivate the relations of the two houses so eagerly, and as if we wished nothing so ardently as to bring more Hamburg blood into the family. . ."

"But Jenny. . ."

"No 'buts,' Treibel. You men don't understand anything about such matters because you don't have an eye for it. I say that's the sort of thing they have in mind and that's why we're to do the inviting. If Helene invites Hildegard it means so little that it's hardly worth the tips and certainly not the new wardrobe. What significance does it have when two sisters see each other again? None at all, they don't even get along and bicker constantly; but if we invite Hildegard it'll mean that the Treibels are infinitely enchanted with their first Hamburg daughter-in-law and would be happy and honored to see such good fortune renewed and doubled with Fräulein Hildegard Munk becoming Frau Leopold Treibel. Yes, friend, that's what it amounts to. It's a perfect plot. Leopold is to marry Hildegard or rather Hildegard is to marry Leopold—because Leopold is passive and just does what he's told. That is what the Munks want, what Helene wants, and what our poor Otto who, Lord knows, hasn't got much to say, will finally have to want too. And because we hesitate and don't really seem to want to come out with an invitation, Helene pouts and lowers at us and acts so reserved and offended and doesn't even give up the role on a day when I've done her a big favor and have invited Mr. Nelson here just so that her irons don't get cold."

Treibel leaned further back in his chair and artfully blew a little ring into the air.

"I don't think you're right. But if you were right, what could happen? Otto has been happily married to Helene for eight years, which is only natural—I can't recall that anyone of my acquaintance has been unhappily married to a Hamburg woman. There's nothing dubious about them whatever; inwardly and outwardly they have such an unusually well-washed quality, and everything they do and don't do supports the theory about the influence of a good upbringing. One never has to be ashamed of them, and they usually come very close to their disputed but always quietly cherished heart's desire, 'to be taken for an Englishwoman.' But let's leave that be. This much in any case is certain, and I have to repeat it: Helene Munk has made our Otto happy and it seems most probable to me that Hildegard Munk would make our Leopold happy too, or even happier. And it wouldn't take witchery either, because there just isn't a better person than our Leopold—he's almost like a sissy. . . ."

"Almost?" Jenny said. "You can pretend to take him seriously! I don't know where both boys got this milksop quality. Two born Berliners and they act as if they'd come out of Pietist schools. Both of them do have something sleepy about them, and I really don't know, Treibel, on whom I can put the blame. . ."

"On me, Jenny, naturally on me. . . ."

"And even though I know very well," Jenny continued, "that it's useless to rack my brains about such things because such characters unfortunately can't be changed, I know too that it's one's duty to help if help can still be given. We neglected it with Otto, and to his own spiritlessness we've added this spiritless Helene, and now you can see the outcome in Lizzi who must be the greatest doll to be seen anywhere. I believe Helene will give her English training down to showing her front teeth. Well, for all I care! But I'll confess to you, Treibel, that I have enough with *one* such daughter-in-law and *one* such granddaughter, and that I'd like to find a more suitable place for this poor boy, Leopold, than the Munk family."

"You want to make a dashing man out of him, a gentleman, a sportsman. . ."

"No, not a dashing man, but simply a man. A man should have passion, and if he could seize a passion, that would be something, that would be a start. And as much as I hate scandal I would almost be pleased if something like that came up, naturally nothing bad, but at least something out of the ordinary."

"Don't speak of the devil, Jenny. I don't know whether it's fortunate or unfortunate, but it doesn't seem very probable to me that he should take up seducing. There have, however, been instances in which individuals who decidedly did not have the stuff for seducing were, as if in punishment, seduced themselves. There are some really devilish women, and Leopold is just weak enough to be lifted into the saddle of a poor and somewhat emancipated noblewoman, whose name could even be Schmidt, and be carried across the border. . ."

"I don't believe it," the Kommerzienrätin said, "he's even too dull for that."

And she was so firmly convinced of the lack of danger in the whole situation that not even the name Schmidt, spoken perhaps by accident, perhaps by intention, startled her. "Schmidt" had just been thrown out in an everyday way, nothing more, and in a half-playful efflorescence of youth the Rätin indulged in quietly picturing an escapade: Leopold, with a mustache added, on his way to Italy and with him a devil-may-care baroness from a declining Pomeranian or Silesian family, the aigrette in her hat and the tartan coat spread out over the slightly shivering lover. She envisioned all that, and almost sadly she said to herself: "The poor boy. Yes, if he had the stuff for *that!*"

When the Treibels had this conversation around nine o'clock, they had no idea that at the same time the young Treibels were also having breakfast on their veranda and reflecting on the previous day's party. Helene looked very lovely, not the least because of her becoming morning gown and a particular liveliness in her otherwise dull and almost forget-me-not blue eyes. It was quite obvious that until this minute she had been zealously preaching at Otto, whose eyes were cast down uneasily; and if all appearances weren't deceiving she was about to continue her charge when she was interrupted by the appearance of Lizzi and her governess, Fräulein Wulsten.

In spite of the early hour Lizzi was already all dressed up. The child's slightly wavy blond hair hung down to her waist; everything else was white, the dress, the long stockings, the turned-down collar. Around her waist, if it could be called that, she wore a wide red sash, which Helene never called a red sash in German but rather a "pink-colored scarf" in English. The way she was, the little girl could immediately have been placed in her mother's linen closet as a symbolic figure, a pure expression of freshly bought linen with a red ribbon around it. Throughout their circle of acquaintances Lizzi was considered a model child, which filled Helene's heart with gratitude to God—and to Hamburg. For added to the gifts of nature that heaven had so visibly bestowed here, there had been a model upbringing such as only the Hamburg tradition could give. This model upbringing had begun right with the first day of the child's life. "Because it was uncomely," Helene could not be persuaded to nurse the infant herself (though Krola, then seven years younger, had disputed this). In the ensuing discussions a Spreewald wetnurse suggested by the old Kommerzienrat had been declined with the remark, "as everyone knows, so much of that is passed on to the innocent child," and they had turned to the sole remaining source of information. The clergyman of the Thomas community had warmly recommended a married woman who then had taken over the feeding with great conscientiousness and with a watch in her hand, and Lizzi thrived so well that for a time she even had little dimples in her shoulders. Everything was normal and almost better than normal. Our Kommerzienrat had never really trusted this business fully, and only considerably later, when Lizzi had cut her finger with a ripping-knife (for which the nursemaid was dismissed), Treibel had exclaimed with relief: "Thank God, as far as I can see, it's real blood."

Lizzi's life had begun in an orderly fashion, and it was continued in an orderly fashion. The undergarments she wore bore the corresponding number of the day throughout the month, so that, as her grandfather said, one could always read the date from her stockings. "Today is the tenth." Her doll's wardrobe had numbered hooks, and all the containers in her doll's kitchen were clearly labelled. When it happened (and this dreadful day was not far past) that Lizzi, otherwise care personified, had put seminola in the container very clearly marked "Lentils," Helene had taken the occasion to explain to her darling how far-reaching such a blunder was.

"That makes a lot of difference, dear Lizzi. Whoever wants to take care of great things must also know how to take care of small things. Just think, if you had a little brother, and the little brother seemed faint, and you wanted to spray him with *eau de cologne* and you sprayed him with *eau de javelle*.[1] Why, Lizzi, then your little brother could become blind or if it went into his blood he could die. And that would still be easier to excuse because both are clear and look like water; but seminola and lentils, my dear Lizzi, that's a strong case of inattentiveness or, which would be even worse, of indifference."

Such was Lizzi, who also, to her mother's great satisfaction, had a cupid's bow mouth. Her two bright front teeth however still were not visible enough to please Helene completely, and so her maternal cares now returned to this important question. She was convinced that the materials so fortunately provided by nature had so far lacked only the proper attention in the child's upbringing.

"You're pursing your lips so again, Lizzi, you mustn't do that. It looks better if the mouth is half open, almost as if to speak. Fräulein Wulsten, I would really like for you to pay a bit more attention to this little matter, which really isn't a little matter. . . . How is the birthday poem coming along?"

"Lizzi is making the greatest efforts."

"Well, then I'll let you have your wish, Lizzi. Invite the little Felgentreu girl over this afternoon. But first your homework, of course. . . . And now, if Fräulein Wulsten permits it"—who nodded—"you can take a walk in the garden, anywhere you want to, just not toward the yard where the boards are lying across the limestone pit. Otto, you should change that; the boards are so rotten anyway."

Lizzi was happy to have an hour free, and after she had kissed her Mama's hand and had also been warned to stay away from the water barrel, she and the Fräulein started out, her parents looking after her as she turned around a few times and gratefully nodded at her mother.

"Actually," said the latter, "I would like to have kept Lizzi here and read a page of English with her; Wulsten doesn't understand it and has a pitiful pronunciation, so low, so vulgar. But I'm forced to let it go until tomorrow because we have to finish our conversation. I don't like to say anything against your parents because I know it isn't proper, and I know too that with your peculiarly obstinate character"— Otto smiled—"it would just strengthen this obstinacy of yours. But one shouldn't put propriety above everything, any more than intelligence. And that is what I would be doing if I kept quiet any longer. Your parents' position on this question is nothing short of insulting for me and almost more so for my family. Now don't be angry with me, Otto, but who are the Treibels after all? It's awkward to touch on such things, and I'd be careful not to do it if you didn't virtually force me to weigh our families against one another."

Otto remained silent and let his teaspoon balance on his index finger, but Helene continued: "The Munks are originally Danish, and one branch, as you know very well, was ennobled as Counts under King Christian. As a Hamburger and the daughter of a Free City, I don't want to make much of that, but it is nonetheless something. And then on my mother's side too! The Thompsons are a guild[2] family. You act as if that were nothing. Fine, let that be as it may, and I just want to say this much more, our ships were already going to Messina when your mother was still playing in that orange store that your father got her out of. Groceries and produce! You call that a merchant too, here. . . . I'm not saying *you*. . . but there are merchants and then there are merchants."

Otto endured it all and looked down into the garden where Lizzi was playing ball.

"Do you intend to answer me at all, Otto?"

"Preferably not, dear Helene. And for what? You can't simply demand that I share your opinion in this affair, and if I don't and say as much, then I irritate you all the more. I find that you're asking for more than you should. My mother is very attentive towards you and only yesterday proved it again, because I doubt very much that the dinner given in honor of *our* guest suited her particularly. You know besides that she's frugal where it doesn't concern her own person."

"Frugal," Helene laughed.

"Call it greed, it's all the same to me. But despite that she never fails in her attentions, and when birthdays come, her presents come too. But all that doesn't change your mind; quite the contrary, your opposition to Mama continues to grow, and all just because through her attitude she's given you to understand that what Papa calls the 'Hamburg business' is not the highest thing in the world and that God didn't create his world for the sake of the Munks. . . ."

"Are those your mother's words or are you adding something of your own? It almost sounds that way; your voice is nearly trembling."

"Helene, if you want us to talk the matter over quietly and weigh both sides reasonably and considerately, then you shouldn't pour oil on the flames constantly. You're so irritated with Mama because she ignores your hints and shows no intention of inviting Hildegard. But you're in the wrong there. If the whole thing is just supposed to be something between sisters, then the one sister should invite the other; then it's a matter with which my Mama has precious little to do. . . ."

"Very flattering for Hildegard and for me too. . . ."

"But if it's to pursue another plan, and you've admitted to me that this is the case, then it has to—as desirable as such a second family connection doubtless would be for the Treibels —then it has to take place under circumstances of a more natural and spontaneous character. If you invite Hildegard and if that led, let's say a month or two later, to an engagement with Leopold, then we have exactly what I call the natural and spontaneous way. But if my Mama writes the invitation to Hildegard and says in it how happy she would be to see her dear Helene's sister visit for a good long time and to share in her sister's happiness, Hildegard would think she were being courted and even pursued, and that the Treibel firm wants to avoid."

"And you approve of that?"

"Yes."

"Well, that's at least clear. But just because it's clear still doesn't mean it's right. If I understand you correctly, everything revolves around the question of who should take the first step."

Otto nodded.

"Well, if that's the way it is, why do the Treibels want to resist taking this step first? Since the beginning of time, the bridegroom or the suitor has been the one who did the courting. . . ."

"Certainly, dear Helene. But we haven't gotten to the courting yet. For the time being it's still a question of beginning, of building bridges, and building such bridges is up to those who have the greater interest in it. . . ."

"Hah," laughed Helene. "We, the Munks. . . and the greater interest! Otto, you shouldn't have said that. I don't care that it disparages me and my family, but it makes the whole Treibel clan, and you especially, appear so ridiculous that it damages the respect you men constantly demand. Yes, friend, you're challenging me, and so I want to tell you plainly: on your side there is interest, profit, honor. And it's up to you to show you realize that; you have to express it unmistakably. That is the first step that I spoke of. And since I'm making confessions, let me tell you, Otto, that beyond their serious, business side these things have a personal side as well, and I'm assuming for now that it couldn't occur to you to compare your brother and my sister in appearance. Hildegard is a beauty and is just like her grandmother Elizabeth Thompson—after whom we baptized our Lizzi—and she has the *chic* of a lady; you yourself admitted that to me earlier. And now look at your brother Leopold! He's a good fellow who's acquired a saddle horse because he thinks it'll make a man of him and now he shortens his stirrups as much as an Englishman. But it doesn't do him any good. He is and always will be below average, in any case, far from a gentleman, and if Hildegard were to take him—I'm afraid she won't take him—that would be the only possible way to make anything near a perfect gentleman out of him. And you can tell that to your Mama."

"I'd prefer you did it."

"If you're from a good family you avoid disputes and scenes. . ."

"And make them in front of your husband instead. . ."

"That's something different."

"Yes," Otto laughed. But there was something melancholy in his laughter.

Leopold Treibel, who was employed in his older brother's business while he lived in his parents' house, had wanted to serve his year in the guard dragoons, but because of his weak chest he had not been accepted, which deeply offended the whole family. Treibel himself finally got over it, less so the Kommerzienrätin, and least of all Leopold himself, who—as Helene liked to stress at every opportunity and had done again this morning—had taken riding lessons to attempt to blot out his defeat. Every day he was in the saddle for two hours, and because he really made an effort he cut quite a passable figure.

Today too, on the same morning that the old and the young Treibels had their arguments about the same dangerous subject, Leopold had, without the least idea of being the cause and object of such touchy conversations, begun his usual morning excursion in the direction of Treptow. Riding from his parents' home down Köpenick Strasse, which was not very busy at this early hour, he passed first his brother's villa and then the old Engineers' barracks. The barracks' clock was just striking seven as he passed the Silesian gate. If being in the saddle of itself pleased him every morning, it did so particularly today when the events of the preceding evening, chiefly the conversations between Mr. Nelson and Corinna, were having a strong aftereffect, so strong that he could entertain a desire—held in common with the otherwise dissimilar Ritter Karl von Eichenhorst[3]—of "riding himself calm." His mount though was hardly a Danish steed full of strength and fire, but rather a horse from the Graditz stables that had been in the riding school for a long time and could not be expected to do anything extravagant. And so Leopold rode at a walk, as much as he wished to be able to storm off.

Very gradually he fell into a gentle trot and stayed at it until he reached the Schafgraben and immediately afterwards the nearby "Silesian Bush," a small wood in which the evening before two women and a watchmaker had been robbed, as Johann had told him just as he was riding off. "There's just no end to this mischief! Laxness, police negligence!" But in the bright daylight this hardly mattered, and so Leopold was in the agreeable situation of being able to enjoy unhindered the sounds of the blackbirds and finches all around him. Once out of the "Silesian Bush" he enjoyed the open road hardly the less: to his right, cornfields spread out, while on the left the Spree with its adjacent parks bounded the way. All this was so lovely, so morning-fresh, that he let his horse fall into a walk again. But even as slowly as he rode, he soon reached the spot where the small ferryboat came across from the other shore, and when he stopped in order to be able to watch the little drama better, a few other riders came trotting along the avenue from the city, and a horse tram containing, so far as he could see, no morning visitors for Treptow, glided past. That was just what he liked because having breakfast in the open, his regular refreshment here, was only half the pleasure if half a dozen genuine Berliners sat around him and let their terriers jump over chairs or retrieve things from the landing. None of all that was to be feared today, unless this empty car had already been preceded by a fully occupied one.

Around half-past seven he was there and, waving to a half-grown boy with only one arm and the corresponding loose sleeve (which he constantly swung in the air), he now got off and said while giving the reins to the boy: "Take him under the linden tree, Fritz. The morning sun beats down so here."

The boy did as he had been told and Leopold himself walked along a picket fence overgrown with privets towards the entrance of the Treptow establishment. Thank God everything was just as he wished here, all the tables empty, the chairs tipped over, and not even any waiters except for his friend Mützell. This Mützell, a fastidious man in his middle forties, wore an almost spotless tailcoat even in the morning hours and handled the matter of tips with an astonishing *gentilezza*[4] (which was never necessary with Leopold though, since he was always very liberal).

"You see, Herr Treibel," had been his words when their conversation had taken this turn, "most people don't really want to tip and they even try to deny you a share, especially the ladies. But then again a lot of them are good and some even very good, and they know that you can't live on a cigar, and the wife at home with her three children sure can't. And you see, Herr Treibel, these people, and especially the little ones that don't have much themselves, they give. Just yesterday there was a fellow here who gave me a fifty-pfennig piece by mistake because he thought it was a ten-pfennig piece, and when I told him, he didn't take it back and just said: 'That was meant to be that way, my friend and copperminer; now and then Easter and Pentecost fall on the same day.' "

It had been weeks ago that Mützell had begun to talk to Leopold Treibel in this way. They both were inclined to chat, but what was even more pleasant for Leopold than this chatting was that he didn't have to talk about things that went without saying. When Mützell would see the young Treibel enter the restaurant and walk across the freshly raked gravel towards his place immediately by the water, he would simply salute from the distance and then promptly withdraw into the kitchen from which he would reappear under the front trees three minutes later with a tray bearing a cup of coffee, some English biscuits, and a large glass of milk. The large glass of milk was the main thing because the Sanitätsrat Dr. Lohmeier had said to the Kommerzienrätin after the last auscultation: "My dear Madam, it doesn't mean anything yet, but one should take preventive measures, that's what we're here for; for the rest our knowledge is piecework. So if I may ask you—as little coffee as possible and every morning a quart of milk."

At Leopold's appearance this morning the daily meeting ritual had been reenacted: Mützell had disappeared towards the kitchen and now emerged again in front of the house, balancing the tray on the five fingers of his left hand with an almost acrobatic virtuosity.

"Good morning, Herr Treibel. Lovely morning, this morning."

"Yes, my dear Mützell. Very lovely. But a bit brisk. Especially here by the water. I'm actually shivering, and I've already walked up and down. Let's see, Mützell, if the coffee is warm."

And before the waiter, addressed in such a friendly way, could set the tray on the table, Leopold had taken down the little cup and emptied it in one draught.

"Ah, splendid. That does an old fellow good. And now I'll drink the milk, Mützell, but with devotion. And when I'm finished with that—the milk is always a bit clabbery, but that's not a reproach, good milk should always be a bit clabbery—when I'm finished with that I'd like to have another..."

"Coffee?"

"Of course, Mützell."

"But, Herr Treibel..."

"Well, what is it? You're looking awfully embarrassed, Mützell, as if I'd said something peculiar."

"Well, Herr Treibel, when your Frau Mama was here the day before yesterday and the Herr Kommerzienrat too, and the lady's companion, and you, Herr Leopold, had gone to the Sperl and the carousel, your Frau Mama told me: 'Listen, Mützell, I know he comes here almost every morning, and I'm making you responsible... *one* cup, never more.... Sanitätsrat Lohmeier, who treated your wife once too, told me confidentially but in all seriousness: 'two is poison...'"

"So... and did my Mama perhaps say anything more?"

"Frau Kommerzienrätin also said: 'It won't be to your

disadvantage, Mützell. . . . I can't say that my son is a passionate fellow, he's a good fellow, a dear fellow. . .' You'll pardon, Herr Treibel, that I'm repeating everything your Frau Mama said so plainly. . . 'but he has a passion for coffee. And that's always the bad thing, that people have just the passion they shouldn't have. So, Mützell, one cup may be all right, but not two.' "

Leopold had listened with mixed feelings not knowing whether to laugh or become annoyed. "Well, Mützell, let's not then, no second cup." And with that he sat down again while Mützell withdrew to his post at the corner of the house.

"There I have my life at a single stroke," Leopold said when he was alone again. "I once heard of a fellow who, on a bet at Josty's café, drank down twelve cups of coffee in a row and then fell over dead. But what does that prove? If I eat twelve cheese sandwiches I'll fall over dead too; anything twelvefold kills a person. But what reasonable person takes his food and drink twelvefold? You have to assume of every reasonable person that he would avoid such madness and consult his health and not destroy his body. I can vouch for myself at least. And my good Mama should know that I don't require such supervision and shouldn't appoint my friend Mützell as guardian so naively. But she always has to have all the strings in her hand, she has to decide everything, arrange everything, and if I want a cotton jacket it has to be a woolen one."

He now turned to the milk and had to smile when he picked up the tall glass in which the foam had just subsided. "My proper drink. 'The milk of human kindness,' Papa would say. Oh, it's irritating, everything is irritating. Everyone making decisions for me, worse than if I'd just been confirmed yesterday. Helene knows everything better, Otto knows everything better, and then Mama! She'd really like to dictate whether I should wear a blue or a green tie and a straight or a slanting part. But I'm not going to be irritated. The Dutch have a saying: 'Let it puzzle you, but don't let it irritate you.' And I'll even get out of the habit of that."

He continued talking to himself like this, alternately deploring people and circumstances, until he suddenly directed all his displeasure at himself: "Foolishness. The people, the circumstances, that isn't it; no, no. Others also have mothers jealous of ruling their house and still they do what they want; it's my fault. 'Pluck, dear Leopold, that's it,' that's what the good Nelson said in parting just yesterday, and he's quite right. That's what it is, nothing else. I lack energy and courage, and I've certainly never learned to rebel."

While saying this he looked down and flicked little pieces of gravel away with his riding crop and drew letters into the freshly strewn sand. When he looked up again after a while he saw numerous boats coming over from the Stralau shore and in between them a Spree barge with a large sail traveling downriver. His glance seemed to follow it yearningly.

"Ah, I've got to get out of this miserable state, and if it's true that love gives you courage and determination, then everything will still have to turn out well. And not just well, it has to become easy for me too, and absolutely force me and press me to take up the fight and to show them all, Mama most of all, that they've really misjudged and underestimated me. And if I fall back into irresolution, which God forbid, then *she* will give me the necessary strength. Because she has all those things I lack, and knows everything and can do everything. But am I sure of her? There I've come to the main question again. Of course, now and then it seems to me as if she did concern herself with me and as if she were speaking really only to me when she's speaking to others. That's the way it was yesterday evening again, and I saw too how Marcell changed color because he was jealous. It couldn't have been anything else. And all that. . ."

He interrupted himself because the sparrows gathering

around him were becoming more insistent with every moment. A few came up onto the table and admonished him, by picking at the table and looking at him boldly, that he still owed them their breakfast. Smiling, he broke up a biscuit and threw them the pieces, with which they triumphantly flew back into the linden trees. But the intruders were hardly gone before his old reflections were back again.

"Yes, that about Marcell, that I can interpret to my benefit, and quite a few other things too. But it could all have been just a game and a whim. Corinna doesn't take anything seriously and actually she always just wants to shine and attract the admiration or the amazement of her listeners. And if I consider this part of her character, I have to think of the possibility that I might in the end be sent home and laughed at too. That's bitter. But still I must risk it. . . . If only I had someone in whom I could confide, who would advise me. Unfortunately I have no one, no friend; Mama saw to that too, and so I have to get a double 'yes' all by myself without advice and support. First from Corinna. And when I have this first 'yes,' I still don't have the second one by a long way. I see that all too clearly. But the second one I can at least win by fighting for it and I will do it. . . . There are enough people for whom all this would be an easy matter, but for me it's difficult; heroes are born and I know I'm not one of them. 'Each according to his own powers,' Direktor Hilgenhahn always said. Ah, I almost find that more is placed on my shoulders than I can bear."

A steamer full of people was coming up the river at that moment and went on towards the "Neuen Krug" and "Sadowa" establishments without putting in at the landing; there was music on board and all sorts of songs were being sung. When the ship had passed the landing and then the Isle of Love, Leopold started out of his musings and saw, looking at his watch, that it was high time to leave if he still wanted to reach the office punctually and spare himself a reprimand or,

even worse, a sarcastic remark from his brother Otto. With
a friendly greeting he therefore walked past Mützell, who was
still standing at his corner, and on to the spot where the one-
armed boy was holding his horse. "There you are, Fritz!" And
now he got into the saddle, made his way back at a good trot,
and turned, once he had passed the Gate and the Engineers'
barracks again, to the right into a narrow passage. This ran
alongside the Treibel lumberyard, bordered by a picket fence,
and beyond it one could see the front yard and the villa set
between the trees. His brother and sister-in-law were still
sitting at breakfast. Leopold greeted them: "Good morning,
Otto; good morning, Helene!" Both returned the greeting,
but smiled because they found his daily riding routine rather
ridiculous. And especially for Leopold! Just what did he think
he was doing.

Leopold himself had meanwhile dismounted and now gave
the horse to a servant who was already waiting at the back-
stairs of the villa to take it up the Köpenick Strasse to his
parents' factory yard and the stable belonging to it—"stable-
yard," Helene always called it in English.

Chapter Nine

A week had passed and the Schmidt house was overcast with ill humor; Corinna was angry with Marcell because he was angry with her (or so she interpreted his staying away), and the good Schmolke in turn was angry with Corinna herself because of her anger at Marcell.

"It's not good, Corinna, to reject such a fine opportunity. Believe me, that kind of opportunity doesn't come back when it's chased away. Marcell is a treasure, a jewel—Marcell is just the way Schmolke was."

That was said every evening. Schmidt alone noticed nothing of the cloud settled over his house; instead he became more and more deeply involved in his study of the gold masks and decided, in an increasingly vehement dispute with Distelkamp, that one of them was most definitely Aegisthus. After all, Aegisthus had been Clytemnestra's husband for seven years, and was a close relation of the house besides. Schmidt did have to admit that the murder of Agamemnon argued somewhat against his Aegisthus hypothesis, but then it shouldn't be forgotten that the murder was more or less an internal affair, purely a family matter, so to speak. And for that reason the question of an official public burial ceremony couldn't actually be discussed. Distelkamp was silent and withdrew from the debate with a smile.

At the old and the young Treibels, too, something of a bad mood prevailed: Helene was dissatisfied with Otto, Otto with Helene, and Mama in turn with both. But the most dissatisfied, even if only with himself, was Leopold. Only the elder Treibel noticed precious little, or didn't want to notice anything, of the ill humor surrounding him, and instead he enjoyed an unusually good mood. That this was so was because, like Wilibald Schmidt, he was able to exercise his hobbyhorse the whole time, and could pride himself on several triumphs already attained.

Immediately after the dinner held in his and Mr. Nelson's honor, Vogelsang had left for the electoral district to be conquered for Treibel, in order to probe, in a sort of preliminary campaign, the hearts and minds of the Teupitz-Zosseners and the position they might take in the decisive hour. It must be said that in the execution of this assignment he not only had been remarkably active, but had also sent numerous, almost daily telegrams in which he gave, depending on the significance of the action, longer or shorter reports on the results of his expedition. It had not escaped Treibel that these telegrams were desperately similar to those of the erstwhile Bernau war correspondent[1] who was always pressed for money, but he had not taken exception to them, particularly because he only paid attention, after all, to what pleased him personally. One of these telegrams said: "Everything going fine. Cable money to Teupitz, please. Your V." And then: "The villages by Scharmützel Lake are ours. Thank God. Everywhere the same attitude as at Lake Teupitz. Cable hasn't arrived yet. Urgent, please. Your V."—"To Storkow tomorrow! There it will have to be decided. Cable received meanwhile. But just covers past expenditures. Montecuccoli's remark[2] about war holds for election campaigns too. Cable more to Gross-Rietz. Your V." His vanity flattered, Treibel considered the electoral district secured for him, and only one bitter drop fell into the cup of his joy: he knew how critically Jenny objected to this business, and therefore saw himself forced to enjoy his happiness alone. Friedrich, generally his confidant, was once more "the only feeling breast under all the masks,"[3] a quotation he did not tire of repeating to himself. But there remained a certain emptiness. It struck him, moreover, that the Berlin newspapers reported nothing at all, and this seemed all the more striking to him because there wasn't, according to Vogelsang's reports, any sharp opposition to speak of. The Conservatives and the National Liberals, and perhaps even a few professional parliamentarians might be against him, but what did that mean? According to a rough estimate Vogelsang had made and addressed to him in a registered letter to the Treibel villa, the whole district had only seven National Liberals: three secondary school teachers, one district judge, one rationalist clergyman who was district superintendent, and two educated farm owners; while the number of orthodox Conservatives came to fewer than even this modest bunch. "Serious opposition—*vacat*." So ended Vogelsang's letter, and the *vacat* was underlined. That sounded most encouraging, but in the midst of sincere joy a trace of disquiet persisted. When a week had passed after Vogelsang's departure, the important day that ultimately justified this recurring anxiety began. His instinctive worries would not be substantiated immediately, not right at the first moment, but the respite was a short one measured to the minute.

Treibel was sitting in his room and having breakfast. Jenny had let herself be excused because of a headache and a bad dream. "Could she have dreamed of Vogelsang again?" He had no idea that this mockery would be revenged within the very same hour. Friedrich brought the mail which included few cards and letters this time, but many more newspapers in their wrappers, some of which—so far as could be distinguished outwardly—were embellished with strange emblems and city-arms.

Closer examination soon confirmed Treibel's assumptions, and when he had removed the wrappers and had spread the soft newsprint out on the table he read the various titles with a certain cheerful devotion: *The Watch on the Wendish Spree, Disarmed—Dishonored, Forever Onward,* and *The Storkow Messenger*—two of them came from this side of the Spree and two from the other side. Treibel was ordinarily an enemy of overhasty reading since he expected only harm to come of all blind eagerness, but this time he got at the papers with notable rapidity and skimmed the places marked in blue. Lieutenant Vogelsang (it said in each one, repeated word for word), a man who had taken his stand against the revolution and had trampled the head of the Hydra[4] in '48, had presented himself to the district on three successive days, not on his own behalf but on that of his political friend, Kommerzienrat Treibel, who would visit the district later. At that opportunity he would repeat the principles enunciated by Lieutenant Vogelsang, which—and this much could be said now—may be viewed as the warmest recommendation of the actual candidate. For the Vogelsang program alleged that there was too much governing, particularly too much that looked out for personal interests, and it accordingly proposed that all the costly "middle steps" should be dropped (which in turn amounted to a reduction in taxes), and that nothing should remain of these current complexities, incomprehensible as they often are, but a free lord and a free people. This, of course, meant that the program had two midpoints or focuses but that was of no harm to the matter. For whoever had plumbed the depths of life or even just skimmed them, knew that there was really no simple midpoint—the word "center" was deliberately avoided—and that life did not move in a circle but rather in an ellipse. And for that reason two focal points were what was necessary.

"Not bad," said Treibel, when he had finished reading, "not bad. It has something logical about it—a bit crazy but still logical. The only thing that puzzles me is that it all sounds as if Vogelsang had written it himself. The trampled Hydra, the reduced taxes, the awful wordplay with the center and finally the nonsense about the circle and the ellipse, all that is Vogelsang. And the correspondent of the four Spree papers is naturally Vogelsang as well. I know my man."

And with that Treibel pushed *The Watch on the Wendish Spree* and all the rest off the table down onto the sofa and took in hand half of the *National News* which had come in wrappers along with the others, but to judge by the handwriting and the whole address, it had to have been sent by someone else. Earlier the Kommerzienrat had been a subscriber and eager reader of the *National News*, and even now there were times every day when he regretted the change in his reading.

"Let's see now," he finally said, opening the paper and scanning the three columns—and right, there it was: "Parliamentary News. From the District of Teupitz-Zossen." When he had read the headline he interrupted himself. "I don't know, it sounds so peculiar. And then again, how could it sound otherwise after all? It's the most natural beginning in the world; forward then."

And so he read on: "Our quiet district, usually undisturbed by political battles, has for the last three days witnessed the beginnings of election preparations. These are being made by a party which has apparently resolved to make up for what it lacks in historical knowledge and political experience—why, one might well say, in good common sense—with 'deftness.' This very party, which knows nothing else, apparently knows the fairy tale of 'The Hare and the Hedgehog',[5] and seems to intend, on the day that the race with the real parties is to begin, to receive each of these with the familiar call of the hedgehog in the fairy tale, 'I'm here already.' This is the only way we can explain their being on the spot so prematurely. It seems that all places are to be occupied, as at theater premieres, by Lieutenant Vogelsang and his following. But that will prove a deception. This party may have the face to present its principles to us, but it lacks the mind to convince us."

"Confound it," Treibel said, "he starts in sharply. . . . Where it touches me it's not exactly pleasant, but I don't begrudge Vogelsang getting it. There is something in his program that dazzles, and he took me in with it too. But the more I look at it, the more questionable it seems to me. Among these broken-down soldiers who fancy they trampled the Hydra forty years ago, there are several circle-squarers and perpetual motion-seekers—always the sort who want to bring about the impossible, the contradictory. Vogelsang is one of them. Maybe it's just a question of good business—if I add up what this week. . . But I've only gotten through the first paragraph of the article; the second half will probably make an even sharper attack on him, or maybe even on me."

And Treibel read on: "The gentleman who favored us with his presence yesterday and the day before—not to mention his previous activities in our district—in Markgraf-Pieske, and then in Storkow and Gross-Rietz can hardly be taken seriously, and the more serious his face, the less credible he is. He belongs to that class of Malvolios, the solemn fools, whose number is unfortunately greater than is generally assumed. If his gibberish has no name as yet, one could teach him the song of the three full C's, because the Cabinet, Churbrandenburg,[6] and Cantonal freedom are the three big C's with which this cure-all wants to save the world. A certain method in it cannot be denied, though there is method in madness too. Lieutenant Vogelsang's song displeased us in the extreme. Everything in his program is publicly dangerous. But what we deplore most is that he did not speak for himself and in his own name, but in the name of one of our most respected Berlin industrialists, the Kommerzienrat Treibel (Berlin blue factory, Köpenick Strasse), of whom we would have expected something better. New evidence that one can be a good man and still a bad musician, and likewise evidence of where political dilettantism leads."

Treibel folded the paper up again, slapped his hand on it, and said: "Well, this much is certain—that wasn't written in Teupitz-Zossen. That's Tell's arrow. That's at close range. That's by that National Liberal secondary school teacher who didn't just oppose us at Buggenhagen's recently but tried to deride us as well. Didn't get through, though. All in all, I don't want to be unjust to him, and I like him better than Vogelsang in any case. Besides, at the *National News* they're halfway a Court party and go along with the Free Conservatives. It was stupid of me, or at least over-hasty, that I turned away. If I had waited, I could now—in much better company—stand on the side of the government. Instead of that I'm sworn to that stupid fellow and his ridiculous principles. But I'll pull myself out of the whole affair, and that forever; the burned child dreads the fire. . . . Actually I could still congratulate myself on having gotten off with about a thousand marks, or at least not much more, if only my name hadn't been mentioned. My name. That's awkward. . . . And he opened the paper again. "I want to read that part once more: 'one of our most respected Berlin industrialists, the Kommerzienrat Treibel'—yes, that I like, that sounds good. And now thanks to Vogelsang's good graces I'm a laughable figure."

And with these words he got up to take a walk in the garden and to get rid of his anger as best he could in the fresh air.

But it did not seem quite meant to succeed, because at the same moment that he turned around the corner of the house into the backyard, he saw Fräulein Honig who, as on every morning, was leading the little Maltese around the fountain.

Treibel recoiled, because a conversation with the stiff Fräulein did not suit him at all just now. But she had already seen and greeted him, and since great politeness and even more great kindheartedness counted among his virtues, he pulled himself together and cheerfully went up to Fräulein Honig, in whose knowledge and judgment he did after all have sincere confidence.

"Very pleased, my dear Fräulein, to meet you alone once and at such a good hour. . . . For a long time I've had this and that on my chest and would like to get it off. . . ."

Fräulein Honig turned red because, despite the good reputation Treibel enjoyed, a feeling of sweet anxiety had run over her at his remarks, though it became almost cruelly clear the next moment that it was totally unjustified.

"What's been occupying me is my dear little granddaughter's upbringing, in which I see those Hamburg methods being executed—I'm choosing this scaffold expression intentionally—to a degree that fills me with a good deal of concern, from my simple Berlin standpoint."

The Maltese, called Czicka, pulled on the leash at that moment and seemed to want to run after a guinea hen that had strayed into the garden from the yard—but Fräulein Honig was not to be trifled with and gave the dog a slap. Czicka let out a yelp and tossed its head back and forth so that the little bells sewn onto its jacket (actually just a belt) started ringing. But then the little animal calmed down again and the promenade around the fountain began anew.

"You see, Fräulein Honig, that's how Lizzi is being brought up too. Always on a leash that her mother holds in her hand, and if a guinea hen happens to come and Lizzi wants to get away, she'll get a slap too, though a very, very little one. The difference is only that Lizzi doesn't let out a yelp and toss her head and naturally doesn't have a set of bells that can start ringing."

"Little Lizzi is an angel," said Fräulein Honig, who had

learned caution in what she said in her sixteen-year career as a governess.

"Do you really believe that?"

"I really believe that, Herr Kommerzienrat, assuming that we agree on the meaning of 'angel.' "

"Very good, Fräulein Honig, now that's perfect. I had just wanted to talk about Lizzi with you and now I hear something about angels too. On the whole, there is not much opportunity to form a firm judgment about angels. Now tell me, what do you mean by angel? And don't come out with wings."

Fräulein Honig smiled. "No, Herr Kommerzienrat, nothing about wings, but I should like to say "untouched by anything earthly,' that is an angel."

"That sounds good. Untouched by anything earthly, not bad. Why, more than that, I'll let it stand as it is and think it fine. And if Otto and my daughter-in-law Helene would clearly and methodically resolve to bring up a genuine little Genevieve or a chaste little Susanna—pardon me, but I can't find a better example at the moment—or, let's say, if everything were aimed at producing an imitation of Saint Elizabeth to marry some Thuringian landgrave or, as far as I'm concerned, one of God's lesser creatures, I wouldn't have anything against it. I find it very difficult to carry out such a task, but not impossible, and as someone said so well, and it's still said, just to have wanted such things is great in itself."

Fräulein Honig nodded, perhaps because she was thinking of her own efforts towards this goal.

"You agree with me," Treibel continued. "Well, that pleases me. And I think we should stay of one mind on the second part too. You see, my dear Fräulein, I understand perfectly, even though it contradicts my personal taste, that a mother wants to raise her child to be a genuine angel; one can never know how these things really stand, and to be able, when it comes to the end, to stand before one's judge so completely without doubt—who shouldn't wish himself that? I'd almost like to say I wish it for myself. But, my dear Fräulein, there are angels and then there are angels. If the angel is nothing more than a wash-angel and the spotlessness of the soul is calculated according to the soap consumption, and the whole purity of the growing person lies in the whiteness of her stockings, then I'm filled with a slight feeling of dread. And then, if it's his own grandchild whose flaxen hair is already halfway like an albino's from too much care, then an old grandfather gets a mortal fear. Couldn't you get after Wulsten a bit? She's an understanding person and inwardly, I think, rebels against this Hamburg business. I'd be glad if you were to find occasion to. . ."

At this moment Czicka became restless again and yelped more loudly than before. Treibel, who did not like to see himself interrupted in discussions of this sort, was going to become annoyed, but before he could do so, three young ladies came into view from the villa, two of them dressed completely alike in a straw-colored summer fabric. It was the two Felgentreus, followed by Helene.

"Goodness, Helene," said Treibel, who turned first—perhaps because he had a bad conscience—to his daughter-in-law, "goodness, it's nice to see you once again. You were just now the subject of our conversation, or rather your dear little Lizzi was, and Fräulein Honig declared that little Lizzi was an angel. You can imagine I didn't contradict her. Who doesn't like being the grandfather of an angel? But, ladies, what gives me the honor this early? Or is it for my wife? She has her migraine. Should I have her called. . .?"

"Oh, no, Papa," Helene said with a friendliness that she didn't always show. "We're coming to *you*. The Felgentreus are planning an outing to Lake Halen, but only if all the Treibels, not just Otto and I, take part."

The Felgentreu sisters confirmed this by waving their parasols while Helene continued.

"And not later than three. So we have to try to give our lunch a bit of a dinner quality or to postpone our dinner until eight o'clock in the evening. Elfriede and Blanca still want to go to the Adlerstrasse to invite the Schmidts too, at least Corinna; perhaps the Professor will come later then. Krola has already accepted and wants to bring a quartet, with two junior officials from the Potsdam administration in it. . . ."

"And lieutenants in the reserves," added Blanca, the younger Felgentreu.

"Reserve lieutenants," Treibel repeated earnestly. "Why that, ladies, that turns the scales. I don't believe that a family man living hereabouts—even if a cruel fate has denied him daughters of his own—would have the courage to decline an outing into the country with two reserve lieutenants. Gladly accepted. And three o'clock. My wife will of course be upset that final decisions have been made over her head, and I'm almost afraid of an immediate increase in her *tic douloureux*.[7] Despite that I'm certain of her. A country outing with a quartet and of such a social composition—the pleasure over it will remain the predominating feeling. No migraine can stand up to that. May I show you my melon beds, by the way? Or should we rather have a light snack, very light, without seriously endangering lunch at all?"

All three gratefully declined, the Felgentreus because they wanted to go directly to Corinna's, Helene because she had to get back home on account of Lizzi. Wulsten was not careful enough, and let things pass that she could only call "shocking." Fortunately Lizzi was such a good child, otherwise she would have to be seriously concerned about it.

"Little Lizzi is an angel, just like her mother," Treibel said and while saying it, exchanged glances with Fräulein Honig who had stood off to the side in a rather reserved pose the whole time.

Chapter Ten

THE Schmidts had accepted too, Corinna with especial joy because since the day of the dinner at the Treibels' she had been heartily bored in her domestic solitude; she had long known the old man's great speeches by heart, and the same went for the good Schmolke's stories. "An afternoon at Lake Halen" therefore sounded almost as poetic as "four weeks on Capri," and Corinna consequently decided to do her best on this occasion to be able to hold her own next to the Felgentreus in appearance. For in her soul a vague notion had dawned that this country outing would not take an ordinary course but would bring something great. Marcell had not been invited to take part, which, after the attitude he had maintained for a whole week, suited his cousin perfectly well. Everything promised a cheerful day, especially in view of the composition of the party. After rejecting Treibel's suggestion of a Kremser partywagon, "which was always the thing," and thus doing without the drive together, it was settled that the main point to be agreed upon was to oblige each and everyone to be at Lake Halen at four o'clock on the dot or in any case not to exceed the academic quarter.[1]

And at four o'clock all had actually gathered, or almost all anyway. The old and the young Treibels as well as the Felgentreus had come in their carriages, while Krola, accompanied by his quartet, had for unexplained reasons taken the new steam rail, and Corinna, altogether alone, had taken the city trolley. Of the Treibels only Leopold was missing and he had let himself be excused in advance for coming half an hour late because he absolutely had to write to Mr. Nelson. Corinna was momentarily put out, until it occurred to her that it was probably better this way—short encounters are richer than long ones.

"Well, dear friends," Treibel began, "everything in proper order. First question, where shall we settle ourselves? We have various choices. Shall we stay here on the ground floor between these formidable rows of tables, or shall we move to the neighboring veranda which, if you set great store by it, you can also call a balcony or terrace? Or would you perhaps prefer the discreetness of the inner chambers, of some medieval bower of Lake Halen? Or finally, fourth and last, are you for climbing the tower and do you feel an urge to see this wonderworld in which no human eye has yet been able to discover a fresh blade of grass—do you feel an urge, I say, to see this great desert panorama interspersed with asparagus beds and railway embankments spread out at your feet?"

"I think," said Frau Felgentreu who, though only in her late forties, already had the *embonpoint* and the asthma of a sixty-year-old, "I think, dear Treibel, we'll stay where we are. I'm not for climbing, and besides I think one should always be satisfied with what one happens to have."

"A remarkably modest woman," Corinna said to Krola, who for his part answered simply by citing in figures what she did have, adding quietly, "but in talers."

"Good then," Treibel continued, "we'll stay below. Why strive for the higher. One must be satisfied with what fate has determined, as my friend Frau Felgentreu has just declared. In other words: 'Enjoy happily what you have.' But my dear fellow revellers, what shall we do to enliven our cheerfulness, or more properly and politely, to make it last? For to speak of enlivening our cheerfulness would mean to call its existence into question—a blasphemy I won't commit. Country outings are always cheerful. Isn't that right, Krola?"

Krola confirmed it with an arch smile, which was supposed to express to the initiated a quiet yearning for some Siechen or the heavier Wagner.[2]

And that was how Treibel understood it. "Country outings are always cheerful, and then we have the quartet ready and have Professor Schmidt to look forward to and Leopold as well. I find that this in itself establishes a program." And signalling a nearby middle-aged waiter after these introductory words, he continued talking, apparently to the waiter, but in reality to his friends: "I think, Waiter, we should push a few tables together, here between the well and the lilac shrubs; there we'll have fresh air and some shade. And then, friend, as soon as the question of locale has been settled and the field of action has been marked off, several portions of coffee—let's say five for the time being—and with double sugar and something in the way of cake, no matter what, except for old German pound cake which always admonishes me to make an earnest and honest effort with the new Germany. The beer question we can settle later when our reenforcements have arrived."

These reenforcements were now in fact nearer than any of the party could have dared hope. Schmidt, coming along in a cloud, was gray as a miller from the dust of the road and had to put up with being brushed clean by the rather coquettish young ladies. And hardly had he been put into good condition again and placed in the circle of the others, when Leopold also came into view in a cab slowly trotting up, and both Felgentreus (Corinna held herself back) ran down on the road to greet him, waving the same little cambric handkerchiefs with which they had just restored Schmidt and made him socially acceptable again.

Treibel had also risen and watched his youngest drive up.

"Strange," he said to Schmidt, "strange—it's always said, 'like father, like son.' But now and then that's not at all the case. All of nature's laws are wavering nowadays. Science is setting on them too severely. You see, Schmidt, if *I* were Leopold Treibel—with my father it was different, he was still old-fashioned—even a devil wouldn't have kept me from riding up here today high on a horse and I would have swung myself out of the saddle gracefully—after all, we had our day too, Schmidt—gracefully, I say, and brushed off my boots and unmentionables with my riding switch, and would have appeared here, at a modest estimate like a young god, with a red carnation in my buttonhole, just like the *Legion d'Honneur* or similar nonsense. And now look at that boy. Isn't he coming up as if he's to be executed? That's not even a cab, that's a cart, a sledge. Heaven knows, if you haven't got it in you, it won't come to you either."

During these remarks Leopold had come up, arm in arm with the two Felgentreus, who seemed resolved to provide for the "country atmosphere" *à tout prix*. Corinna, as one can imagine, inclined to disapprove of this intimacy and said to herself, "Silly things!" But then she too got up to greet Leopold with the others.

The cab was still stopped outside, which the older Treibel finally noticed. "Say, Leopold, why is he still stopping there? Is he counting on a return trip?"

"I believe he wants to feed, Papa."

"Well and good. Of course he won't get far with his bag of chaff. More energetic means of invigoration have to be applied here, otherwise something will happen. Waiter, could

you give the horse a pint. But make it Löwenbräu. That's
what he needs most."

"I bet," said Krola, "the patient won't want to have anything to do with your medicine."

"I'll vouch for the contrary. There's something in that
horse; it's just run down."

And while this conversation continued, they followed what
was going on outside and saw how the poor parched animal
greedily drank down the pint and broke out into a weak
neighing of joy.

"There we have it," Treibel exulted. "I'm a good judge of
men; that one has seen better days and with this pint old times
came back to him again. And memories are always the best.
Isn't that right, Jenny?"

The Kommerzienrätin answered with a long drawn-out
"Yes, Treibel," and indicated by her tone that he would do
better to spare her such observations.

An hour passed with all sorts of chatting, and anyone not
talking for a moment let the view spread out before him have
its effect. There was a terrace running down to the lake, and
coming from the other shore one could hear the weak report
of a few Tesching guns used for target shooting at a gallery
established there, while from relatively nearby one could hear
the sound of rolling balls and the shouts of the pin boys at a
two-lane bowling alley running along the near shore. But one
couldn't see the lake itself very well, which at last made the
Felgentreu girls impatient.

"Why, we've got to see the lake. We can't have been at
Lake Halen without having seen the lake."

And they pushed two chairs together back to back and
climbed up so that they could perhaps catch a glimpse of the
water in this way.

"Oh, there it is. A bit small."

"The 'eye of the landscape' has to be small," said Treibel. "An ocean isn't an eye anymore."

"And where could the swans be?" asked the older Felgentreu sister curiously. "I can see two swan huts."

"Why, dear Elfriede," Treibel said, "you're asking too much. It's always that way: where there are swan huts there are no swans. The one has the purse, the other the money. You'll observe that repeatedly in life, my young friend. Let me assume not to your disadvantage."

Elfriede looked at him in surprise: What does that refer to, and to whom? To Leopold? Or to an old tutor with whom she still corresponded, but just so that it didn't end altogether? Or to the Engineer Lieutenant? It couldn't refer to all three. Leopold has the money. . . Hm.

"Anyway," Treibel continued, now addressing the whole party, "I did read somewhere once that it's always best not to exhaust pleasure but to bid enjoyment farewell in the midst of the enjoyment. And this thought is coming back to me now. There is no doubt that this spot is among the most pleasant the north German lowlands possess. It's perfectly suited to be glorified in song and painting, if it hasn't been done already— since we now have a Mark Brandenburg school, from whom nothing is safe. And they're illumination artists of the first order, no matter whether in words or colors. But just because it's so beautiful, let's recall the statement quoted earlier, which cautioned against complete exhaustion, in other words, let's occupy ourselves with the thought of breaking up. I say 'breaking up' deliberately, not going back, not prematurely going back into the old tracks—far be it from me; this day hasn't had its last word yet. But just to leave this particular idyll, before it ensnares us completely! I propose a forest promenade to Paulsborn or, if this should appear too daring, to Hundekehle. The prosaic quality of that name is balanced by the poetic quality of its being much nearer. Perhaps this modification will earn me the special thanks of my friend Frau Felgentreu. . . ."

Frau Felgentreu, to whom nothing was more annoying than allusions to her portliness and shortwindedness, contented herself with turning her back on her friend Treibel.

"Thanks from the House of Austria.[3] But that's the way it is, the righteous always have to suffer. On a discreet forest path I'll make an effort to take the sharp edge off your lovely displeasure. May I have your arm, my dear friend?"

And all of them rose to go down the terrace in groups of twos or threes and to walk toward the half-dusky Grunewald, some on one side of the lake and some on the other.

The main column kept to the left. Led by the Felgentreu couple (Treibel had separated from his friend) it consisted of Krola's quartet and the Felgentreu sisters. Elfriede and Blanca had joined them in such a way that they walked between the two officials and the two young businessmen, one of whom was a famous yodeler and wore the appropriate hat. Then came Otto and Helene while Treibel and Krola brought up the rear.

"There just isn't anything better than a real marriage," Krola said to Treibel and pointed to the young couple in front of them. "You must be sincerely pleased when you see your eldest walk so happily and so tenderly beside this pretty and always spick-and-span woman. Up above they were already sitting close together, and now they're walking arm in arm. I almost think they're quietly squeezing one another."

"Sure proof to me that they had a quarrel this morning. Otto, the poor fellow, now has to pay forfeit money."

"Oh, Treibel, you're forever a mocker. Nobody can do right for you, and least of all the children. Fortunately you're just saying that without really believing it. With a lady who was that well brought-up one can't have a quarrel at all."

At that moment the yodeler was heard emitting a few

warbles, but they were so genuinely Tirolean that the echo of the Pichel hills saw no occasion to answer them.

Krola laughed. "That's young Metzner. He has a remarkably good voice, at least for an amateur, and he's really the one who holds the quartet together. But as soon as he scents a pinch of fresh air it's all over with him. Then Fate seizes him with an overpowering force, and he has to yodel. . . . But we don't want to get off the children"—Krola was always curious and liked to hear intimacies—"you're not going to try to tell me that the two in front of us there are unhappily married. And as far as quarreling goes, I can only repeat, Hamburg women have a level of culture that precludes quarreling."

Treibel rocked his head back and forth. "Well, you see, Krola, now you're such an intelligent fellow and know women, well, how shall I say, you know them as only a tenor can know them. For a tenor is far ahead of a lieutenant. And yet in the specific matter of marriage, which is a subject in itself, you're revealing a dreadful gap. And why? Because in your own marriage, whether it's to your wife's credit or to yours, you've hit it exceptionally well. And as your case proves, that can happen too. But the consequence is simply that you —even the best things have a bad side—that you, I say, are not a normal husband, that you have no full knowledge of the matter; you know the exception but not the rule. Only those who have fought through it can talk about marriage, only the veterans who can show their scars. . . . How did it go? 'To France marched two Grenadiers,/Their heads were hanging down'[4]. . . There you have it."

"Oh, that's just claptrap, Treibel. . ."

"And the worst marriages are those, my dear Krola, where they argue in a dreadfully 'cultured' way, where, if you'll permit the expression, war is carried on with velvet gloves, or more correctly, where they throw confetti into one another's faces as they do during the Roman carnival. It looks pretty, but it still hurts. And at this pleasant-looking confetti-throwing my daughter-in-law is a master. I'll bet that my poor Otto has often thought to himself, if she'd only scratch, if she'd only get completely beside herself once, if she'd only say once: monster or liar or miserable seducer. . . ."

"But Treibel, she can't say that. That would just be non-sense. Otto isn't a seducer, and so he's not a monster either."

"Oh, Krola, that's not what matters at all. What matters is that she has to be able to think such things at least, she has to have a jealous impulse, and at a moment like that it has to break out of her wildly. But everything about Helene is, at best, comparable to the temperature of the Uhlenhorst River. She has nothing but an unshakable faith in virtue and Windsor Soap."

"Well, all right. But if that's the way it is, how can there be quarrels?"

"There still are. They just show up differently, differently but not better. No thunderstorms, just little words with the poison content of half a mosquito bite, or instead silence, mute-ness, sulking—the inner fortifications of marriage—while on the outside the face doesn't show a single crease. Those are the forms the quarreling takes. And I'm afraid all the tender-ness we see parading in front of us there, and that appears so very one-sided, is nothing but penance—Otto Treibel in the courtyard of Canossa with snow under his feet. Just look at the poor fellow; he's constantly turning his head to the right and Helene doesn't stir and doesn't get out of that straight Hamburg line. . . But now we have to be quiet. Your quartet is just beginning. What is it?"

"It's Heine's familiar 'I know not what it should mean.' "[5]

"Oh, that's right. A good question to ask anytime, espe-cially on country outings."

Only two couples were going around the right side of the lake, old Schmidt and the friend of his youth, Jenny, in front, and at some distance behind them, Leopold and Corinna.

Schmidt had extended an arm to his lady and at the same time asked to be permitted to carry her mantilla for her because it was a bit warm under the trees. And Jenny had accepted the offer gratefully; but when she noticed that the good Professor constantly let the lace trim drag behind and get caught alternately in junipers and heather, she asked for the mantilla again.

"You're still just the way you were forty years ago, dear Schmidt. Gallant, but not successfully so."

"Yes, my dear Madam, I cannot exonerate myself of that fault, and it proved to be my destiny at the same time. If I had been more successful with my homage, imagine how completely different my life and yours as well would have been. . . ."

Jenny sighed softly.

"Yes, my dear Madam, then you would never have begun the fairy tale of your life. For all great fortune is a fairy tale."

"All great fortune is a fairy tale," Jenny repeated slowly and full of feeling. "How true, how beautiful! But you see, Wilibald, this envied life that I lead denies my ear and my heart such words, and it's rare that utterances of such poetic depth reach me. And that is an eternally gnawing pain for a person whose nature has turned out like mine. And there you speak of fortune, Wilibald, even of great fortune! You can believe me—because I've lived through all this—these much-coveted things are worthless to the person who has them. Often when I can't sleep and think over my life, it becomes clear to me that fortune, which apparently did so much for me, did not lead me on the paths that were suited to me, and that I probably would have become happier in plainer circumstances and as the wife of a man of ideas and especially of ideals. You know how good Treibel is and that I have a grateful feeling for his goodness. But despite that I'm sorry to say that I lack that high joy of subordination to my husband, which is, after all, our greatest fortune and therefore really means the same as genuine love. I can't tell anyone that; but to pour out my heart to you, Wilibald, is, I believe, my perfect human right and perhaps even my duty. . . ."

Schmidt nodded in agreement and then uttered a simple "Oh, Jenny. . ." with a tone in which he sought to express all the pain of a misspent life. Which he did succeed in doing. He listened to the sound of it and quietly congratulated himself that he had played his little part so well. Jenny, despite all her cleverness, was still vain enough to believe in the "oh" of her former admirer.

Thus they walked side by side, silent and apparently immersed in their feelings, until Schmidt felt the need to break the silence with some question. Here he decided on the old expedient of steering the conversation towards the children.

"Yes, Jenny," he began with a voice still veiled, "what's been missed has been missed. And who feels that more deeply than I do. But a woman like you, who understands life, can find solace in life itself, especially in the pleasure of fulfilling daily obligations. There are always the children; why, there's already a grandchild too, all lilies and roses, dear little Lizzi, and that must be, I would think, the support that comforts women's hearts. And even if I can't speak of your actual marital bliss, my precious friend—since we seem to agree on what Treibel is and is not—I can still say that you are a fortunate mother. You've had two sons grow up, healthy, or what's usually considered healthy at least, well-educated and well-mannered. And consider what this last factor alone means nowadays. Otto has married according to his inclination and has given his heart to a beautiful and wealthy lady who, so far as I know, is the object of universal admiration; and if I'm correctly informed, a second engagement is being prepared in the Treibel house, and Helene's sister is at the point of becoming Leopold's bride. . . ."

"Who says that?" Jenny shot out, falling suddenly out of her sentimental reverie into a tone of most pronounced reality. "Who says that?"

Because of this tone Schmidt found himself in a slight predicament. He had thought it to be this way or perhaps had even heard something similar and now stood rather helplessly before the question of "who said that?" Fortunately it wasn't meant all too seriously, so that Jenny, without waiting for an answer, continued with great animation:

"You have no idea, my friend, how all that irritates me. That's the lumberyard's favorite way of going over my head. You, my dear Schmidt, are passing on what you hear, but those who spread such things around as if by chance—with them I have a serious bone to pick. That's insolence. And Helene had better look out."

"But, Jenny, dear friend, you shouldn't get so excited. I just said that because I took it as a matter of course."

"As a matter of course," Jenny repeated mockingly and while saying it tore off her mantilla again and threw it over the Professor's arm. "As a matter of course. So the lumberyard has gotten so far that your closest friends view such an engagement as a matter of course. But it isn't a matter of course, it's quite the contrary, and when it occurs to me that Otto's know-it-all wife is supposed to be a mere shadow next to her sister Hildegard—and I'll readily believe it, because even in her teens she had a downright ridiculous arrogance—then I must say that I have quite enough with one Hamburg daughter-in-law from the Munk House."

"But, my precious friend, I don't understand you. There isn't any doubt that Helene is a beautiful woman and, if I may put it that way, she is uncommonly dainty. . . ."

Jenny laughed.

"Dainty enough to eat, if you'll permit the expression," Schmidt continued, "and she has the singular charm traditional to those in constant proximity to water. But above all I have no doubt that Otto loves his wife, that he's even in love with her. And *you*, Otto's own mother, dispute this happiness and resent perhaps seeing this happiness doubled in your house. All men are subject to feminine beauty; I was too, and would almost like to say I still am, and if now this Hildegard even surpasses Helene, then I don't know what you could have against her. Leopold is a good boy, perhaps not of all too fiery a temperament, but I imagine he couldn't have anything against marrying a very pretty woman. Very pretty and rich as well."

"Leopold is a child and can't marry according to his own wishes at all, but least of all according to his sister-in-law Helene's. That's all I need, that would mean abdicating and retiring to the back of the house for me. If it were a question of some young lady for whom one might feel a desire to subordinate oneself—a baroness or a real, I mean a proper, Geheimrat's[6] daughter or the daughter of a senior Court Chaplain. . . . But an insignificant young thing who knows nothing but to drive out to the Blankenese resort, and fancies she can run a household or even raise children with a gold thread in her embroidering needle, and really believes seriously that we can't distinguish between sole and turbot here, and is always using the English for lobster, and treats curry powder and soy sauce as the utmost secrets—such a conceited tattle, dear Wilibald, that's not for my Leopold. Leopold, despite all he lacks, has to do better than that. He's a bit ordinary, but he's good, which gives him a claim too. And therefore he should have a clever wife, a really clever one; knowledge and cleverness and the higher things in general—that's what counts. All else doesn't amount to a fig. Misery, that's all these externals are. Happiness, happiness! Oh, Wilibald, at a time like this it would have to be you to whom I must confess this—happiness, that lies here alone!"

And at that she put her hand on her heart.

Leopold and Corinna had followed at a distance of about fifty paces and had carried on their conversation in the usual way, that is, Corinna had been talking. But Leopold was firmly determined to have a word too, for better or worse. The tormenting pressure of the last days had made him face what he had planned with much less fear than before—he simply had to put himself at ease. A couple of times already he had been close at least to asking a question that would lead to his goal; but when he would see the stately figure of his mother striding on in front of him, he would give it up again. Finally he suggested that they cut diagonally across a clearing just now in front of them in order that they would be in the lead once instead of always following. He realized that as a result of this maneuver he would get Mama's glance from the back or from the side, but with something of the attitude of an ostrich, he found relief in the feeling of not having his mother before his eyes, constantly laming his courage. He wasn't able to account for this peculiar nervous state and simply chose what seemed to him the lesser of two evils.

Using the diagonal had worked; they were now as much ahead as they had been behind earlier, and dropping an indifferent and somewhat forced conversation revolving around the asparagus beds at Lake Halen as well as their cultivation and their sanitary significance, Leopold made a sudden beginning and said:

"Do you know, Corinna, that I have greetings for you?"

"From whom?"

"Guess."

"Well, let's say Mr. Nelson."

"There's something odd going on here—why that's just like clairvoyance; now you can read letters that you don't even know have been written."

"Yes, Leopold, I could just leave it at that now and establish myself as a seeress before you. But I'll beware of that. For healthy people have a dread of everything that's as mystical and hypnotic and spiritualist as that. And I don't like to instill dread. I prefer to win good people's hearts."

"Oh, you don't even need to wish for that. I can't imagine a person whose heart you wouldn't win. You should just read what Mr. Nelson has written about you; he begins with 'amusing,' and then comes 'charming' and 'high-spirited' and he concludes with 'fascinating.' And only then come the greetings, which seem, after all that's gone before, almost prosaic and everyday. But how did you know that the greetings came from Mr. Nelson?"

"I haven't encountered an easier riddle in a long time. Your Papa informed us that you would be coming late because you had to write to Liverpool. Now, Liverpool means Mr. Nelson. And if you've got Mr. Nelson, the rest comes out by itself. I believe clairvoyance is very much like that. And you see, Leopold, with the same ease with which I read Mr. Nelson's letters, with the same sureness I can read your future, for example."

A sigh of relief was Leopold's answer, and his heart rejoiced in a feeling of happiness and salvation. For if Corinna read correctly, and she had to read correctly, then he was spared all the inquiries and all the anxieties connected with it, and *she* would then speak out what he still couldn't find the courage to say. Blissfully, he took her hand and said:

"You can't do that."

"Is it that hard?"

"No, it's really easy. But easy or hard, Corinna, let me hear it. And I'll say honestly, too, whether you've hit it or not. But nothing about the distant future, only the near, the very nearest."

"Well then," Corinna began roguishly, with added emphasis here and there, "what I see is this: first of all, a beautiful September day, and in front of a beautiful house a lot of beautiful coaches are stopping, and the foremost one, with a wigged coachman on the box and two servants on the back, is a bridal

coach. And the roadway is full of people who want to see the
bride, and now comes the bride, and the bridegroom walks
beside her, and this bridegroom is my friend Leopold Treibel.
And now the bridal coach, with the other carriages following,
drives along a wide, wide river. . ."

"But Corinna, you're not going to call our Spree between
the Lock and the Jungfern Bridge a wide river, are you? . . ."

"Along a wide river and finally stops in front of a Gothic
church."

"The Twelve Apostles Church. . ."

"And the bridegroom gets out and offers his arm to the
bride and so the young couple walks up to the church, in
which the organ is playing and the lights are already burning."

"And now. . ."

"And now they're standing before the altar and after the
exchange of rings the blessing is spoken and a song is sung, or
the last verse anyway. And now it's back again, along the
same wide river, but not towards the town house from which
they had driven off, but further and further into the open,
until they stop in front of a little villa. . ."

"Yes, Corinna, that's how it should be. . ."

"Until they stop in front of a little villa before a triumphal
arch with a giant wreath at its highest point, and in the wreath
glow the two initials L and H."

"L and H?"

"Yes, Leopold, L and H. And what else could it be? For
the bridal coach came from the Uhlenhorst and drove along
the Alster River and afterwards down the Elbe, and now
they're stopping in front of the Munk villa out in Blankenese,
and L means Leopold and H means Hildegard."

For a moment Leopold seemed overcome with genuine ill
humor. But quickly recollecting himself he gave the pretended
seeress a little love pat and said:

"You're always the same, Corinna. And if the good Nelson,
who is the best fellow and my only confidant, if he had heard

all this, he'd be full of enthusiasm and talk of 'capital fun,'
because you so graciously want to give my sister-in-law's
sister over to me."

"I am a prophetess, after all," Corinna said.

"Prophetess," Leopold repeated. "But this time a false one.
Hildegard is a beautiful girl, and hundreds would think themselves fortunate. But you know my Mama's stand on that
question; she suffers under the constant better-than-thou attitude of those relatives and has sworn surely a hundred times,
that *one* Hamburg daughter-in-law, *one* representative of the
great house of Thompson-Munk is quite enough for her. She
very honestly half hates the Munks, and if I came to her with
Hildegard like that, I don't know what would happen; she
would say no and we'd have a dreadful scene."

"Who knows," said Corinna, who now knew the decisive
word to be very near.

"She would say 'no' and 'no' again and again, that's as sure
as the 'Amen' in church," Leopold continued with his voice
raised. "But that situation can never arise at all. I won't come
to her with Hildegard, and instead I'll make a closer and
better choice. . . . I know, and you know too, that the picture
you painted there was just fun and sport. You know above
all that if a triumphal gate is built at all for this poor fellow,
the wreath would have to bear a letter altogether different
from the Hildegard-H, and that in hundreds and thousands
of flowers. Do I have to say which one? Oh, Corinna, I can't
live without you, and this hour must decide for me. And now
say yes or no."

And with these words he took her hand and covered it with
kisses. For they were walking in the protection of a hazel
hedge.

After confessions such as these, Corinna had every right to
view the engagement as a *fait accompli*, and she wisely re-
frained from any further discussion. Directly she said:

"But one thing, Leopold, we can't conceal from ourselves, we have some hard struggles ahead of us. Your Mama has enough with one Munk, that I can see; but whether a Schmidt will be right for her is still very much a question. She has now and then made allusions, as if I were an ideal in her eyes, perhaps because I have what you lack and perhaps what Hildegard lacks too. I say 'perhaps' and cannot stress this qualifying word enough. For love, I can see clearly, is humble, and I can feel how my faults are falling from me. That is supposed to be characteristic. Yes, Leopold, a life of happiness begins and love lies before us, but it presupposes your courage and your firmness, and here under this forest cupola with its mysterious rustling and gleaming, here, Leopold, you must swear to me that you want to persevere in your love."

Leopold solemnly asserted that he not only wanted to but that he would. For if love made one humble and modest, which was certainly right, it surely also made one strong. If Corinna had changed, he felt himself to be another person too.

"And," he concluded, "one thing I may say—I've never talked idly, and even my enemies won't accuse me of boasting; but believe me, my heart is leaping so high, so happily, that I almost wish difficulties and struggles on myself. I feel an urge to show you that I'm worthy of you. . . ."

At that moment the crescent moon became visible between the treetops, and from the Grunewald castle, at which the quartet had just arrived, voices rang out across the lake:

> When oft in vain I've peered
> Into the night for you,
> Life's dark stream appeared
> Stopped in mourning too.[7]

And now they were silent—or the evening wind that had come up carried the sounds to the other side.

A quarter of an hour later everyone halted by Paulsborn. After they had greeted each other and had taken a short rest during which creme de cacao made the rounds (Treibel himself doing the honors), they finally broke up—the carriages had followed from Lake Halen—to begin the return trip. The Felgentreus bid a moving farewell to the quartet, now keenly lamenting that they had declined the Kremser party-wagon Treibel had suggested.

Leopold and Corinna also separated, but not before they had once more firmly and discreetly pressed each other's hands in the shadow of the tall reeds.

Chapter Eleven

WHEN they left, Leopold had to be satisfied with a seat on the box of his parents' landau. All in all, however, he preferred this to sitting inside the carriage itself under the eye of his mother, who might after all have noticed something, either in the forest or during the short rest in Paulsborn. Schmidt again used the train, while Corinna got in with the Felgentreus. She was placed, as well as could be, between the Felgentreu couple who filled out the backseat of the carriage rather well; and because, after all that had happened, she was less inclined to chat than otherwise, it suited her excellently to find Elfriede as well as Blanca doubly talkative and still quite occupied and delighted with the quartet. The yodeler, a very good match, seemed to have carried off a decisive victory over the summer lieutenants who had of course appeared in mere civilian clothes. For the rest, the Felgentreus insisted on driving to the Adlerstrasse and dropping their guest off there. Corinna thanked them cordially and, waving once more, went up the three stone steps and then up the old wooden staircase across the hall.

She had not taken along the latchkey to the apartment so there was nothing for her but to ring, which she did not like to do. And presently Schmolke appeared; she had used the absence of "master and mistress," as she now and then said with emphasis, to smarten herself up a bit with her Sunday best. The most conspicuous thing again was the bonnet whose frills seemed to have just come out of the crimping iron.

"Why, dear Schmolke," said Corinna while pulling the door shut again, "what's the matter? Is it your birthday? But no, I know when that is. Or is it his?"

"No," said Schmolke, "it's not his either. And then I won't put on a scarf like this and a ribbon like this."

"But if it's not a birthday, what is it then?"

"Nothing, Corinna, does there have to be something if you tidy yourself up a bit? See, it's easy for you to talk; every day God grants us you sit in front of the mirror for half an hour, and sometimes even longer, and heat up those curls of yours. . ."

"But dear Schmolke. . ."

"Yes, Corinna, you think I don't see it. But I see everything and more still. . . . And I can tell you too, Schmolke once said he thought it was actually pretty, curly hair like that. . . ."

"But was Schmolke that way?"

"No, Corinna, Schmolke was *not* that way. Schmolke was a decent man, and if you can say something as strange and actually as wrong as this, he was almost *too* decent. But now give me your hat and your mantilla. Lord, child, the way these things look! Is there such terrible dust? It's lucky that it didn't rain too, then the velvet is done for. And a professor doesn't have that much either, and even if he's not exactly complaining, he's not made of money."

"No, no," Corinna laughed.

"Now listen, Corinna, there you go laughing again. But it's not to be laughed at. The old man plagues himself enough, and when he brings those bundles of homework into the house and the strap sometimes isn't long enough, there are so many, it sometimes hurts me right here. Because Papa is a very good man and his sixty years are beginning to weigh on him a bit. He naturally doesn't want to admit it and still acts as if he were twenty. But nothing doing. And the other day he jumped down from the trolley, and I just happened to come along—I thought right away I was going to have a stroke. . . . But now tell me, Corinna, what should I bring you? Or have you eaten already and will be glad not to see anything more. . . ."

"No, I haven't eaten anything. Or as good as nothing anyway; the crackers you get are always so old. And then in Paulsborn a little sweet liqueur. That can't be counted, though. But then I don't have any real appetite, and my head is so giddy; maybe I'm going to get sick. . . ."

"Oh, that's silly stuff, Corinna. That's just another one of your whims; if your ears are ringing or your forehead's a bit hot once, you talk about nervous fever right away. And that's really godless, because you shouldn't speak of the devil like that. It was probably a bit damp, a bit foggy, an evening mist."

"Yes, it was foggy when we were standing beside the reeds, and the lake actually couldn't be seen anymore. It's probably from that. But my head is really giddy, and I'd like to go to bed and wrap myself up. And I don't want to talk anymore either when Papa comes home. And who knows when that'll be, and whether it won't be too late.

"Why didn't he come along right away?"

"He didn't want to and he's having his 'evening' today too. I believe at Kuh's. And there they usually sit for a long time because his daughters 'coo' along with them. But with you, dear, good Schmolke, I'd like to chat for another half hour. You've always got something special about you. . . ."

"Oh, don't talk like that, Corinna. Why should I have something special about me? Or actually, why shouldn't I have something special about me. You were still a child when I came into the house."

"Well, something special or not," said Corinna, "I'll be sure to like it. And when I'm lying down, dear Schmolke, let me have my tea in bed, the little Meissen pot—you take the other little pot—and just a couple of tea sandwiches, sliced very thin and not too much butter. Because I have to watch out for my stomach, otherwise I'll have gastric trouble and it'll mean six weeks in bed."

"It's all right," Schmolke laughed and went into the kitchen to put the kettle back on the fire. For there was always hot water, it just wasn't boiling yet.

A quarter of an hour later Schmolke came back in and found her darling already in bed. Corinna was sitting more than lying and received Schmolke with the consoling assurance that she felt much better already—what was said in praise of a warm bed was really true, and she now almost believed that she would pull through once more and survive everything happily.

"I believe it too," said Schmolke while she set the tray on the little table standing at the head of the bed. "Now, Corinna, from which one shall I serve you? This one with the broken spout has steeped longer and I know you like it strong and bitter so that it already tastes a bit like ink. . . ."

"I'll have the strong of course. And then lots of sugar; but very little milk; milk always gives you gastric trouble."

"Lord, Corinna, why don't you drop this gastric business. You're lying there looking like a Borsdorf apple and always talk as if death were already right at your nose. No, little Corinna, it doesn't go that fast. And now take a tea sandwich. I sliced them as thin as could be. . . ."

"That's fine. But you brought in a big ham sandwich too."

"For me, little Corinna. I want to eat something too."

"Oh, dear Schmolke, then I'd like to invite myself to be

your guest. These tea sandwiches look like nothing at all, and that ham sandwich is really smiling at me. And everything already sliced so appetizingly! I'm just now beginning to notice that I'm actually hungry. Give me a little slice, if you don't mind too much."

"How you talk, Corinna. How can I mind? I just keep house here and I'm just a servant."

"It's lucky that Papa can't hear you. You know that he doesn't like it when you speak of being a servant like that, and he calls it false modesty. . . ."

"Yes, yes, that's what he says. But Schmolke, who was a pretty smart man too, even if he wasn't educated, he always said, 'listen, Rosalie, modesty is good, and false modesty— modesty is really always false—is still better than none at all.' "

"Hm," said Corinna, who felt a twinge at this herself, "there's something to that. Your husband, my dear Schmolke, must really have been an excellent man. And you did say earlier that there was something very decent about him, al- most *too* decent. You see, I like to hear that sort of thing, and I'd like to have some idea of it. In what way was he so very decent. . . . And then, he was with the police. Now frankly, I am happy that we have the police, and I'm pleased with every policeman that I come up to to ask for directions and information, and it must be true that all of them are polite and well-mannered, at least I always found it that way. But that about decency and about *too* decent. . ."

"Yes, dear Corinna, that was right. But there are differences, and what they call departments. And Schmolke was in such a department."

"Of course. He can't have been everywhere."

"No, not everywhere. And he happened to be in the hardest of all, the one that has to provide for decency and good morals."

"There is such a thing?"

"Yes, Corinna, there is such a thing, and there has to be.

Now when a—and people do things like that, women and girls too, which you must have seen and heard since Berlin children see and hear everything—when a poor unfortunate creature—and many of them really are just poor and unfortunate—does something that's against decency and good morals, then she'll be interrogated and punished. And there where the interrogation is, that's exactly where Schmolke sat. . . ."

"Strange. But that's something you've never told me about. And Schmolke you say was involved in that? Really, very strange. And you mean because of that he was so very decent and so steady?"

"Yes, Corinna, that's what I mean."

"Well, if you say so, dear Schmolke, then I'll believe it. But isn't it really astounding? Because your Schmolke was still young, or anyway a man in his best years then. And many of our sex, and especially those, are often very pretty. And now a fellow sits there just as Schmolke sat there, and always has to look strict and honorable, just because he happens to be sitting there. I can't help myself, I find that difficult. Because that's just like the tempter in the desert—'All this power will I give thee.' "

Schmolke sighed. "Yes, Corinna, I'll admit it outright, I did cry sometimes, and my terrible ache, right here in my neck, that's from those times. And between the second and the third year we were married I lost almost five pounds, and if we'd had all those weighing machines then, it would probably have been more, because when I got around to weighing I was already beginning to gain again."

"Poor woman," Corinna said. "Why, yes, those must have been difficult days. But how did you get over it? And if you began to gain again there must have been something to calm and console you."

"There was, Corinna dear. And since you know everything now, I'll tell you how that was too, and how I got my peace of mind again. Because I can tell you, it was awful, and sometimes I didn't close an eye for weeks. Well, finally you do sleep a bit; nature wants it and it's finally even stronger than jealousy. But jealousy is very strong, much stronger than love. With love it's not so bad. But what I wanted to say, when I was really down and just hanging there and just had enough strength that I could set his mutton and his beans in front of him—that is, he didn't like cut ones and always said you could taste the knife—then he saw that he'd have to have a talk with me. Because *I* didn't talk, I was much too proud for that. So he wanted to have a talk with me, and when the time had come and he'd seen his chance, he took a little four-legged stool that always stood in the kitchen—and it seems like yesterday to me—and pulled the stool up to me and said: 'Rosalie, now tell me, what's bothering you?' "

Corinna's mouth lost every expression of mockery; she pushed the tray aside somewhat, supporting herself on the table with her right arm while drawing herself up and said: "Go on, dear Schmolke."

" 'So, what's bothering you?' he said to me. Well, the tears just started rolling out and I said: 'Schmolke, Schmolke,' and I looked at him as if I wanted to get to the very bottom of him. And I can say that it was a sharp look, but it was still friendly. Because I did love him. And then I saw that he stayed perfectly calm and didn't change color at all. And then he took my hand, stroked it very tenderly and said: 'Rosalie, that's all nonsense, you don't understand anything about it, because you're not in the Morals Department. Because I can tell you that anybody who has to sit there in Morals day in and day out gets more than his fill, his hair stands on edge over all the misery and all the wretchedness. And when some of them come in completely starved besides, which happens too, and we know very well that the parents sit at home there and fret day and night about the shame because they still love the poor thing, who's often enough come to this in a very strange way, and they want to help and to save if helping and saving are still humanly possible—I tell you, Rosalie, if you have to see that every day and have a heart in your body and have served in the First Guard Regiment and are for propriety and discipline and healthiness, well, I tell you, then it's all over with seduction and all that, and you want to go out and cry, and a couple of times I did it too, old fellow that I am, and there's none of that caressing and "my little miss" any more, and you go home and you're happy if you get your mutton and have a good wife whose name is Rosalie. Are you satisfied now, Rosalie?' And then he gave me a kiss. . . ."

Schmolke, whose heart had been very much affected during her story, went to Corinna's dresser to get herself a handkerchief. And when she had straightened herself up again so that her words no longer stuck in her throat, she took Corinna's hand and said:

"See, that's how Schmolke was. What do you say to that?"

"A very decent man."

"You see!"

At this moment the bell sounded. "Papa," Corinna said, and Schmolke got up to let the Professor in. She was back again soon and said that Papa had been surprised not to find Corinna up; what had happened? Just because of a little headache one doesn't go to bed right away. And then he had lighted his pipe and taken the newspaper in hand and had said: "Thank God, dear Schmolke, that I'm back again; parties are all nonsense; that's a statement I'll bequeath to you for life." But he had looked perfectly jolly, and she was convinced that he had really enjoyed himself very much. For he had the fault that so many had, and the Schmidts especially: they talked about everything and knew everything better. "Yes, Corinna dear, in this respect you're a perfect Schmidt too."

Corinna gave the good woman her hand and said: "You're

probably right, dear Schmolke, and it's really good that you
tell me that. If it hadn't been for you, who would have told
me anything at all. No one. I grew up running wild, and it's
still really astounding that I didn't become even worse than I
am. Papa is a good professor but not too good a parent, and
then he always was too prejudiced in my favor and would
say, 'the Schmidt in you will take care of itself,' or 'it'll break
through eventually.' "

"Yes, he's always saying something like that. But now and
then a good slap is better."

"For God's sake, dear Schmolke, don't say anything like
that. That frightens me."

"Oh, you're silly, Corinna. What's there to frighten you.
You're a grown and spirited person and have long worn out
your baby shoes and could already have been married for
six years."

"Yes," Corinna said, "that I could have if somebody had
wanted me. But stupidly enough no one has wanted me yet.
And so I had to look after myself. . . ."

Schmolke didn't think she had heard right and said: "You
had to look after yourself? What do you mean by that, what's
that supposed to say?"

"It's supposed to say, dear Schmolke, that I got engaged
this evening."

"Lord in heaven, is it possible! But don't be mad if I start
so. . . Because it's actually a good thing. Well then, to whom?"

"Guess."

"To Marcell."

"No, not to Marcell."

"Not to Marcell? Why, Corinna, then I don't want to know
either. But then I'll have to know in the end anyway. Who is
it then?"

"Leopold Treibel."

"Goodness gracious me!"

"Do you find that bad? Do you have something against it?"

"Heavens no, how could I. And wouldn't be proper for me anyway. And then the Treibels, they're all good and respectable people, especially the old Kommerzienrat, who's always so droll and always says 'the later the evening, the nicer the people' and 'another fifty years like today' and things like that. And the oldest son is very good too and Leopold too. A bit skinnier, that's true, but marrying isn't like joining the circus. And Schmolke often said, 'Listen, Rosalie, never mind that, you can be fooled by that, you can be wrong there— the thin ones and the ones who look so weak, often they're not so weak at all.' Yes, Corinna, the Treibels are good, and just the Mama, the Kommerzienrätin—well, I can't help myself, but the Rätin, she's got something that doesn't suit me right, and always puts on so, and when some teary story is told about a poodle that's pulled a child out of the canal, or when the Professor is preaching about something and mutters in his bass voice, 'as the immortal. . .' and then there's always a name that not a soul knows and the Kommerzienrätin I'm sure doesn't either—then her tears always come and they always just sit there and don't want to roll down at all."

"It's really a good thing that she can cry like that though, dear Schmolke."

"Yes, with some it's a good thing and shows a tender heart. And I don't want to say anything more either and would rather beat my own breast, and I should because my tears sit in there pretty loose too. . . . Lord, when I think of when Schmolke was still alive, why then a lot of things were different, and he had tickets for the third gallery every day and sometimes for the second one too. And then I'd get all dressed up, Corinna, because I wasn't even thirty yet and still in very good shape. Lord, child, when I think about that. There was an actress then, her name was Erhart,[1] who afterwards married a count. Oh, Corinna, I cried many a good tear then. I can say good tear because it relieves you. And with *Maria Stuart* there were the most tears. There was so much snorting and sniffling that you couldn't understand anything at all anymore—I mean just at the end though, when she takes leave of all her servants and her old nurse, all completely in black, and she herself always with the cross just like a Catholic. But this Erhart woman wasn't one. And when I think about all that again and how I just didn't run out of tears, then I can't really say anything against the Kommerzienrätin either."

Corinna sighed, half in jest and half in earnest.

"Why are you sighing, Corinna?"

"Yes, why am I sighing, dear Schmolke? I'm sighing because I believe you're right and that nothing can actually be said against the Rätin, just because she cries so easily or always has a glistening eye. Lord, a lot of people have that. But the Rätin is of course a very peculiar woman and I don't trust her, and poor Leopold actually has a great fear of her and doesn't yet know how he's going to get out of that. There'll just have to be all sorts of hard struggles yet. But I'll take my chances and hold on to him, and if my mother-in-law is against me, it won't do much harm in the end. Mothers-in-law are actually always opposed, and every one of them thinks her little pet is too good for anyone. Well, we'll see; I have his word, and a way must be found for the rest."

"That's right, Corinna, hold on to him. Actually I got quite a shock, and believe me, Marcell would have been better, because you go together. But that's something I'll say only to you. And since you've got the Treibel fellow now, well, then you've got him and it can't be helped, and he's got to hold still and the old lady too. Yes, the old lady especially. Serve her right."

Corinna nodded.

"And now go to sleep, child. A night's sleep is always good, because you can never know what's going to come or what you're going to need your strength for the next day."

Chapter Twelve

ABOUT the same time that the Felgentreu carriage stopped in the Adlerstrasse to drop off their passenger, the Treibel carriage stopped in front of the Kommerzienrat's residence and the Rätin together with her son Leopold got out while the elder Treibel stayed in his seat and accompanied the young couple—who had again spared their horses—down Köpenick Strasse to the lumberyard. From here, after a hearty kiss (because he liked to play the tender father-in-law) he had himself driven to Buggenhagen's where there was a party meeting. He did want to see once more how things stood and also, if necessary, to show that the report in the *National News* had not crushed him.

The Kommerzienrätin, who usually treated Treibel's political errands with a slightly scornful smile if not with occasional suspicion, today blessed Buggenhagen's and was glad to be alone for a few hours. The walk with Wilibald had stirred up so much in her. The certainty of seeing herself understood—that was really the higher thing.

"Many people envy me, but what do I have in the end?

Stucco and gold borders and Fräulein Honig with her sweet-sour face. Treibel is good, particularly to me; but his prosaic nature weighs on him like lead, and if he doesn't feel it, I feel it. ... And then Kommerzienrätin and forever Kommerzienrätin. It's been almost ten years now, and we don't seem to get any higher up, despite all the effort. And if it stays that way, and it will stay that way, then I really don't know if the other title, which suggests art and learning, doesn't have a finer ring to it after all. Yes, that it has. ... And these eternal 'better circumstances!' I can only drink one cup of coffee and when I go to bed, what counts is that I sleep. Birch grain or walnut doesn't make any difference, but sleeping or not sleeping, that does, and sometimes I can't get any sleep— which is life's best thing because it lets us forget life. ... And the children would be different too. When I look at Corinna, just bubbling over with joy and life, why, she can put both of them in her pocket with a flick of her wrist— there's not much to Otto, and nothing at all to Leopold."

While immersing herself in sweet self-deceptions such as these, Jenny went to the window and looked alternately at the frontyard and the street. In the house opposite, high up in the open garret, like a silhouette in bright light, someone stood running an iron over the board with a sure hand—why, it seemed to her she could hear the girl singing. The Kommerzienrätin could not take her eye off the charming picture, and something like genuine envy came over her.

She only looked away when she noticed that the door behind her was moving. It was Friedrich, who was bringing the tea.

"Set it down, Friedrich, and tell Fräulein Honig she won't be needed."

"Very well, Frau Kommerzienrätin. But there is a letter here."

"A letter?" the Rätin started. "From whom?"

"From the young master."

"From Leopold?"

"Yes, Frau Kommerzienrätin. . . . And an answer is. . ."

"A letter. . . an answer. . . . He's not all there," and the Kommerzienrätin tore open the envelope and glanced over the contents.

"Dear Mama! If it would suit you at all, I would like to have a brief talk with you before the end of the day. Let me know through Friedrich, yes or no. Your Leopold."

Jenny was so struck that her sentimental indulgences were dispelled on the spot. This much was certain—all this could only signify something rather awkward. But she pulled herself together and said:

"Tell Leopold I'm expecting him."

Leopold's room lay above hers; she heard clearly how he walked up and down quickly and shut a few drawers with a loudness altogether unusual for him. And right after that, if she wasn't mistaken, she heard his steps on the stairs.

She had heard rightly, and now he came in and was going to walk up to her across the whole length of the room (she still stood near the window) in order to kiss her hand; but the look with which she met him so warded him off that he stopped still and bowed.

"What's the meaning of this, Leopold? It's now ten, time to be asleep at night, and here you write me a note and want to talk with me. It's new to me that you have something on your chest that wouldn't bear postponement until morning. What do you have in mind? What do you want?"

"To get married, Mother. I've become engaged."

The Kommerzienrätin started back, and it was fortunate that the window by which she stood gave her support. She hadn't expected anything good, but an engagement over her head, that was even more than she had feared. Was it one of the Felgentreus? She considered both of them silly things and the whole Felgentreu clan far beneath their station.

He, the old Felgentreu, had been the warehouse manager in a large leather business and had finally married the pretty housekeeper of the owner, a widower who frequently changed his feminine surroundings. That was the way the affair had begun, and in her eyes it left much to be desired. But compared with the Munks, it wasn't the worst by a long way, and so she said:

"Elfriede or Blanca?"

"Neither of them."

"So. . ."

"Corinna."

That was too much. Almost fainting, Jenny began to totter and she would have fallen on the floor before her son if he had not rushed up and caught her. She was not easy to hold and even less easy to carry; poor Leopold, however, rose to the occasion and proved himself physically by carrying Mama to the sofa. Then he wanted to press the button to ring the electric bell; but Jenny, like most women who have fainted, was not faint enough not to know exactly what was going on around her, and so she grasped his hand as a sign that the bell should not be rung.

She recovered very quickly, reached for the flask of *eau de cologne* standing in front of her and said, after she had dabbed her forehead with it: "So, with Corinna."

"Yes, Mother."

"And not just in fun. But really to get married."

"Yes, Mother."

"And here in Berlin and in the Luisenstadt Church in which your good, upright father and I were wed?"

"Yes, Mother."

"'Yes, Mother,' and again and again 'Yes, Mother.' It sounds as if you're speaking on command and as if Corinna had told you, always just say 'Yes, Mother.' Well, Leopold, if that's the way it is we can learn our roles by heart very quickly.

You just keep saying 'Yes, Mother,' and I'll just keep saying 'No, Leopold.' And then we'll see which holds out longer, your Yes or my No."

"I find that you're making it somewhat easy for yourself, Mama."

"Not that I know of. But if that's the way it's supposed to be, then I've just learned well from you. In any case, it's proceeding without much ado when a son comes up to his mother and simply declares, 'I've become engaged.' That's not the way it's done in our circles. That may be how it is in the theater or perhaps even in the world of art and learning, in which the clever Corinna has been brought up—some even say that she corrects homework for the old man. But however that may be, it may pass there, for all I care; and if she's surprised the old Professor, her father—a man of honor, by the way—with this 'I've become engaged' herself, well, then let *him* be pleased; he has reason for it too, because Treibels don't grow on trees and can't be shaken down by everybody that passes by. But I, I am not pleased and I forbid you this engagement. You've shown again how completely immature you are, yes, I'll say it, Leopold, how childish."

"Dear Mama, if you could have a bit of consideration for me. . ."

"Consideration for you? Did you have any consideration for me when you agreed to this nonsense? You've become engaged, you say. Whom are you trying to tell that? *She's* become engaged, and you've merely been engaged. She's toying with you, and instead of refusing that, you kiss her hand and let yourself be caught like some bird. Well, I haven't been able to prevent that, but the rest I can prevent and will prevent. Get engaged as much as you want to, but discreetly and secretly; coming out with it can't be thought of. There'll be no announcements, and if you want to make announcements yourself, you can receive the congratulations in a *hôtel garni*. No engagement and no Corinna exist in my house.

That's all over. Now I'm getting to know the old story of ingratitude myself and I see that it's unwise to spoil people and raise them above their own social level. And with you it's no better. You too could have spared me this grief and this scandal. That you've been misled only half excuses you. And now you know what my will is, and I may well say, your father's will too, because as many follies as he commits, in *those* questions where the honor of his house is at stake, he can be depended on. And now go, Leopold, and sleep, if you can sleep."

Leopold bit his lip and smiled bitterly to himself.

"And whatever you might be planning—since I've never seen you smile and stand there so defiantly before, but that's just that other, foreign spirit and influence—whatever you might be planning, Leopold, don't forget that the blessing of the parents builds the houses of the children.[1] If I may advise you, be sensible, and don't deprive yourself of life's foundations, without which there is no real happiness, for the sake of a dangerous person and a fleeting whim."

Much to his own astonishment, Leopold had not felt at all crushed this time, and for a moment he appeared to want to answer; a glance at his mother, whose agitation had only increased while she had spoken, let him perceive, however, that every word would only increase the difficulty of the situation; he therefore bowed quietly and left the room.

He was hardly out when the Kommerzienrätin got up from her place on the sofa and began to walk up and down across the carpet. Every time she came near the window again she stood still and looked over at the garret and the woman still ironing in the full light until her glance would drop again and turn to the colorful activities in the street before her. Here in her frontyard her housemaid, a pretty blonde who had almost not been hired out of consideration for Leopold's morals, stood with her left arm propped on the lattice railing from

inside, laughing and speaking animatedly to a "cousin" standing outside on the sidewalk; but then she withdrew when the
Kommerzienrat, just now coming from Buggenhagen's drove
up in a cab and walked towards the villa. Throwing a glance
at the row of windows, Treibel saw immediately that only
his wife's room was still lighted, and that encouraged him to
go to her right away to report on the evening and his various
experiences. The dull mood he had initially encountered at
Buggenhagen's as a result of the *National News* report had
quickly given way under the influence of his charm, and that
all the more because he had abandoned Vogelsang, who was
little liked here too, with a grin.

Though he knew where Jenny stood on these things, he
felt compelled to tell of his victory; but when he entered and
became aware of his wife's quite visible agitation, his jovial
"Good evening, Jenny" died on his lips, and extending his
hand to her he merely said:

"What has happened, Jenny? You look like the Passion
of. . . no, no blasphemy. . . you look as if your apple-cart had
been upset."

"I believe, Treibel," she said while she continued pacing
back and forth in the room, "you could look a little higher
for your similes; 'apple-cart' has an excessively rural, not to
say peasant taste to it. I see that the Teupitz-Zossen business
is already bearing its fruits. . ."

"Dear Jenny, the fault lies, I believe, less with me than with
the words and images in the German Nation's vocabulary.
All the phrases we have for depressions and sorrows seem
expressly lower class, and all I can think of other than that
is the one about the tanner whose hides have washed away."

He stopped short because such an angry look struck him
that he would be well-advised to forgo searching for further
similes. Then too Jenny took up the conversation and said:

"Your consideration for me always stays at the same level
too. You see that I've had a shock, and the form in which

you garb your concern is that of tasteless similes. What the
basis of my agitation is doesn't seem to awaken your curiosity particularly."

"But of course, Jenny. . . . You shouldn't take that amiss;
you know me, and you know how all that is meant. Shock!
That's a word I don't like to hear. Surely something with
Anna again, giving notice or having an affair. If I'm not
mistaken, she was. . ."

"No, Treibel, that's not it. Anna can do what she wants to
and as far as I'm concerned end her life in the Spree forest.
Her father, the old schoolmaster, can then teach his grandchild what he neglected with his daughter. If love affairs are
going to shock me, they have to come from another side. . . ."

"So it is love affairs after all. Now tell me who?"

"Leopold."

"Well, I'll be. . ." And one couldn't tell from this whether
Treibel had been more struck with alarm or pleasure at the
sound of this name. "Leopold? Is it possible?"

"It's more than possible, it's certain; because a quarter of
an hour ago he was here himself to let me know about this
love affair."

"Strange boy. . ."

"He's become engaged to Corinna."

It was quite unmistakable that the Kommerzienrätin expected this information to have a great effect, but this effect
failed to appear. Treibel's first feeling was one of somewhat
cheerful disappointment. He had expected something with a
little soubrette, perhaps even with a "maiden of the people,"
and now stood before an announcement which, to his more
unbiased views, called forth anything but alarm and dismay.

"Corinna," he said, "and engaged just like that and without
asking Mama. A devil of a fellow. One always underestimates
people and most of all one's own children."

"What are you saying, Treibel? This is hardly a proper
time for you to deal with serious questions in a mood that still

smacks of Buggenhagen's. You come home and find me in great agitation and the moment I tell you the reason for this agitation you find it appropriate to make all sorts of peculiar jokes. You must be able to feel, after all, that that is the same as ridiculing my person and my feelings, and if I understand your whole attitude correctly, you're far from seeing a scandal in this so-called engagement. And I would like to be certain of that before we talk further. Is it a scandal or not?"

"No."

"And you won't call Leopold to account about it?"

"No."

"And you're not disgusted with this person?"

"Not in the least."

"With this person who has made herself absolutely unworthy of your and my kindness and now wants to bring her bedstead—there can't be much of anything else after all—into the Treibel house."

Treibel laughed. "See, Jenny, there's a successful turn of expression, and if I picture the pretty Corinna in my imagination—this misfortune of mine—bringing her bedstead, harnessed, so to speak, between its boards, over here into the Treibel house, I could laugh for a quarter of an hour. But I had better not laugh, and have, since you're so much for the serious, a serious word with you.

"Everything that you've blared out here is firstly nonsensical and secondly disgusting. And what else besides—blind, forgetful, arrogant—I don't even want to talk about. . ."

Jenny had gone completely pale and trembled because she knew very well what the "blind and forgetful" was aimed at. But Treibel, who was a good and quite clever fellow too, and sincerely rose up against all this pride, now continued:

"You speak of ingratitude and scandal and disgrace, and only the word 'dishonor' is lacking and you'd have scaled the peak of glory. Ingratitude! Do you want to hold her to account for the dates and oranges she, with her graceful hand, has taken from our Majolika bowl with its Venus and Cupid on it—a ridiculous daubing, incidentally—this clever, always cheerful, always entertaining person, who's a match for at least seven Felgentreus—not to mention close relatives. And weren't we ourselves guests at the good old Professor's, at Wilibald's, who is usually the apple of your eye otherwise, and didn't we drink his Brauneberger wine, which was just as good as mine or at least not much worse? And weren't you in perfectly high spirits, and didn't you sing your old songs at the old piano that's standing in the parlor there? No, Jenny, don't come to me with stories like that. Then I can get really angry for once too."

Jenny took his hand and wanted to keep him from saying more.

"No, Jenny, not yet, I'm not finished yet. I've only just wound up. Scandal you say, and disgrace. Well, I'll tell you, watch out that this purely imagined disgrace doesn't become an actual one and that—I say this because you like such images —the arrow doesn't fly back at the marksman. You're well on your way to dragging us into immortal ridiculousness. Who are we, after all? We're neither the Montmorencys nor the Lusignans—from whom, I might add, the beautiful Melusine is supposed to come, which may interest you—we're not the Bismarcks or the Arnims or anything else in the Brandenburg nobility either; we're the Treibels, potassium ferro-cyanide and ferrous sulphate, and you're born a Bürstenbinder from the Adlerstrasse. Bürstenbinder is quite good, but the first Bürstenbinder can't possibly have stood any higher than the first Schmidt. And so I ask you, Jenny, no exaggerations. And if it can be done, drop the whole war plan and accept Corinna with as much composure as you accepted Helene. It's not necessary after all that mother-in-law and daughter-in-law love each other terribly; they don't marry each other. It's up to those who have the courage to subject themselves to this serious and difficult task in their very own person. . . ."

During this second half of Treibel's philippic, Jenny had become remarkably quiet; the reason for this was her thorough knowledge of her husband's character. She knew that he habitually had to speak his mind and that he could be talked to again only once he had gotten certain feelings off his chest. Ultimately it was perfectly all right with her that this act of inner self-liberation had begun so quickly and so thoroughly; what had been said now wouldn't need to be said tomorrow; it had been done with, and permitted the prospect of more peaceful negotiations. Treibel was very much the man to consider all things from two sides, and so Jenny was fully convinced that overnight he would get to looking at this whole engagement of Leopold's from the opposite side too. She therefore took his hand and said:

"Treibel, let's continue the conversation tomorrow morning. I believe that with calmer blood you won't mistake the justice of my views. In any case, I'm not counting on changing my mind. I naturally didn't want to anticipate you, as the man who has to act, in this affair either; but if you decline to act at all, then I'll act. Even at the risk of your disagreement."

"Do what you want."

And with that he threw the door shut and went over into his room. As he threw himself down into the easy chair he muttered to himself: "And if she were right in the end!"

And could it be otherwise? The good Treibel was after all himself the product of three generations who had gotten richer and richer in the manufacturing business, and regardless of all the good inclinations of the mind and of the heart, and despite his political guest performance on the stage of Teupitz-Zossen—the bourgeois was deep in his blood as it was in his sentimental wife's.

Chapter Thirteen

THE next morning the Kommerzienrätin was up earlier than usual and had Treibel informed that she wanted to have breakfast alone in her room. Treibel attributed this to the ill humor of the preceding evening, but was mistaken since Jenny actually planned to use the half hour freed by staying in her room to write a letter to Hildegard. There were simply more important things today than having coffee leisurely and peacefully, or perhaps even with a continued waging of war. And, indeed, she had hardly emptied the little cup and pushed it back on the tray, before she exchanged the sofa for her seat at the desk and let her pen glide with great speed over various little sheets each of which was only the size of a hand, but, thank goodness, had the usual four sides. Letters were easy for her to write when she was in the proper mood, but never more so than today. Before the little console clock had struck the ninth hour, she pushed the sheets together, straightened them out on the table top like a deck of cards and, half aloud, read over what she had written.

"Dear Hildegard! For weeks we've been thinking about fulfilling our long-cherished wish to have you under our roof again. Well into May we had bad weather and one could hardly call it spring, which is to me the most beautiful season. But for almost two weeks it has been different, and in our garden the nightingales are singing, which you, as I remember very well, like so much, and so we ask you affectionately to leave your beautiful Hamburg for a few weeks and to grant us your company. Treibel sends his wishes with mine and Leopold joins in them too. To mention your sister Helene here would be superfluous, for you know her affectionate feelings for you as we know them, and, if I've observed correctly, those feelings have been constantly growing, especially recently. The situation is such that I want to speak to you about it more fully, insofar as that is possible in a letter. Sometimes, when I see her so pale—as well as such paleness becomes her—it hurts me in my innermost heart, and I don't have the courage to ask the cause. It is *not* Otto, I'm sure of that, because he is not only good but also considerate, and I sense that in all likelihood it can't be anything other than homesickness. Oh, that's all too understandable for me, and then I always want to say, 'go, Helene, go today, go tomorrow, and be assured that I'll see to the household in general and to the linen ironing particularly to the best of my ability, just as much as—why even more than—if it were for Treibel, who is also very difficult in these matters, more difficult than many other Berliners.' But I don't say all that because I know Helene would rather forgo any other happiness than the happiness that lies in the knowledge of fulfilled duty. Especially towards the child. To take Lizzi along on the trip when her lessons would have to be interrupted is almost as unthinkable as to leave Lizzi behind. The sweet child! How glad you'll be to see her again, assuming, of course, that my request is not in vain. For photographs do give only a very insufficient picture, especially with children whose whole charm lies in a transparent skin color; the complexion isn't just a nuance of the expression, it's the expression itself. For as Krola, whom you perhaps still recall, just recently claimed again, the relationship between complexion and soul was downright remarkable. What can we offer you, my sweet Hildegard? Little—nothing actually. You're familiar with the limitations of our rooms; and besides Treibel has formed a new passion. He wants to have himself elected, and that in a district whose peculiar, somewhat Wendish-sounding name I won't expect from your geographical knowledge though I know very well that your schools—as Felgentreu (not an authority in this area, of course) assured me again quite recently—are superior to ours. At the moment there's actually nothing here but an anniversary exhibition for which the firm of Dreher from Vienna has taken over the catering and is being attacked vehemently. But what would the Berliners not attack—that the beer mugs are too small can mean little to a lady—and I would hardly know anything that would be safe from the conceit of our populace. Not even your Hamburg, of which I can't think without my heart rejoicing. Oh, your glorious Buten-Alster! And in the evening when the lights and the stars glimmer in it—a sight that lifts those granted it above everything earthly. But forget that, dear Hildegard, otherwise we won't have much of a prospect of seeing you here, which would produce sincere regrets in all the Treibels, most of all in your most loving friend and aunt,

Jenny Treibel."

"*Postscript*: Leopold is riding a great deal now—to Treptow and to the Egg Hut every morning. He complains that he has no company. Do you still have your old passion? I can still see you flying along like that, you madcap you. If I were a man, I would live only to capture you. I'm sure, by the way, that others think so too, and we would long have

had the proof of it in hand if you were less choosy. Don't be
that any longer and forget all the demands you could make."

Jenny folded the little sheets and put them in the envelope
which, perhaps to announce outwardly her desire for peace,
showed a white dove with an olive branch. This was all the
more in order since Hildegard carried on a lively correspondence with Helene and knew very well what, up until now
at least, the true feelings of the Treibels and particularly of
Frau Jenny had been.

The Rätin had just risen to ring for Anna—the girl briefly
under suspicion the evening before—when she happened to
direct her glance at the frontyard and saw her daughter-in-law
quickly walking up to the house from the lattice railing. A
second-class cab, closed and with the window drawn shut
though it was very warm, was stopped outside.

A moment later Helene came in to her mother-in-law and
embraced her impetuously. Then she threw her summer coat
and garden hat aside and said, repeating her embrace:

"Is it true? Is it possible?"

Jenny nodded mutely and only now saw that Helene was
still in her dressing gown and that her hair was still plaited.
So, just as she was at the moment the great news became
known at the lumberyard, she had immediately gotten under
way in the first cab to come along. That meant a good deal,
and in view of this fact, Jenny felt the ice that had girded
her mother-in-law's heart for eight years melt away. And
tears came to her eyes.

"Helene," she said, "what has stood between us is gone.
You're a good child and you share our feelings. I was sometimes against this and that, let's not examine whether justly or
unjustly; but in things like this you can be depended on, and
you can distinguish sense from nonsense. Unfortunately, I
can't say that of your father-in-law. But I think that's just a

passing thing, it'll soon be all right. In all events, let us hold firm. This has nothing to do with Leopold personally. But we must arm ourselves against her—she's a dangerous person, who shies away from nothing and has enough self-confidence to outfit three princesses. Don't believe she's going to make it easy for us. She has all the presumption of a professor's daughter and could be capable of imagining that she's even doing the Treibel house an honor."

"A terrible person," Helene said. "When I think of that day with dear Mr. Nelson. We were deathly afraid that he would postpone his departure and ask for her hand. What would have come of that I don't know; with Otto's connections with the Liverpool firm it might have been disastrous for us."

"Well, thank God that it's behind us. Perhaps it's still better this way, since we can settle it *en famille*. And I'm not afraid of the old Professor, I've got a hold on him from earlier days. He has to come over to our camp. And now, child, I've got to do my toilette. . . . But one more main point. Just now I wrote to your sister Hildegard and asked her to pay us a visit soon. Please, Helene, add a few words to your mother and put both things in the envelope and address it."

With that the Rätin left and Helene sat down at the desk. She was so absorbed in her task that it never occurred to her to feel triumphant because Hildegard had been invited at last. No, in view of the common danger, she only felt in sympathy with her mother-in-law as the "support of the house" and full of hatred for Corinna. What she had to write was written quickly. And now she addressed it in lovely English handwriting with the usual round lines and flourishes: "Frau Konsul Thora Munk, née Thompson. Hamburg. Uhlenhorst."

When the address had dried and the fairly considerable letter had had two stamps put on it, Helene rose, knocked lightly on Frau Jenny's dressing room and called to her:

"I'm leaving now, dear Mama. I'll take the letter along."

And right after that she crossed the frontyard again, woke up the cab driver and got in.

Between nine and ten two pneumatic post[1] letters had arrived at the Schmidts—an unprecedented event, two such letters at once. One of them was directed to the Professor and had the following contents:

"My dear friend! May I count on meeting you in your apartment today between twelve and one? No answer, good answer. Your most devoted Jenny Treibel."

The other, not much longer letter was addressed to Corinna and read:

"Dear Corinna! Late yesterday evening I had a talk with Mama. I hardly need to tell you that I met resistance, and I'm more certain than ever that we face difficult struggles. But nothing shall separate us. A lofty joyfulness abides in my soul and gives me courage for everything. That is the secret as well as the power of love. This power shall also lead me and strengthen me further. Despite all cares, Your overly happy Leopold."

Corinna put the letter down. "Poor boy! What he's writing there is meant honestly, even that about the courage. But a white feather seems to show through anyway. Well, we'll have to see. Hold on to what you have. *I* won't give in."

Corinna spent the morning in continued conversation with herself. Periodically Schmolke would come in, but said nothing or limited herself to minor household questions. The Professor, for his part, had to give two classes, one Greek—Pindar, and one German—the Romantic School (Novalis), and was back soon after twelve. He paced back and forth in his room, occupied alternately with the absolutely incomprehensible closing phrase of a poem by Novalis and the solemnly announced visit of his friend Jenny. It was shortly before one when the rattling of a carriage on the bad stone pavement below led him to assume she had come. And she had come, this time alone, without Fräulein Honig and without the Maltese. She opened the carriage door herself and then slowly and deliberately, as if once more rehearsing her role, climbed up the stone steps of the exterior stairway. A minute later Schmidt heard the bell go off, and presently Schmolke announced:

"Frau Kommerzienrätin Treibel."

Schmidt went to meet her, somewhat less at ease than usual, kissed her hand and asked her to take a seat on the sofa whose deepest depression was now somewhat levelled by a large leather pillow. He took a chair for himself, sat down opposite her and said:

"To what do I owe the honor, my dear friend? I assume something special has occurred."

"Exactly, my dear friend. And your words leave me no doubt that Fräulein Corinna has not yet seen fit to acquaint you with what has occurred. Namely, that yesterday evening Fräulein Corinna engaged herself to my son Leopold."

"Ah," said Schmidt in a tone that could equally well have expressed joy or alarm.

"Yes, yesterday on our Grunewald excursion—which perhaps should never have taken place—Fräulein Corinna engaged herself to my son Leopold, not the other way around. Leopold does not take any step without my knowledge and my approval, least of all such an important step as an engagement. With the utmost regret I therefore find myself forced to speak of a plot or a trap, yes, if you'll pardon me, my dear friend, of a well-considered ambush."

These strong words restored not only Schmidt's composure but also his usual cheerfulness. He saw that he had not been deceived by his old friend, that she, completely unchanged despite poetry and elevated feelings, was still the Jenny Bürstenbinder of old, exclusively concerned with externals. And he saw that for his part, though naturally preserving the politest forms and seeming completely cooperative, he would now have to assume a tone of superior haughtiness for the debate that was very probably going to ensue. That much he owed to himself and to Corinna.

"An ambush, my dear Madam. Perhaps you're not altogether incorrect in calling it that. And it did have to be on just that terrain. It's strange enough that things of this sort seem inalienably to attach to very particular localities. All attempts at quiet reform to get at the matter peacefully by means of swan huts and bowling greens, prove useless, and the earlier character of these areas, especially that of our ill-reputed Grunewald, always breaks through again. Time and again, just like that. Permit me, my dear Madam, to call in this cavalier of the female genus so that we can hear a first-hand confession of guilt in this affair."

Jenny bit her lip and regretted the careless words that now exposed her to mockery. But it was too late to turn back, and so she only said:

"Yes, my dear Professor, it will be best to hear from Corinna herself. And I think she will admit with some pride to having taken the lead over the poor boy in this game."

"Very possible," Schmidt said, got up, and called into the hall: "Corinna."

He had hardly returned to his place when Corinna appeared in the door, bowed politely towards the Kommer-zienrätin and said: "You called, Papa?"

"Yes, Corinna, I did. But before we go on, take a chair and sit some distance from us. Because I want it to be outwardly apparent too that for the present you are the accused. Move into the window corner, we can see you best there. And now tell me, is it a fact that yesterday evening in the Grunewald, you, in all the cavalier arrogance of a born Schmidt, robbed a good burgher's son by the name of Leopold Treibel, going his way peacefully and unarmed, of his best asset?"

Corinna smiled. Then she stepped from the window to the table and said: "No, Papa, that's completely wrong. Everything took its customary course, and we're as properly engaged as one can possibly be."

"I don't doubt that, Fräulein Corinna," Jenny said. "Leopold too considers himself your fiancé. I'm saying only that the feeling of superiority which your years. . ."

"Not my years. I'm younger. . ."

". . . which your cleverness and your character have given you, that you used this superiority to make the poor boy lose his will, and to win him for yourself."

"No, my dear Madam, that's not quite right either, at least not for the first. It might be right in the end, but you'll have to permit me to come back to that later."

"Good, Corinna, good," said the old man. "Go right ahead. So, for the first. . ."

"So, for the first, incorrect, my dear Madam. For how did it come about? I talked with Leopold about his immediate future and described a wedding procession to him, intentionally in indefinite outlines and without using names. And when I finally had to use names, it was at Blankenese where guests were gathering for the wedding feast, and it was the beautiful Hildegard Munk, dressed like a queen, sitting as the bride beside her bridegroom. And this bridegroom was your Leopold, my dear Madam. But this same Leopold didn't want to hear of any of this and seized my hand and proposed to me in due form. And after I had reminded him of his mother and had had no success with this reminder, we became engaged. . . ."

"I believe that, Fräulein Corinna," the Rätin said. "I sincerely believe that. But ultimately all this is really just a farce. You knew perfectly well that he would give you preference over Hildegard, and you knew only too well that the more you put the poor child, Hildegard, into the foreground, the more definitely—though not to say the more passionately, because he is not actually a man of passion—the more definitely, I say, he would side with and favor you."

"Yes, my dear Madam, I knew that, or at least I almost knew it. Not a word had passed between us on this subject, but I nevertheless believed, and had for some time, that he would be pleased and happy to call me his bride."

"And with that calculated and cleverly chosen story of the Hamburg wedding day you knew you could bring about his declaration. . . ."

"Yes, my dear Madam, that I did, and I think I was perfectly within my rights. And though you may seriously wish to protest that right—as you seem to intend—don't you hesitate to expect, to demand, that I should refrain from influencing your son in any way? I'm no beauty, I'm only just above average. But assume for a moment, as difficult as it may be for you, that I really were something of a beauty, whom your good son could not resist. Would you have demanded that I destroy my face with acid, just so that your son, my fiancé, wouldn't fall into a trap set by my beauty?"

"Corinna," the old man smiled, "don't be too sharp now. The Rätin is our guest."

"You would not have demanded that I do that, or so I'll assume for the moment at least, perhaps overestimating your friendly feelings for me; and yet you do demand of me that I renounce what nature has given me. I have a good mind and am open and free and thereby have a certain effect on men, sometimes even on those who lack what I have—should I divest myself of that? Should I hide my talent? Should I hide the little light that's been given me under a bushel? Do you demand that I sit there like a nun when I'm with your son, just so that the House of Treibel is preserved from an engagement with me? Permit me, my dear Madam—and you must attribute my words to the agitated feelings you've provoked—permit me to tell you that I find that not only arro-

gant and highly reprehensible, but most of all absolutely
ridiculous. After all, who are the Treibels? Berlin blue manu-
facturers with the title of Kommerzienrat, and I, I'm a
Schmidt."

"A Schmidt," old Wilibald repeated cheerfully, presently
adding: "And now tell me, my dear friend, shouldn't we
rather stop here and leave everything to the children and
to a certain quiet historical development?"

"No, my dear friend, that we should not. We should leave
nothing to historical development and much less to the decision of the children, which would mean the same as leaving
the decision to Fräulein Corinna. And that's what I'm here to
prevent. I had hoped, what with the memories that live between us, to be certain of your agreement and support, and
I see I was deceived and will have to confine my influence,
which has proven unavailing here, to my son Leopold. . . ."

"I fear," said Corinna, "that it will fail there too. . . ."

"Which will solely depend on whether he sees you or not."

"He will see me!"

"Perhaps. Perhaps not though."

And with that the Kommerzienrätin got up and without
giving the Professor her hand went towards the door. Here
she turned around once more and said to Corinna:

"Corinna, let us talk reasonably. I'll forget everything. Let
the boy go. He's not even suitable for you. And as far as the
House of Treibel is concerned, you just characterized it in
such a way that it can't cost you much of a sacrifice to do
without it."

"But my feelings, my dear Madam. . ."

"Bah," Jenny laughed, "that you can talk like that shows
me clearly that you don't have any, and that all this is pure
wantonness or perhaps even willfulness. For your sake and for
ours I wish you would give up this willfulness. For it can't
lead to anything. A mother can also influence a weak person,
and it seems doubtful to me that Leopold would want to

spend his honeymoon in an Ahlbeck fisherman's hut. And you can be sure that the house of Treibel will not provide you a villa on Capri."

And with that she bowed and stepped out into the hall. Corinna remained behind, but Schmidt escorted his friend to the stairs.

"Adieu," the Rätin said here. "I regret that this had to come between us and disturb the cordial relations of so many, many years. It isn't my fault. You've spoiled Corinna, and the little daughter now adopts a mocking and overbearing tone and ignores the years, if nothing else, that separate me from her. Impiety is the character of our time."

Schmidt, a rogue, was pleased to put on a sad face at the word "impiety."

"Oh, my dear friend," he said, "you may well be right, but now it's too late. I regret that it was given to our house to inflict a grief, not to say an insult, such as this on you. Of course, as you've so rightly observed, the times. . .everybody wants to rise above himself and to attain heights providence obviously did not intend."

Jenny nodded. "God help it."

"Let us hope so."

And with that they separated.

Back in the room Schmidt embraced his daughter, gave her a kiss on the forehead and said: "Corinna, if I weren't a professor I'd become a Social Democrat in the end."

At the same moment Schmolke came in too. She had heard only the last words, but guessing what it was all about, she said:

"Yes, that's what Schmolke always said too."

Chapter Fourteen

THE next day was a Sunday, and the mood of the Treibel household could only add considerably to the usual dreariness of the day. Everyone avoided one another. The Kommerzienrätin occupied herself with arranging letters, cards, and photographs; Leopold sat in his room and read Goethe (it need not be said what);[1] and Treibel himself walked around the fountain in the garden and talked, as he mostly did in such cases, with Fräulein Honig. He went so far as to ask her quite seriously whether there would be war or peace, though with the precaution of giving a sort of preliminary answer himself. First and foremost it was certain that no one knew, "not even the leading statesmen" (he had accustomed himself to this phrase in his public speeches), and just because no one knew, one had to depend on intuition, and in that no one was greater and more reliable than women. It couldn't be denied; the intuition of the feminine sex had a Pythian quality which set it apart from the run-of-the-mill oracles. Fräulein Honig, when she finally had a chance to speak, summed up her political diagnosis in this way: towards the West she saw a clear sky, while in the East it was ominously brewing, and that on top as well as on bottom.

"On top as well as on bottom," Treibel repeated. "Oh, how true. And the top determines the bottom, and the bottom the top. Yes, Fräulein Honig, with that we've hit it."

And Czicka, the little dog, naturally there too, yelped to all that.

Thus the conversation went to their mutual satisfaction. But Treibel seemed disinclined to continue drawing upon this well of wisdom, and after a time withdrew to his room and his cigar, cursing all of Lake Halen which had conjured up this domestic discord and this Sunday's extra tedium.

Towards noon a telegram addressed to him arrived:

"Thanks for letter. I'm coming tomorrow with the afternoon train. Your Hildegard."

He sent the telegram, from which he found out for the first time that an invitation had even been extended, over to his wife, and though he found her independent procedure somewhat strange, he was still sincerely glad to have something to occupy his imagination. Hildegard was very pretty, and the idea of having a face other than that of Fräulein Honig around him on his garden walks during the next weeks did him good. He had something to talk about now too, and while the conversation at noon would probably have taken a rather wretched course or perhaps failed to take place altogether without this message, it was now at least possible to ask a few questions. He actually did ask these questions too, and everything went quite tolerably; Leopold alone didn't say a word and was glad when he could get up from the table and return to his reading.

Leopold's whole attitude generally let it be understood that he was no longer willing to have decisions made for him; nevertheless it was clear to him that he could not evade the formal duties of the house and fail to meet Hildegard at the railroad station the next afternoon. He was there punctually, greeted his beautiful sister-in-law, and disposed of the ritual of questions after her health and the family's summer plans while one of the porters he had engaged took care of the cab and then the baggage. This consisted only of a single trunk with brass bindings, but it was of such a size that when it had been hoisted up it gave the rolling cab the appearance of a two-story building.

Underway Leopold resumed the conversation, but it achieved its purpose only imperfectly because his excessive self-consciousness only gave his sister-in-law reason for mirth. And now they stopped in front of the villa. The whole Treibel clan was standing at the railing, and once affectionate greetings had been exchanged and essential toilette arrangements had been made in a flying rush—that is, fairly leisurely— Hildegard appeared on the veranda where coffee had been served in the meantime. She found everything "heavenly," which indicated that she had received strict instructions from Frau Konsul Thora Munk, who probably had recommended the suppression of everything Hamburgish and a regard for Berlin sensitivities as the first rule. No comparisons were made and right away the coffee service, for example, was roundly admired.

"Your Berlin patterns are leading everything in the field now, even Sèvres. How charming, this *Grecborte!*"

Leopold was standing at a distance and listening until Hildegard suddenly broke off, and to all she had said added only:

"Don't scold me, by the way, because I keep talking of things for which there would be time tomorrow too— *Grecborte* and Sèvres and Meissen and Blue Onion.[2] But it's Leopold's fault; he conducted such a strictly scientific conversation in the cab that I was almost uncomfortable; I wanted to hear about Lizzi, and just imagine, he only talked about radial systems and connections, and I was embarrassed to ask what it was."

Old Treibel laughed; but the Kommerzienrätin didn't move a muscle, while Leopold's pale face was momentarily flushed.

Thus passed the first day, and Hildegard's unconstrained ease, which they were very careful not to disturb, seemed to promise further tolerable days as well, all the more so since the Kommerzienrätin encouraged her by attentions of every sort. Why, she ventured so far as to give her quite valuable gifts, which was not her way usually. And though these efforts appeared at least partially successful, if not more closely examined, no one really seemed genuinely comfortable, not even Treibel, whose rapidly returning good mood was counted on with a kind of certainty, what with his happy disposition. This good mood failed to appear for a variety of reasons, one of which happened to be that the Teupitz-Zossen election campaign had ended with the total defeat of Vogelsang, with which the personal attacks on Treibel grew in number. Initially, because of his great popularity, Treibel had been considerately left out of the question until the tactlessness of his agent made it impossible to spare him further.

"It is doubtless a misfortune," thus it said in the organ of the opposing party, "to be as limited as Lieutenant Vogelsang, but to take such a limited individual into one's service is to disrespect the healthy common sense of our district. The candidacy of Treibel will founder on this affront."

Things did not look all too cheerful at the older Treibels', and Hildegard gradually began to feel this so much that she spent great parts of the days at her sister's. The lumberyard was nicer than the factory anyway and Lizzi was altogether charming with her long white stockings. And once they were even red. When she would come up and greet Aunt Hildegard with a curtsy, the latter would whisper to her sister: "Quite English, Helene," and they would smile at each other happily. Yes, these were bright spots. But when Lizzi was gone again, there would be no more easy conversation between the sisters to speak of, because their talk could not touch on the two most important points: Leopold's engagement and the desire to get out of this engagement with good grace.

Yes, things did not look too cheerful at the Treibels', but not at the Schmidts' either. The old Professor was not actually troubled or out of humor, since he was firmly convinced that now everything would turn to the better; yet it seemed quite essential to him to let this process take its course quietly, and so he condemned himself—which wasn't easy for him—to a qualified silence. Schmolke was naturally of quite the opposite opinion and thought extraordinarily much of "speaking out," like most older Berlin women, and the more and the oftener, the better. But her attempts in this direction had no effect, and Corinna couldn't be moved to speak when Schmolke would begin: "Well, Corinna, what's it actually going to be now? What do you actually think?"

There was no real answer to all that, and instead Corinna stood as if at the roulette wheel and waited with her arms crossed for where the ball would stop. She was not unhappy, but extremely restless and annoyed, especially when she thought of the vehement scene in which she had perhaps said too much after all. She felt quite clearly that everything would have come out differently if the Rätin had shown somewhat less harshness and she herself somewhat more accommodation. Yes, then peace could have been made without particular effort and some guilt could have been confessed, since everything had indeed been pure calculation. But of course at the same moment that she accused herself first and foremost—while regretting the Rätin's haughty attitude—at that same moment she also had to tell herself that even an unquestionably clear conscience about her own role in this affair would not have improved anything in the eyes of the Rätin. This terrible woman was not reproaching her seriously for toying with emotions, even though she constantly acted and spoke as if she did. That was an incidental matter, that wasn't it. And even if Corinna had sincerely and whole-heartedly loved this dear and good man, which was certainly possible, the offense would have been precisely the same.

"This Rätin with her arrogant 'No' didn't catch me where she could have caught me; she's not rejecting this engagement because I'm lacking heart or love, no, she's rejecting it only because I'm poor, or at least not likely to double the Treibel fortune; for nothing, nothing else. And if she declares to others or perhaps even persuades herself that I'm too self-confident and too professorial, she's only saying that because it just happens to suit her. Under different circumstances being professorial would not only not damage me, but would mean she would have the highest admiration for me."

Thus ran Corinna's words and thoughts. To elude them as much as possible she did what she hadn't done for a long time and paid visits to the old and the young professors' wives. Best of all she again liked Frau Rindfleisch who, completely occupied with her domestic economy because of her many boarders, went to the large market hall every day and always knew the best sources and the cheapest prices—which, later communicated to Schmolke, would first arouse her anger but finally her admiration for a higher economic power. She also called on Frau Immanuel Schultze and found her, perhaps because Friedeberg's impending divorce provided a very profit-able subject, strikingly nice and talkative. Immanuel himself, however, was so boastful and cynical again that she felt she would not be able to repeat the visit. And because the week had so many days, she finally had to resort to the Museum and the National Gallery. But she wasn't in the right mood for it. In front of the large mural in the Cornelius Room only the very little predella, with a man and a woman sticking their heads out from their bedcover, interested her, and in the Egyptian Museum she found a strange resemblance between Ramses and Vogelsang.

When she came home she would ask each time if anyone had been there, which meant "Has Leopold been here?", to which Schmolke regularly answered, "No, Corinna, not a soul." Really, Leopold did not have the courage to come and confined himself to writing a little letter every evening which would then be lying on her breakfast table the next morning. Schmidt would overlook it with a smile and Corinna would then get up as if by chance in order to read the letter in her room.

"Dear Corinna. This day has gone like all others. Mama seems to want to persevere in her opposition. Well, we'll see who wins. Hildegard is at Helene's a great deal because there is no one here who really pays any attention to her. I can well feel sorry for her, such a young and pretty girl. All of it the result of this sort of scheming! My soul longs to see you, and during the next week the decisions I'll make will create perfect clarity. Mama will be surprised. Just this much now—I'll shy away from nothing, not even the utmost. All that about the Fourth Commandment is fine, but it has its limits. We have obligations to ourselves too and above all else to those whom we love, who signify life and death in our eyes. I'm still wavering about where to, but I think England; there we have Liverpool and Mr. Nelson, and in two hours we're at the Scottish border. It's all the same, after all, by whom we're outwardly united, since we've long been so within ourselves. How my heart beats at this! Forever yours, Leopold."

Corinna tore the letter into little strips and threw them into the stove outside. "It's best this way; then I'll forget again what he wrote today and won't be able to compare tomorrow any more. It seems to me as if he were writing the same thing every day. Strange engagement. But should I reproach him for not being a hero? And my fancying I would transform him into a hero is all over too. This must be the beginning of my defeat and humiliation. Deserved? I'm afraid so."

A week and a half had gone by, and still nothing had changed in the Schmidts' house; the old man remained silent now as before, Marcell didn't come, much less Leopold, and only his morning letters appeared with great punctuality. Corinna had long since stopped reading them; she only skimmed them and then put them into her dressing gown pocket where they would become wrinkled and crumpled up. She had nothing to console her but Schmolke, whose healthy presence really was good for her, even if she did still avoid speaking to her.

But there was a time for that too.

The Professor had just come home, at eleven, because it was Wednesday when his classes ended an hour earlier. Both Corinna and Schmolke had heard him come in and shut the door noisily, but neither took any occasion to be further concerned with him and they both stayed in the kitchen with the bright July sun shining in and all the windows open. At one of the windows stood the kitchen table. Outside, on two hooks, hung a boxlike flower shelf, one of those odd creations of the woodcarver's art that are peculiar to Berlin: little holes in a starwort pattern and all painted dark green. In this box were several pots of geraniums and wallflowers through which the sparrows would flit and then, in their big-city boldness, sit on the kitchen table by the window. Here they merrily picked around at everything, and no one would have thought of disturbing them. Corinna, with the mortar between her knees, was busy pounding cinnamon, while Schmolke was slicing green cooking pears lengthwise and dropping the halves into a large brown bowl, a so-called chafing dish. Of course these halves weren't really equal ones, nor could they be because naturally only one half had the stem, and this stem then became the occasion for Schmolke to begin the conversation she had been longing for.

"See, Corinna," she said, "this one here, this long one, that's a stem just after your father's heart. . . ."

Corinna nodded.

"He can pick it up like a macaroni and hold it up and eat it all up from the bottom. . . . He really is a peculiar man. . ."

"Yes, that he is!"

"A peculiar man and full of eccentricities and you have to study him out first. But the most peculiar thing must be this business with the long stems and that we can't peel them when we're going to have bread pudding and pears, and that the whole core with the seeds and all has to stay in. He is a professor and a very smart man, but I'll have to say, Corinna, if I had come to my good Schmolke, who was just a plain man, with these long stems and the whole core in them, why, then something would have happened. Because as good as he was, if he thought 'she probably thinks that's good enough,' then he'd get cross and make his on-duty face and look as if he wanted to arrest me. . . ."

"Well, dear Schmolke," Corinna said, "that's simply the old story about taste, and you can't argue about tastes. And then it's probably habit too, and perhaps it's even for the sake of health."

"For the sake of health," Schmolke laughed. "Why listen, child, when those pips get in your throat like that and you swallow wrong and sometimes have to ask a complete stranger, 'Could you hit me on the back a couple of times, hard between the shoulders here'—no, Corinna, then I'd much rather have a cored Malvasian pear that goes down like butter. Health. . . ! Stem and peel, what that has to do with health, I don't know."

"But yes, dear Schmolke. Fruit doesn't agree with some people and they feel uncomfortable, especially if, like Papa, they spoon up the sauce afterwards too. And there's only one remedy for that: everything has to stay on, the stem and the green peel. Those two, they have the astringent. . ."

"What?"

"The astringent, that means that which draws together—first the lips and the mouth, but this process of drawing together continues throughout the whole inside of a person, and that's what then puts everything in order again and protects from harm."

A sparrow had been listening, and as if penetrated by the rightness of Corinna's explanation, he took a stem that had broken off accidentally into his beak and flew over to the next roof with it. The two women, however, fell silent and took up the conversation again only after a quarter of an hour.

The scene was no longer quite the same because Corinna had meanwhile cleared off the table and had spread a blue sugar wrapper over it on which numerous old rolls were lying with a large grater beside them. The latter she now took in her hand, propped it against her left shoulder and began her grating activity with such vehemence that the grated rolls scattered out over the whole blue wrapper. Now and then she interrupted herself and poured the crumbs together into a little mound in the center, but immediately afterwards she would begin anew, and it really sounded as if she were having all sorts of murderous thoughts during this work.

Schmolke watched her from the side. Then she said: "Corinna, who is it you're actually grating up there?"

"The whole world."

"That's a lot. . . and yourself with it?"

"Myself first of all."

"That's good. Because when you're all good and grated up and worn down, then you'll probably come to your senses again."

"Never."

"One should never say 'never.' That was one of Schmolke's main principles. And it must be true, because I've always found that every time somebody says 'never,' then he's just about to tip over. And I wish it were like that with you too."

Corinna sighed.

"Look, Corinna, you know that I was always against it. Because it's really plain as can be that you have to marry your cousin Marcell."

"Dear Schmolke, not a word about *him*, please."

"Yes, that sounds familiar, that's the feeling of being in the wrong. But I don't want to say any more and just want to say what I've already said, that I was always against it, I mean against Leopold, and that I got a shock when you told me. But when you told me then that the Kommerzienrätin would be angry, I thought it'd serve her right and 'why not? Why shouldn't it work? And even if Leopold is just a baby, little Corinna will nurse him up to full strength.' Yes, Corinna, that's what I thought and what I told you too. But it was a bad thought because you shouldn't make your fellowman angry, even if you don't like him, and what came to me first, the shock of your engagement, that was the right thing after all. You have to have a smart husband, one who's actually smarter than you—you're not all that smart, for that matter —and one who's got something manly about him, like Schmolke, and for whom you'll have respect. And you can't have any respect for Leopold. Do you really love him still?"

"Oh, I wouldn't think of it, dear Schmolke."

"Well, Corinna, then it's time to put an end to it. You can't just want to turn the whole world on its head and spoil your and other people's happiness—which includes your father and your old Schmolke—just to play a nasty trick on the old Kommerzienrätin with her puffed-up hairdo and her diamond earrings. She's a purse-proud woman who's forgotten the fruit store and always just acts finicky and gives the old Professor soulful looks and calls him 'Wilibald' too, as if they were still playing hide-and-seek in the attic and standing behind the peat—in those days they still kept peat in the attic, and when you came down you always looked like a chimney sweep. Yes, you see, Corinna, all that is right, and something like this would have served her right as far as I'm concerned, and she's probably had trouble enough with it. But as the old Pastor Thomas said to Schmolke and me in our wedding sermon, 'Love one another, for man should not set his life on hatred, but on love'—and Schmolke and I were always heedful of it too—so, my dear Corinna, I'll say the same to you; you shouldn't set your life on hatred. Do you really hate the Kommerzienrätin like that, I mean, thoroughly?"

"Oh, I wouldn't think of it, dear Schmolke."

"Well, Corinna, then I can just tell you once more that it's high time that something happens. Because if you don't love *him* and don't *hate* her, then I don't know what the whole business is about."

"I don't either."

And with that Corinna embraced the good Schmolke, and the latter saw in the glistening in Corinna's eyes that everything was over now and that the storm had broken.

"Well, Corinna, then we'll make it all right, and everything can still come out fine. But now give me the mold so we can put it in because it does have to cook an hour at least. And before dinner I won't say a word to your father because he won't be able to eat for joy. . ."

"Oh, he'd eat anyway."

"But after dinner I'll tell him, even if it does him out of his nap. And I've already dreamed it too and just didn't want to tell you anything about it. But now I can do it. Seven carriages, and the two daughters of Professor Kuh were bridesmaids. Naturally everybody wants to be a bridesmaid because everybody looks at them even more than the bride since she's already out of the running, and because they will get their turn pretty soon too. I couldn't recognize the pastor for sure. It wasn't Thomas. But maybe it was Souchon; it's just that he was a bit too stout.

Chapter Fifteen

THE pudding appeared at two o'clock on the dot, and Schmidt ate it with relish. In his contented mood it escaped him entirely that Corinna only smiled mutely to everything he said; for he was a lovable egoist, and like most of his sort he did not concern himself particularly with the mood of his surroundings so long as nothing happened that was likely to directly disturb his own good humor.

"And now have the table cleared, Corinna; before I stretch out a bit I want to write a letter to Marcell—or at least a few lines. He did get the position. Distelkamp, who's kept up some of his old connections, let me know this morning."

And while the old man said this he looked over at Corinna because he wanted to observe the effect this important news would have on his daughter's feelings. But he saw nothing, perhaps because there was nothing to be seen or perhaps because he was not a very sharp observer, not even when for once he wanted to be.

When the old man rose Corinna also got up and went out to give Schmolke the necessary directions for clearing the table. When the latter came in soon afterwards, she stacked the plates and silverware with that intentional and wholly unnecessary racket with which old servants like to express their dominating position in the house; and she did this in such a way that the tips of the knives and forks pointed out in all directions, and then she pressed this spiked tower firmly to herself the moment she prepared to leave.

"Don't get hurt now, dear Schmolke," said Schmidt, who enjoyed allowing himself such familiarity now and then.

"No, Professor, there's no being hurt anymore, there hasn't been for a long time. And with the engagement, it's all over too."

"All over. Really? Did she say something?"

"Yes, when she was grating the rolls for the pudding it came out all at once. It'd been gnawing at her heart for a long time, and she just didn't want to say anything. But now she's tired of it, this business with Leopold. Always just these little billets with a forget-me-not outside and a violet inside; there she can see now that he doesn't have any real courage, and that his fear of Mama is even greater than his love for her."

"Well, I'm glad. I didn't expect anything else either. And you probably didn't either, dear Schmolke. Marcell is of a different cut, after all. And as for a good match, Marcell is an archeologist."

"Of course," said Schmolke, who on principle never confessed unfamiliarity with foreign words before the Professor.

"Marcell, I say, is an archeologist. For the time being he's moved into Hedrich's position. After all, he's been in everyone's good graces for a while now. And then he'll go to Mycenae with a leave and a stipend."

Here too Schmolke expressed her complete understanding as well as agreement.

"And perhaps," Schmidt continued, "to Tiryns too, or wherever Schliemann happens to be. And when he's gotten back from there and brought me a Zeus for this room. . .", and he automatically pointed above the stove where the only vacant spot for Zeus was left, "when he's gotten back from there, I say, he's certain of a professorship. The old ones can't live forever. And you see, dear Schmolke, that is what I call a good match."

"Of course, Professor. What are the exams and all that for after all? And Schmolke, even if he wasn't educated, did always say too. . ."

"And now I want to write to Marcell and then lie down for a quarter of an hour. And coffee at half-past three. But no later."

The coffee came at half-past three. The letter to Marcell, a pneumatic post letter which Schmidt had decided on after some hesitation, had been gone for at least half an hour, and if everything went well and Marcell was at home he was perhaps already reading the three lapidary lines from which he could learn of his victory. Assistant Master at the Gymnasium! Until today he had been merely a German literature instructor at a senior girls' school and had occasionally laughed grimly to himself when he had talked about the *Codex argenteus*,[1] at which words these young things always giggled, or about *Heliand*[2] or *Beowulf*. A few obscure phrases regarding Corinna had also been inserted, and all in all it could be assumed that within very little time Marcell would appear to express his thanks.

And indeed, five o'clock had not quite arrived when the bell rang and Marcell came in. He thanked his uncle heartily for his patronage, and when the latter declined all this with the remark that if anything of the sort were to be said at all, any claims of gratitude should fall to Distelkamp, Marcell replied:

"Well, then to Distelkamp. But I should be able to thank you for writing me about it right away. And by pneumatic post too!"

"Yes, Marcell, that about the pneumatic post, that could give me a claim; because before we old fellows come around to something new that costs thirty pfennigs, a lot of water has to flow down the Spree. But what do you say to Corinna?"

"Dear Uncle, you used such an obscure phrase there. . . I didn't really understand it. You wrote: 'Kenneth of Leopard is retreating.' Does that mean Leopold? And is Corinna now going to feel punished for Leopold's turning away from her, when she believed she had him so surely?"

"It wouldn't be all that bad if it were that way. For in that case the humiliation, as we can surely call it, would be a degree greater. And as much as I love Corinna, I have to admit that she could certainly use a lesson."

Marcell tried to put in a word for her.

"No, don't defend her, she would have deserved it. But the gods have milder plans for her and instead of the complete defeat of Leopold himself wanting to retreat, they dictate only half a defeat—it's only the mother who doesn't want it and it's my good Jenny, in spite of poetry and obligatory tears, who is proving more powerful to her son than Corinna."

"Perhaps only because Corinna reconsidered in good time and didn't use all her ammunition."

"Perhaps that's so. But however it may be, Marcell, we now have to resolve where you're going to stand in this whole tragicomedy, here or there. Are you disgusted with Corinna, whom you wanted to defend so generously earlier, or not? Do you find that she really is a dangerous person, superficial and vain, or do you think that it all wasn't so bad and serious, really just a caprice that can be forgiven. That is what matters."

"Yes, dear Uncle, I think I know where I stand in this. But I'll frankly admit to you that I would like to hear your opinion first. You've always meant well with me and you won't praise Corinna more than she deserves. Just out of selfishness you wouldn't, because you'd like to keep her in the house. And you are just a bit of an egoist. Forgive me, I only mean now and then and in some things. . ."

"Go ahead and say in all things. I know that too, and I comfort myself with the fact that it occurs frequently in the world. But that's digressing. I'm supposed to talk about Corinna and will do so. Well, Marcell, what is there to say? I believe she went at it quite earnestly. She frankly and freely explained as much to you at the time, and you believed it too, even more than I. That was the state of affairs, that was the way it was a few weeks ago. But now, I'll make a bet, now she's completely transformed, and if the Treibels wanted to set their Leopold among all sorts of jewels and gold bars, I believe she wouldn't take him anymore. She actually has a healthy and honest and sincere heart, a fine point of honor, and after a short aberration it's suddenly become clear to her what it actually means when, with two family portraits and a paternal library, one wants to marry into a wealthy family. She's made the mistake of imagining that 'it would be all right' because they constantly nourished her vanity and acted as if they were courting her. But there's courting and then there's courting. Socially that's all right for a while, just not for life. One might be able to get into a ducal family, but not into a bourgeois family. And even if *he*, the bourgeois, had the heart to do it, his bourgeoise certainly wouldn't, least of all if her name is Jenny Treibel, née Bürstenbinder. To put it plainly, Corinna's pride has finally awakened—let me add 'thank God'—and no matter whether she could still have prevailed or not, she doesn't like it and doesn't want it anymore. She's fed up. What had been half calculation, half willfulness before she now sees in a different light, and it has now become a matter of principle for her. There you have my wisdom. And now let me ask you once again, what position do you intend to take? Do you have the desire and the strength to forgive her her folly?"

"Yes, dear Uncle, that I have. Of course, this much is right—

I'd much prefer the whole business had never taken place, but now that it has, I'll take the good that's come of it. Surely Corinna has abandoned this modern obsession with externals now, and has learned to appreciate the ways of life she grew up in and which she has been ridiculing."

The old man nodded.

"Many a person," Marcell continued, "would take a different stand on this, that's completely clear to me; people are simply different, one sees that every day. Just recently, for instance, I read a charming little story by Heyse[3] in which a young scholar—why if I'm not mistaken it was one infected by the archeological bug, a sort of special colleague of mine— loves a young baroness and is affectionately and sincerely loved in return; he just doesn't really know it for certain. And in this uncertain condition he hears, as he happens to be hidden by a hedge, how the baroness makes all sorts of confessions to a friend promenading in the park with her. Chatting of her happiness and her love with this friend, she unfortunately doesn't refrain from making some jokingly willful remarks about her love. And to hear this and to pack his bag and to take to his heels are all one and the same for the lover and archeologist. Completely incomprehensible to me. I, dear Uncle, would have done it differently, *I* would have just heard the love in it and not the joking and not the mockery; and instead of leaving I would have fallen at my beloved baroness's feet, insanely happy, speaking of nothing but my infinite happiness. There you have my situation, dear Uncle. Naturally one can do otherwise too; I for my part am heartily glad that I'm not one of the solemn sort. Respect for a point of honor, certainly; but too much of it is perhaps an evil everywhere, and in love quite certainly."

"Bravo, Marcell. Didn't really expect otherwise and can see in that again that you're my own sister's son. See, that's the Schmidt in you that can speak like that; no pettiness, no vanity, always the right thing, the whole thing. Come here, boy, and give me a kiss. One is really not enough, because when I consider that you're my nephew and colleague and will soon be my son-in-law—for surely Corinna won't say no —then even two kisses on the cheek are hardly enough. And *this* satisfaction you shall have, Marcell; Corinna must write to you and, so to speak, confess and ask you to forgive her her sins."

"For God's sake, Uncle, don't do anything like that. First of all she won't do it, and if she wanted to do it, I still couldn't stand to see her do it. The Jews, Friedeberg just recently told me, have a law or a saying according to which it is considered particularly punishable to shame a fellow man, and I find that that's a tremendously fine law and almost even Christian. And if one shouldn't shame anybody, not even one's enemies, why, dear Uncle, how could I possibly shame my dear cousin Corinna, who may not know where to hide because of embarrassment. For when the unembarrassed once become embarrassed, then they do so to an extraordinary degree; and when a person is in as awkward a position as Corinna's, then it's one's duty to build golden bridges for that person. *I* will write, dear Uncle."

"You're a good fellow, Marcell; come here, another one. But don't be too good, women can't bear that, not even Schmolke."

Chapter Sixteen

A
ND Marcell really did write, and the next morning two letters addressed to Corinna lay on the breakfast table, one in a small format with a little landscape picture in the left corner, a pond and a weeping willow, in which Leopold spoke, as he had done, oh, how many times, of his "unflinching resolve," the other without artistic ornament, from Marcell. It said:

"Dear Corinna: Papa spoke with me yesterday and to my sincerest joy let me know that—forgive me, these are his own words—'reason is beginning to speak again.' 'And,' he added, 'proper reason comes from the heart.' Can I believe that? Has a change come about, the conversion I had hoped for? Papa at least assured me of that. He was also of the opinion that you would be prepared to say this to me, but I protested against that most solemnly, because I have no wish to hear admissions of wrong or guilt; what I now know, even if not from your own mouth, is fully enough for me, makes me infinitely happy and extinguishes all bitterness in my soul. Many would not be able to follow me in this feeling, but where my heart speaks I don't feel the need to speak to an angel; on the contrary, perfection oppresses me, perhaps because I can't believe in it; failings that I can humanly understand are congenial to me, even if I suffer because of them. I still know all that you told me when I accompanied you home from that Mr.-Nelson-evening at the Treibels', of course, but it exists only in my ear, not in my heart. In my heart there is only the one thing which has always been in it, from the beginning, from childhood on.

I hope to see you this very day. As always, your Marcell."

Corinna passed the letter to her father. He read it too and blew double steam clouds; but when he was finished he got up and gave his darling a kiss on the forehead.

"You're a lucky child. See, that's an example of the higher, the truly ideal, not the ideal of my friend Jenny. Believe me, the classical ideas that are being ridiculed so much now, they are what make the soul free, and there's nothing petty about them; they anticipate Christianity and teach us to forgive and forget, because we all come short of the glory.[1] Yes, Corinna, there are classical sayings just like the Biblical ones. Sometimes they even go beyond those. There is for example the saying, 'Become what you are,'[2] words that only a Greek could say. Of course this process of becoming, postulated here, must be worthwhile, but if my paternal bias isn't deceiving me, it is worthwhile with you. This Treibel business was a mistake, a 'step off the path,'[3] as a comedy is now titled, as you must know, one by a member of the Supreme Court at that. The Supreme Court, thank God, was always literary. Literature makes one free. . . . Now you've found the right thing again and yourself as well. . . . 'Become what you are,' the great Pindar says, and for that reason too, in order to become what he is, Marcell has to go out into the world, to the great places and particularly to the very old ones. The very old ones—that's always like the Holy Sepulchre; that's where the crusades of scholarship go, and once you're both back from Mycenae—I say 'both' because you'll accompany him, Frau Schliemann is always there too—there would have to be no justice at all if there weren't a lecturer's or instructor's post within the year for you two."

Corinna thanked him for appointing her along with Marcell, but for the time being she was more for a home and children. Then she took her leave and went into the kitchen, sat down on a stool and let Schmolke read the letter.

"Well, what do you say, dear Schmolke?"

"Why, Corinna, what should I say? I'll just say what Schmolke always said: 'God lets some people have it in their sleep.' You acted perfectly irresponsibly and almost horribly and now you're still going to get him. You're a lucky child."

"That's what Papa told me too."

"Well, then it must be true, Corinna. Because what a professor says is always true. But no more humbug now and no little jokes, we've had enough of that now with this poor Leopold. I could actually feel sorry for him because he can't help the way he's made, and in the end people are the way they are. No, Corinna, now we want to be serious. And when do you think it'll start or get into the paper? Tomorrow?"

"No, dear Schmolke, it doesn't happen that fast. I do have to see him first, and give him a kiss. . . ."

"Of course, of course. Before that it can't be done. . . ."

"And then I have to write Leopold first too. He did just assure me again today that he wants to live and die for me. . . ."

"Oh, goodness, the poor fellow."

"He'll probably be quite glad too in the end. . . ."

"It's possible."

On the very same evening, as his letter had indicated, Marcell came and first of all greeted his uncle who was absorbed in reading the newspaper. For that reason—and perhaps because he considered the engagement question settled—

he approached Marcell, newspaper in hand, rather absent-mindedly with the words:

"And now tell me, Marcell, what do you say to this? *Summus Episcopus*.[4]. . . The Kaiser, our old Wilhelm, is divesting himself of the office and doesn't want to have it anymore, and Koegel will get it. Or perhaps Stöcker. . ."

"Oh, dear Uncle, first I don't believe it, and then, I'll hardly be married in the Cathedral. . . ."

"You're right. I have the fault of all nonpoliticians—sensational news, which always turns out to be wrong afterwards, makes me forget everything more important. Corinna is sitting over there in her room waiting for you, and I imagine it'll probably be best if you arrange everything between yourselves; I'm not quite finished with the paper either, and a third person only gets in the way, even if it is the father."

When Marcell came in, Corinna came towards him cheerfully and amiably, somewhat embarrassed, but at the same time visibly intent on treating the matter in her own way, that is, with as little of the tragic as possible. From beyond, the evening glow fell into the window, and when they had sat down she took his hand and said:

"You're so good, and I hope that I'll always be mindful of that. What I wanted was just foolishness."

"But did you really want it?"

She nodded.

"And did you love him quite seriously?"

"No. But I wanted to marry him quite seriously. And more than that, Marcell, I don't believe that I would have become very unhappy either. But who is happy? Do you know anybody? I don't. I would have taken painting lessons and perhaps riding lessons too and would have become acquainted with a few English families on the Riviera, some with a 'pleasure yacht' of course, and would have gone to Corsica or to Sicily with them, always in pursuit of blood feuds. For surely I would have felt a need for excitement for the rest of my life—Leopold is a bit sleepy. Yes, that's how I would have lived."

"You never change and you always picture yourself worse than you are."

"Hardly. But of course not better either. I hope you will believe me if I assure that I'm glad to be out of all that. I've always had an inclination toward externals and may have it yet, but gratifying that can be paid for too dearly—I've learned to appreciate that now."

Marcell wanted to interrupt once more, but she wouldn't allow it.

"No, Marcell, I have to say a few words more. You see, all this with Leopold, that might have been all right—why not, after all? To have a weak, good, insignificant person at your side can even be pleasant, it can mean an advantage. But that Mama, that dreadful woman! Certainly, property and money have their magic, if it weren't that way I would have been spared my error; but if money is everything and confines heart and mind, and on top of that goes hand in hand with sentimentality and tears—that gets to be disgusting, and to accept *that* would have been hard on me, even if I could perhaps have borne it. Because I assume that man can bear quite a lot in a good bed and in good care."

The second day after that it was in the newspapers, and along with the public announcement, cards arrived. At the Kommerzienrats' too. Having glanced into the envelope, Treibel strongly sensed the importance of this news and the influence it would have upon the restoration of domestic peace and a tolerable mood, and he did not delay going over into the boudoir where Jenny was breakfasting with Hildegard. Even while coming in he held the letter up high and said:

"What do I get if I tell you the contents of this letter?"

"Make your demands," said Jenny, perhaps with a dawning hope in her.

"A kiss."

"Don't be silly, Treibel."

"Well, if it can't be from you, then at least from Hildegard."

"Granted," said the latter. "But now read."

And Treibel read: " 'I have the honor today of announcing the engagement of my daughter. . .' yes, ladies, which daughter? There are many daughters. Once again, then, guess. I'm doubling the price I set. . . so, 'my daughter Corinna to Dr. Marcell Wedderkopp, Assistant Master and Lieutenant in the Reserve of the Brandenburg Fusilier Regiment Nr. 35. Respectfully, Dr. Wilibald Schmidt, Professor and Assistant Master at the Gymnasium of the Holy Ghost.' "

Jenny, restrained by Hildegard's presence, contented herself with casting a triumphant glance at her husband. Hildegard herself, however, who was immediately searching for a formal error, said only:

"Is that all? So far as I know, the engaged couple customarily says a word too. But the Schmidt-Wedderkopps seem to have done without."

"Not at all, precious Hildegard. On the second sheet, which I've been suppressing, the bridal pair has spoken too. I will leave this document to you as a souvenir of your stay in Berlin and as proof of the gradual progress of our local culture. Naturally we're still a good way behind, but it's coming gradually. And now I'll ask for my kiss."

Hildegard gave him two, and so tempestuously that their significance was clear. This day signified *two* engagements.

The last Saturday in July had been set as Marcell's and Corinna's wedding day; "just no long engagements," Wilibald Schmidt emphasized, and the bridal pair understandably had no objections to speeding up the procedure. Schmolke alone, who had been in such a hurry with the engagement, didn't want to hear of any such speeding-up and said that it was barely three weeks until then, only just time enough for the banns to be called three times, and that wouldn't do, that was too short, people would talk about it; but finally she rested content with it or at least comforted herself with the thought that there would be talk anyway.

On the twenty-seventh there was a little wedding-eve party at the Schmidts' apartment, and the next day a wedding banquet in the "English House." Pastor Thomas performed the ceremony. At three o'clock the carriages drove up in front of the Nicolai church—six bridesmaids, among them the two Kuhs and the two Felgentreus. The latter, it may be revealed here, became engaged during a pause in the dancing to the two junior officials from the quartet, the same young gentlemen who had been along on the Lake Halen party. The yodeler, who had naturally been invited too, was vigorously set upon by the Kuhs, but being accustomed to two-sided assaults from owning cornerhouse property, he was able to resist them. The Kuh daughters accepted this check gracefully—"he was not the first, he won't be the last," Schmidt said—and only the mother appeared strongly out of humor to the last.

Otherwise it was a thoroughly cheerful wedding, which in part was due to the fact that from the start everything was taken lightly. One wanted to forget and forgive, on one side and on the other, and so it happened that the Treibels had not only all been invited, but, with the sole exception of Leopold who had ridden out to the Egg Hut that afternoon, they all actually appeared. The Kommerzienrätin had indeed wavered strongly at first, and had even spoken of tactlessness and affront, but her second thought had then been to take the whole incident as a mere bit of childishness and thereby to put an end, in the easiest way, to the talk people had started here and there. And she stayed with this second thought; the

Rätin, smiling and amiable as always, appeared *in pontificali-bus*[5] and was the uncontested showpiece of the wedding dinner. Even Fräuleins Honig and Wulsten had been invited at Corinna's urgent wish; the former did come, while Fräulein Wulsten excused herself by letter "since she couldn't leave Lizzi, the sweet child, alone after all." Right below the words "the sweet child" there was a spot, and Marcell said to Corinna: "A tear, and I believe a real one." Of the professors, besides the Kuhs mentioned earlier, only Distelkamp and Rindfleisch were present, since those blessed with offspring were all in Kösen, Ahlbeck, and Stolpmünde vacationing. Despite this forfeiture in personnel there was no lack of toasts; Distelkamp's was the best, Felgentreu's the logically most atrocious, for which, though he hadn't intended it, he was rewarded with roaring laughter.

The dessert had begun to go around, and Schmidt was just going from place to place to say all sorts of pleasantries to the older as well as to some of the younger ladies, when the telegram boy who had already appeared numerous times came into the room once more and immediately went up to old Schmidt. The latter, filled with the desire to reward the bearer of so many hearty wishes as royally as Goethe's "Singer,"[6] filled a large glass standing beside him with champagne and handed it to the messenger who, first bowing to the bridal pair, emptied it with a certain flair. Then Schmidt opened the telegram, skimmed it, and said:

"From the kindred tribe of Britain."

"Read it, read it."

" 'To Doctor Marcell Wedderkopp.' "

"Louder."

" 'England expects that every man will do his duty'. . . . Signed 'John Nelson.' "

In the circle of those initiated in the matter and in the language, jubilation broke out, and Treibel said to Schmidt: "I imagine Marcell can vouch to do that."

Corinna herself was exceedingly pleased and cheered by the telegram, but she was already running short of time to express her happy feelings because it was eight o'clock and at half-past nine the train was leaving to take them to Munich and from there to Verona or, as Schmidt preferred to say, "to the grave of Juliet." But this he called a mere trifle and a fore-taste, and generally spoke rather haughtily and oracularly—to Kuh's anger—of Messenia and the Taygetus in which a few more burial chambers would surely be found, if not of Aristomenes himself, then of his father. And when he was finally silent and Distelkamp displayed an amused smile at his friend once again riding his hobbyhorse, they noticed that Marcell and Corinna had meanwhile left the room.

The guests stayed on. But towards ten o'clock their ranks had thinned strongly; Jenny, Fräulein Honig, and Helene had left, and with Helene, Otto too, of course, though he would have liked to stay another hour. Only the Kommerzienrat had emancipated himself and sat beside brother Schmidt, drawing one anecdote after another out of the "Treasury of the German Nation," all of them like jewels, though it would be presumptuous to speak of their "pure gleam." Even with Gold-ammer missing, Treibel found himself supported from various sides, most liberally by Adolar Krola, to whom even story-telling experts would probably have awarded the prize.

The lights had been burning for a long time, cigar clouds wreathed up in large and small rings, and young couples were more and more withdrawing into a few corners where, for no real reason, four or five laurel bushes formed a hedge protecting them from irreverent glances. Here the Kuh girls were seen, perhaps at their mother's advice, once more under-taking an energetic advance on the yodeler, but again to no avail. At the same time someone had begun to play the piano, and it was evident that the point was near at which the young people would assert their good right to dance.

Schmidt, who had begun addressing everyone familiarly and saying "brother," seized upon this threatening moment with a certain fieldmarshal's skill and said, while pushing a box of new cigars towards Krola:

"Listen, Singers and Brothers, *carpe diem.* We Latinists put the accent on the last syllable. 'Use the day.' A few minutes more and some piano drummer will control the whole situation and let us old fellows feel how superfluous we are. So once again, whatever you want to do, do soon. The moment has come—Krola, you must do me a favor and sing Jenny's song. You've accompanied it a hundred times and will surely know how to sing it too. I don't believe there are any Wagnerian difficulties in it. And our Treibel won't take it amiss that this song, so dear to his beloved wife's heart, is profaned in a sense —for every exhibition of something sacred is what I call a profanation. Am I right, Treibel, or am I deceived in you? I can't be deceived in you, you have a clear and open face. And now come, Krola. 'More light'[7]—that was what our Olympian said; but we don't need anymore, at least not here, here we have lights enough and to spare. Come. I want to conclude this day as a man of honor and in friendship with all the world and not least of all with you, with Adolar Krola."

The latter, who had become weatherproof at a hundred tables and, in comparison to Schmidt, was still tolerably capable, walked towards the piano without much resistance, while Schmidt and Treibel followed him arm in arm, and before the rest of the party could even have an inkling that a song was to be performed Krola laid his cigar aside and began:

> Fortune, of your thousand dowers
> There is only one I want.
> What good is gold? I love flowers
> And the rose's ornament.

And I hear the rustling branches,
And I see a flutt'ring band—
Eye and eye exchanging glances,
And a kiss upon your hand.

Giving, taking, taking, giving,
And the wind plays in your hair.
That, oh that alone is living,
When heart to heart is paired.

Jubilation rang out everywhere for Krola's voice was still full of strength and resonance, at least compared with what one otherwise heard in this circle. Schmidt cried to himself. But all of a sudden he came around again.

"Brother," he said, "that did me good. *Bravissimo*. Treibel, our Jenny is right after all. There is something to it, it has got something in it; I don't know exactly what, but that's just it —it's a real song. All real lyrics have something mysterious. I should have stuck to it after all. . . ."

Treibel and Krola looked at one another and then nodded in agreement.

"And poor Corinna. Now she's at Trebbin, first stage to Juliet's grave. . . . Juliet Capulet, the way that sounds! It's supposed to be an Egyptian coffin, incidentally, which is actually even more interesting. . . . And then all in all I don't know if it's right to drive through the night like that; in earlier times it wasn't customary to do that; earlier, one was more natural, I should say more moral. Too bad that my friend Jenny is gone, she should decide if that's true. For me personally it's established—nature is morality and the most important thing altogether. Money is nonsense, science is nonsense, everything is nonsense. Professor too. Whoever disputes it is a *pecus*.[8] Right, Kuh. . . Come, gentlemen, come Krola. . . Let's go home."

Notes

1. *Frau* is simply the German for Mrs. here, but if, as when Frau Schmolke immediately corrects herself, the person addressed has another title, that must be added. As German custom has it, Mrs. Treibel is actually using her husband's title in its feminine form, and *Rat* (fem. *Rätin*) signifies "councilor" while the first half of the compound indicates "of commerce." Titles such as this have been exceedingly valued in German society; they may identify an actual rank within the government's bureaucratic hierarchy (as the *Rechnungsrat*, "councilor of accounts," below) or they may have been granted by a government for a patriotic action or contribution. Ironically undercutting this earnest obsession with titles are the telling names Fontane gives many of his characters. Treibel, for example, coming from the German verb *treiben*—to drive, urge—indicates the energetic drive Jenny displays even as it suggests the social ambitions she nurtures.
2. the Colony: the sizable settlement of French Huguenots in Berlin.
3. *attrappe*: Germanized French word for a dummy container.
4. Hövell or Kranzler: elegant confectioners' establishments.
5. *nécessaire*: a little case or container containing a sewing kit, manicure set, or the like.
6. Mr. Booth: the American actor Edwin Booth (1831-1893) actually did perform in Berlin in 1882.
7. *Parzival*: the medieval epic by Wolfram von Eschenbach (ca.

1170-1220). What with Schmidt's reference to *Tannhäuser* and *Lohengrin* below it should be noted that Richard Wagner's *Parsifal* premièred in Bayreuth on July 26, 1882.

CHAPTER TWO

1. Berlin blue dye: so called because it was first created in Berlin; also known as Prussian blue.
2. Gontard, Knobelsdorff: Karl von Gontard (1731-1791) and Georg Wenzeslaus Knobelsdorff (1699-1753), well-known Berlin architects; the latter built the famous Sans Souci palace for and with Frederick the Great.
3. *bel étage*: the elegant first floor above the ground level.
4. Huster: A. Huster's fashionable "English House" establishment at which a wedding party will be held later and where Fontane's seventieth birthday was celebrated.
5. Socialist: the Social Democrats' party she is referring to was founded in 1869; for many years it was outlawed by Bismarck.
6. *embonpoint*: "in good condition," used politely for plumpness.
7. *Berliner Tageblatt*: a liberal paper, one of the new mass-circulation dailies, founded in 1872 by Rudolf Mosse. Nunne is a comic character feature in Thursday's "Ulk."
8. *Deutsches Tageblatt*: conservative competitor founded in 1880.
9. Teupitz-Zossen: rural constituency south of Berlin.
10. Singer: Paul Singer (1844-1911) Social Democrat leader in Berlin and later in the *Reichstag* (Imperial Parliament).
11. Buggenhagen's: a restaurant not far from the Treibel villa, the meeting place of Treibel's political acquaintances.
12. *Gutta cavat lapidem*: "Drops of water wear away stone."
13. *poveretto*: poor fellow
14. Berlin West: upper class residential section; Charlottenburg refers to a town and summer palace a bit further out west, later incorporated into Berlin.
15. trade names: the corpulent Frau von Ziegenhals' name can be translated as "Goatneck" and the slender Fräulein Bomst's suggests "plump" or "plop." Similarly the two poets mentioned below have particularly unpoetic names. Friedrich Gottlieb Klopstock (1724-1803) is one of the first great modern German poets while Wolfgang Robert Griepenkerl (1810-1868) is a rather obscure dramatist.
16. 'the hart panting after water:' one of Treibel's numerous more or less relevant quotations, from Psalms 42, 2. Such quoting, a popular practice of the age, is to reflect (often ironically) the breadth and depth of a person's culture.

17. Victory and Westminster Abbey: Treibel is playfully referring to Admiral Nelson's flagship and his heroic death, suggesting that the conquest of this Nelson is up to Corinna.

CHAPTER THREE

1. Professor Franz: Julius Franz (1824-1887), well-known Berlin sculptor, rather less famous and fashionable than Reinhold Begas (1831-1911).
2. peculiar song composed on this incident: the ironic doggerel verse in question actually attacks Tschech for missing at such close range in his assassination attempts (July 26, 1844), an irony Vogelsang seems to have missed.
3. Georg Herwegh: (1817-1875) nationalistic poet, eventually exiled in spite of his audience with the king; Vogelsang below refers to his flight after an abortive revolutionary attempt in Baden.
4. Meyerbeer: Giacomo Meyerbeer (1791-1864), opera composer from Berlin who in his day enjoyed great fame there as well as in Paris, where his *Robert le Diable* (from which the "Gold is only a chimera" line comes) had a sensational première in 1831.
5. Ludwig Loewe: (1837-1886) sewing machine and weapons manufacturer, who represented the liberal progressives in the Reichstag after 1878.
6. *l'appétit vient en mangeant*: appetite comes with eating.
7. Father Jahn: Friedrich Ludwig Jahn (1778-1852), known as Turnvater ("father of gymnastics") Jahn, promoted the regeneration of the German nation through his increasingly popular gymnastics movement.
8. school for feminine handicrafts: founded in 1865 by the liberal politician Wilhelm Adolf Lette (1799-1868) as an "Association for the Advancement of the Earning Capacity of the Female Sex."
9. *gonfaloniere*: standard bearer
10. royal democracy: a notion that had arisen within German romanticism and was realized, with devastating irony, in the "ein Volk, ein Führer" (one people, one leader) principle of the Third Reich.

CHAPTER FOUR

1. Molkenmarkt: the "dairy market place" area was one of the oldest parts of Berlin and the site of an old city prison.
2. Kümmel: caraway liqueur

3. Lady Milford: the noble-hearted mistress of the duke in Schiller's *Intrigue and Love.*
4. the Quitzows: Brandenburg nobles who had disputed the rights of, and risen up against, the Hohenzollerns when they were given the Mark Brandenburg as an imperial fief in 1415. *The Quitzows* by Ernst von Wildenbruch (1845-1909), which treated these events, premièred in Berlin in 1888 and was enthusiastically received by the public and favorably reviewed by Fontane.
5. a renunciation of all Catholicism: this mysterious discussion alludes to the so-called *Kulturkampf* ("cultural struggle") of the time, during which Bismarck sought to eliminate Catholic control and influence at all levels of the state.
6. William Tell: the hero of Schiller's play of the same name refuses to salute the cap on the pole, the symbol of Austrian authority, as a required sign of loyal submission; this leads to the apple-shooting scene and triggers the struggle for Swiss independence.
7. *'écrasez l'infâme'*: "crush the infamous (thing)," famous motto of Voltaire directed against superstition and the Catholic Church, Goldammer's Hydra; used by Frederick the Great, the phrase became popular during the later *Kulturkampf.*
8. 'My peace is gone': first line of Gretchen's song in Goethe's *Faust* (Part I).
9. "The Elf-King" (also known as "The Erl-King"), "Lord Henry Sat by the Fowling Floor," and "The Bells of Speier": ballads by Goethe, Johann Nepomuk Vogl (1802-1866), and Max von Oer (1806-1846), respectively; all set to music by Karl Löwe (1796-1869), who had also set Fontane's "Archibald Douglas" ballad.
10. *ex ungue leonem*: you can tell the lion by his paw—Treibel puns on the composer's and the politician's name.
11. "Brooklet, leave your murmuring be," "I'd carve it into every tree": from a cycle of romantic poems by the poet of *Wanderlust*, Wilhelm Müller (1794-1827), set by Franz Schubert.
12. Milanollos: Theresa and Marietta enchanted all of Vienna with the virtuosity of their violin and vocal performances in 1843.

CHAPTER FIVE

1. "Be always true and honest": from a song by Ludwig Hölty (1748-1776) that the bells played every hour to the music of the Papageno aria in Mozart's *Magic Flute* (II, 5), articulating Papageno's wish for a wife.
2. the Canadian who wasn't yet familiar with Europe's white-washed politeness: from a poem by Johann Gottfried Seume (1763-1810) in which a Huron Indian encounters European social hypocrisy.

3. Ruppin print: very popular bold and colorful broadsheet representations of current events from Fontane's birthplace, Neuruppin.
4. 'Corinne au Capitole': Book II of Madame de Staël's (1766-1817) novel *Corinne ou l'Italie*, in which Corinne is crowned with laurel at the Capitol for her poetic success.
5. Bonwitt & Littauer: most fashionable dressmakers in Berlin, purveyors to the Empress.
6. Madai: Guido von Madai (1810-1892) became Police Commissioner (*Polizeipräsident*) of Berlin in 1872.

CHAPTER SIX

1. Gymnasium: secondary school chiefly for university preparation, stressing classical-humanist education.
2. "The Banner of the Upright Seven": novella by the Swiss writer Gottfried Keller (1819-1890), published 1974 by Frederick Ungar Publishing Co.; Schmidt's rejection of this title for the group may be taken as a reflection of Fontane's rather critical attitude toward Keller.
3. the Douglasses were always faithful: Fontane is quoting from a ballad of his own, "The Uprising in Northumberland," part two, "Percy's Death."
4. Eduard von Hartmann: (1842-1906) philosopher influenced by Schopenhauer.
5. *nomen est omen*: the name is an omen
6. veil of Saïs: the veiled image reputed to have been at the ancient Egyptian city of Saïs was supposed to reveal the truth to anyone daring to look behind it.
7. *grandezza*: grandeur
8. Rodigast: Samuel Rodigast (1649-1708), director of the Gray Cloister Gymnasium in Berlin and author of church hymns.
9. 'if you just have faith in yourself, other souls will have faith in you too': quoted from Mephistopheles' advice to the student in Part I of Goethe's *Faust*.
10. Spichern: scene of a Prussian victory in Lorraine (August 6, 1870) in the Franco-Prussian War.
11. 'The old order is collapsing, the times are changing.': from Schiller's *William Tell* (IV, 2) in which the dying Swiss Attinghausen continues, "and new life comes to flower in the ruins."
12. the business of churchmen alone: during the *Kulturkampf* such traditional prerogatives of the church as marriage, for example, had been taken over by the civil authorities. (See Note 4, Chapter Four)
13. Heinrich Schliemann: (1822-1890) "the creator of prehistoric

Greek archeology," after having made his fortune chiefly while an immigrant in the U.S., turned to archeology and excavated sites at Troy and Mycenae; the book referred to appeared in 1878.

14. the cleft skull—Aegisthus' remembrance: Agamemnon's skull; he had been murdered by Aegisthus in conspiracy with the former's wife Clytemnestra.

15. *hic Rhodus, hic salta*: here's Rhodes, now make your jump—the Aesopian advice to a braggart, who claimed that when he was in Rhodes he made an enormous broad jump. Someone then suggested to him that he now prove he had been in Rhodes and duplicate the feat.

16. Teutoburg forest: where the Romans under Varus were defeated in 9 A.D. by Herman (Arminius) the German chieftain.

17. Max Piccolomini: youthful romantic hero in Schiller's *Wallenstein*.

18. Virchow: Rudolf Virchow (1821-1902) famous Berlin pathologist, liberal member of the Reichstag and opponent of Bismarck who, as the founder of the German Society for Anthropology, Ethnology, and Prehistory, assisted Schliemann on a Troy excavation in 1879.

19. *lupus in fabula*: the wolf in the fable—who appears when he is mentioned, as in "speak of the devil."

CHAPTER SEVEN

1. *les défauts de ses vertus*: the defects of one's virtues; a phrase familiar from the French novelist George Sand, pen name for Aurore Dupin (1804-1876), who is also noted for her relationship with the poet Alfred de Musset (1810-1857).

2. *comprendre c'est pardonner*: to understand is to forgive; Madame de Staël had said "tout comprendre, c'est tout pardonner"—to understand all is to forgive all.

3. *méchante*: sorry, wretched.

4. Hohenfriedberg or Leuthen victories: both against Austria, in 1745 (Second Silesian War) and 1757 (Seven Years War), respectively.

5. *petit crevé*: fop, dandy.

6. Freiherr von Rumohr: Karl Friedrich von Rumohr (1785-1843) wrote on the history of art and the pleasures of the table; published *The Spirit of the Art of Cooking* in 1823.

7. Fürst Pückler-Muskau: Hermann Ludwig Heinrich von Muskau (1785-1871) landscape artist, gourmet, and traveler who also re-

corded and published his exotic travel experiences, one of which was to buy and bring home an Abyssinian woman sold as a slave.

8. *jeu d'esprit*: wit, cleverness.

9. "[The] Diver" and "[The Walk] To the Iron Hammer": ballads by Schiller.

10. Brückner, Koegel: two prominent Berlin clergymen the Treibels would infinitely prefer over the combined blacksmith-Justice of the Peace at Gretna Green in Scotland who traditionally married runaway couples from England. Rudolf Koegel (1829-1896) was the Senior Court Chaplain.

CHAPTER EIGHT

1. *eau de javelle*: bleaching and cleaning agent.

2. guild family: a particularly wealthy and influential patrician family representative of the Free Cities in the Hanseatic League.

3. Ritter Karl von Eichenhorst: knightly hero of a ballad, "The Abduction" by Gottfried August Bürger (1747-1794), who has no difficulty carrying off his bride and gaining parental consent.

4. *gentilezza*: superior gentility of manner; delicateness

CHAPTER NINE

1. Bernau war correspondent: comic newspaper character who continually requested advances for making his reports on distant wars without actually ever leaving home.

2. Montecuccoli's remark: the Italian Count and Imperial Field-marshal Raimondo Montecuccoli (1609-1680), quoting Marshall Gian-Jacobo Trivulzio (1448-1518), remarks, "To carry on war, three things are necessary—money, money, and more money."

3. "the only feeling breast under all the masks": Schiller's ballad, "The Diver."

4. Hydra: Vogelsang's, since the revolution in 1848, was the monster of liberal republicanism as he saw it, while Goldammer's Hydra is Catholicism.

5. 'The Hare and the Hedgehog': one of the Grimms' fairy tales in which the hedgehog beats the hare by having his wife stand in his place at the finish.

6. Churbrandenburg: variant of Kurbrandenburg in which "Kur" means the "Electorate" Brandenburg whose rulers were Electors of the Holy Roman Emperor.

7. *tic douloureux*: painful twitch; neuralgia

CHAPTER TEN

1. academic quarter: German university professors begin their lectures at a quarter past the hour announced.
2. some Siechen or the heavier Wagner: as Treibel's comment on "the beer question" suggests, this is generally taken as expressing Krola's wish to be at one of the beer taverns so named (Wagner's serves the heavy Nuremberg beer).
3. "Thanks from the House of Austria": General Buttler in *Wallenstein's Death* by Schiller says this with bitter irony because he feels betrayed by Austria.
4. 'To France marched two Grenadiers,/Their heads were hanging down': first and fourth line of Heine's "The Grenadiers."
5. 'I know not what it should mean': first line of Heine's "Lorelei," set by Franz Liszt and Friedrich Silcher (1789-1860)—see Note 2 above.
6. Geheimrat: a rather higher rank of *Rat*, a privy councilor.
7. When oft in vain I've peered: seventh and penultimate stanza of "Moonlight" by Nikolaus Lenau (1802-1850).

CHAPTER ELEVEN

1. Erhart: Luise Erhart (1844-1916) married Count Karl von der Goltz in 1868 and took her leave of the stage with a performance of Schiller's *Maria Stuart* in 1878.

CHAPTER TWELVE

1. the blessing of the parents builds the houses of the children: this and Jenny's following remark are rather telling variations on the Apocryphal "For the blessing of the father establishes the houses of the children; but the curse of the mother rooteth out foundations" (*The Wisdom of Jesus the Son of Sirach, or Ecclesiasticus*, 3, 9).

CHAPTER THIRTEEN

1. pneumatic post: tubes connecting the different city post offices by which a letter could be pneumatically propelled across town in a matter of minutes.

CHAPTER FOURTEEN

1. (it need not be said what): it would probably have been Goethe's sentimental novel of youthful love frustrated by circumstance, *The Sorrows of Young Werther* (1774).
2. Grecborte and Sèvres and Meissen and Blue Onion: the first and last refer to china patterns, neoclassical ("Grecian border") and a sort of "neo-oriental," usually in, respectively, gold and blue trim; Sèvres and Meissen refer, respectively, to royally instituted china manufacturing establishments in France (1738) and Saxon Germany (1710), a practice followed by Frederick the Great who initiated the production of Royal Berlin china in 1763.

CHAPTER FIFTEEN

1. *Codex argenteus*: sixth-century Gothic Bible manuscript, of a translation by Bishop Ulfilas (311-382), done in silver on purple parchment and preserved in Uppsala, Sweden.
2. *Heliand*: ninth-century Old Saxon epic of the life of Christ.
3. Heyse: Paul Heyse (1830-1914) popular writer of polished stories, such as this "Unforgettable Words"; first German writer to be awarded the Nobel Prize (1910).

CHAPTER SIXTEEN

1. come short of the glory: "For all have sinned, and come short of the glory of God" (*Romans* 3,23).
2. 'Become what you are': Schmidt has slightly altered Pindar's "be what you are" (Second Pythian Ode), though he is surely aware of the implication there—to know the limitations of one's station or condition.
3. *A Step off the Path*: play by Ernst Wichert (1831-1902) who, like E. T. A. Hoffmann, was associated with the Supreme Court in Berlin; premièred in 1873.
4. *Summus Episcopus*: the highest bishop, which title Schmidt thought Adolf Stöcker (1835-1909)—a court chaplain turned politician (member of the Reichstag, founded the reactionary and anti-Semitic Christian Socialist Party in 1878)—might get.
5. *in pontificalibus*: in full episcopal attire; here, dressed to the teeth.
6. Goethe's "Singer": "The Singer," ballad by Goethe in which the minstrel is rewarded with a goblet of wine.

7. 'More light': reputedly the last words of Goethe ("our Olympian") on his deathbed.
8. *pecus*: cattle, single head of cattle; ox or cow here—the name Kuh is also the German word for cow.

Bibliography

The translation is based on the two editions of Theodor Fontane's works published by Nymphenburger Verlagshandlung: Edgar Gross' *Sämtliche Werke* (Munich, 1959) and Kurt Schreinert's more amply annotated *Fontane: Nymphenburger Taschenbuch-Ausgabe* (Munich, 1969). In addition to the latter, the translator consulted H. B. Garland's text edition of *Frau Jenny Treibel* (London: Macmillan, 1968). More generally, the single most useful and commendable background book available in English is Gerhard Masur's *Imperial Berlin* (New York: Basic Books, 1970).

WORKS BY FONTANE AVAILABLE IN ENGLISH INCLUDE:

Across the Tweed: A Tour of Mid-Victorian Scotland (Jenseits des Tweed), tr. by Brian Battershaw. London, 1965.
Beyond Recall (Unwiederbringlich), tr. by Douglas Parmee. London, 1964.
Effi Briest, tr. & abr. by William A. Cooper. New York, 1966.
Effi Briest, tr. by Douglas Parmee. London, 1967.
A Suitable Match (Irrungen, Wirrungen), tr. by Sandra Morris. London and Glasgow, 1968.
"A Woman of My Age" ("Eine Frau in meinen Jahren"), tr. by E. M. Valk. *Transatlantic Review*, 37/38. London and New York, 1970–71.

A Man of Honor (Schach von Wuthenow), tr. by E. M. Valk. New York, 1975.

WORKS ON FONTANE AVAILABLE IN ENGLISH INCLUDE:

Fuerst, Norbert. "The Berlin Bourgeois," *The Victorian Age of German Literature*. London, 1966.

Garland, H. B. "Theodor Fontane," *German Men of Letters*, ed. by Alex Natan. London, 1961.

Hatfield, Henry. "The Renovation of the German Novel: Theodor Fontane," *Crisis and Continuity in Modern German Fiction*. Ithaca, N. Y. 1969.

Hayens, Kenneth. *Theodor Fontane*. London, 1920.

Mann, Thomas. "The Old Fontane," *Essays of Three Decades*, tr. by H. T. Lowe-Porter. New York, 1947.

Pascal, Roy. "Theodor Fontane," *The German Novel*. Manchester, 1956; London, 1965.

Remak, Joachim. *The Gentle Critic: Theodor Fontane and German Politics, 1848–1898*. Syracuse, N. Y., 1964.

Rowley, Brian A. "Theodor Fontane: A German Novelist in the European Tradition?" *German Life and Letters*, 15, 1961.

Samuel, Richard. "Theodor Fontane," *Selected Writings*. Melbourne, 1965.

Stern, J. P. "Realism and Tolerance: Theodor Fontane," *Re-Interpretations: Seven Studies in Nineteenth-Century German Literature*. New York, 1964.

Turner, David. "Coffee or Milk?—That is the Question: On an Incident from Fontane's *Frau Jenny Treibel*," *German Life and Letters*, 21, 1967.

———. "Fontane's *Frau Jenny Treibel*: A Study in Ironic Discrepancy, *Forum for Modern Language Studies*, 8, 1972.